Not Her Daughter

ALSO BY ROBIN MAHLE

REMY FONTAINE THRILLERS
Book 1: Orleans Avenue
Book 2: Terrebonne Bay
Book 3: Baton Rouge
Book 4: River Ranch

STANDALONE
The Chef
The Man in my Attic
The Compound
He's Lying About Everything
Not Her Daughter

NOT HER DAUGHTER

ROBIN MAHLE

JOFFE BOOKS

Joffe Books, London
www.joffebooks.com

First published in Great Britain in 2025

Cover art by Nick Castle

ISBN: 978-1-80573-331-7

PROLOGUE

The first time I found Ben Moore trying to smother his baby sister, he looked me dead in the eye and said, "She's not my sister." His hands covered her mouth as she lay on the play mat with soft toys dangling above her. Of course, she wasn't hurt, and I'd stopped him long before he could do any harm.

I said nothing to the mother because I'd seen sibling rivalry before and discussed with Ben that his actions could have caused his sister harm. Here in the daycare center, this behavior was nothing new. I've learned not to overreact, knowing it could make things worse. Instead, I reminded Ben that he is still important and that just because his mother pays attention to the baby doesn't mean she loves him any less. I thought he'd understood. I thought Ben was like every other child I'd seen before.

But I was wrong.

"Ben?" I see him standing at his sister's crib in the infants' room. "Ben? What are you doing?" I sweep him up, taking him into the other room. "Stay right here." I press the intercom button on the wall. "Brenda, can you come in here a minute? Something's going on with Ben."

Only a moment later, Brenda rushes inside — her short blond hair disheveled, her long cardigan flapping open as she hurries toward me. She's the owner of the facility, and I've come to trust her decisions. A mother and grandmother, Brenda expects only the best from her staff.

Looking slightly panicked, she eyes me. "What happened?"

"I think Ben was sleepwalking or something," I reply, studying Ben, who's coloring at the table. "Maybe he was half asleep, I don't know. But he wandered over to the infants' area, and before I'd realized, he was at Nicky's crib. He was trying to get to her. And I've seen him do this before, just last week, as a matter of fact."

Brenda studies him, her eyes narrowed, hands on her full hips. "Why didn't you tell me the first time? Did he touch her?"

"No. I called out to him, but it was like he couldn't hear me. I had to get him and take him out of the room. And the last time — well, I thought it was just, you know, that he was jealous of the baby. It happens all the time."

"Maybe so, but you should've told me so I could keep watch. Have you said anything to their mother?"

"I haven't, but I think it's time to." I look at Ben, who now appears like any other kid, just coloring away as if nothing had happened. "I don't know if he wants to hurt her, or—"

"Ben?" Brenda approaches him. "Honey, are you feeling okay?"

He looks at her, clutching a crayon in his fist. "Yeah."

"Why did you go see your sister when she was napping?" Brenda asks.

"'Cause I needed to keep her quiet. She can't make any noise."

Brenda glances at me and all I can do is shrug. She turns back to Ben. "Why not? She's a baby and she's your sister. They like to make noise. That's what they do."

He sets down the crayon and tilts his head, creasing his brow. "Because she'll come back, and she'll hurt us."

I see Brenda hesitate, unsure of how to respond. Finally, she continues, "Who? Who's going to come back and hurt you?"

2

CHAPTER 1

The air is heavy with the musky scent of the older man sitting behind his desk, the sole owner of this law firm. I pretend not to notice it, not to swallow the bitter taste that sticks to my tongue or clear my sinuses of the overpowering fragrance — because I need this job. Not many law firms want a woman in her thirties who'd left a promising career in family law to raise her son. Even fewer in a small city like this.

I passed the Pennsylvania State Bar exam after studying harder than I ever did in law school. This law firm is my last shot. I'm running out of money with Derek's life insurance payout barely covering our expenses. And keeping the kids in daycare while I try to find work eats away at it even faster.

"You say you took time off for your son?" he asks, raising his eyes to meet mine.

"Yes, that's right. I'd intended on going back after he was enrolled in school full time, but my husband's unexpected passing hastened my timeline," I reply.

"I'm sorry to hear that. It must be tough being a single mother."

Careful. He's venturing into tricky waters. Looking into his eyes, small and brown-aged, he must know a prospective employer delving into my personal life is generally frowned upon. So I wonder if he's testing me. This isn't Manhattan, Boston, or any other big-city law firm. This is Asheboro, Pennsylvania, and I'm sitting in one of only three law firms in town. The other two are personal injury and estate law. If I don't get this job, I'm out of options. So, I'd better show him what I've got.

"If you'll note the work I've done with my previous firm," I say, crossing my hands in my lap, "you'll see that I've helped many families navigate through difficult jurisdictional waters, and I can assure you that I will continue to do so."

He leans back in his chair with a tight-lipped smile. His thinning gray hair wafts in the air blowing from the ceiling vent. "Deflect and redirect is the name of the game, Ms. Moore," he says. "You seem to have an excellent grasp of the concept. I think you'll fit in just fine here. That being said, I'll have a Notice of Intent drafted this afternoon. Should you agree with the terms of employment, I'm happy to have you start right away. Would that be acceptable to you?"

His words echo in my ears. Was that a job offer? The weight lifts from my shoulders. "Yes, sir. Very much so, thank you." I rise from the chair and offer my hand. "I look forward to working with you, Mr. Goddard."

He rises to meet me, taking my hand with a hearty shake. "Please, call me Tom."

"Thank you, Tom."

I'm escorted out by Tom's assistant and front desk attendant, Lily. The young woman, fresh out of college, opens the door for me.

"Enjoy the rest of your day, Ms. Moore."

"Thank you." I step outside to the warmth of a beautiful spring day. I tilt my face toward the sun, letting it shine down on me. My lips quiver as the reality sets in. I've been offered a job. Oh, I know the pay won't be great, but it'll be enough for now.

After what my children and I have been through these past few months, I wonder if we are finally over the worst of it. The uncertainty. The not knowing. All the fear that came with starting over.

Ben has suffered the brunt of it. The effects still linger in him. Nicole was too young to know or remember any of the horrors. A small miracle.

Now, I've turned the page on a painful past and look forward to this fresh start. And with the law in my corner, I can control the narrative, keeping the truth about my family buried deep. As far as anyone knows, I'm the mother of two. And that's exactly how it will stay.

Not a day goes by that I don't think about Derek. What happened to my husband haunts my dreams as it does my son's. Sometimes, I can still smell his blood on me.

We made a clean break from Beaufort, Connecticut. I sold our house to a young couple who were willing to overlook the tragic events that had occurred inside because they needed an affordable place. And I had it priced to sell.

Josie Brewer had approved of them. I made sure to ask her first. She is alone now, too, and I think having a young family next door to her will do her some good.

Our house here in Asheboro is small, but it's enough for the three of us — Ben, Nicole, and me. They're all the family I have now. I haven't spoken to my mother since Beaufort. She doesn't know about Nicole. Oh, I've sent the occasional email telling her we're all okay, but I can't risk telling her everything. Maybe someday, when I'm sure we're in the clear, but that day hasn't yet come.

I arrive at the daycare feeling good about finally securing this job. As I enter, I see the owner, Brenda, standing in the lobby. Her face wears concern, and I get the feeling that she's been waiting for me. "Is everything okay?"

She places her hand on my shoulder. "You mind if we talk in my office?"

I trail her as she starts on. "Are the kids okay?"

"Yes, yes, they're fine. But we had a small incident that we'd like to discuss."

"We?" I press.

Brenda opens her door, and inside, I see one of the employees. "Hi, Chelsea." Right away, I don't like the look on her face. Worry, concern — shock, even. I've gotten to know her a bit already. A petite thing, she's barely twenty and hasn't yet been stained by the harsh reality of this world. Something's happened, and now my nerves are on end.

"Please take a seat, Ms. Moore," Brenda says, closing the door behind me.

"Okay." I'm left to wonder what the hell is going on while these two look like they're about to tell me the worst news I can imagine . . . though I've imagined the worst, and if that were the case, the cops would be here. "So, what's going on?"

"Chelsea?" Brenda asks.

"Well, we had a little incident with Ben today," she begins before raising a preemptive hand. "He's fine. Everyone's fine. But the thing is . . . he'd gone over to the infants' room, and I found him standing in front of Nicky's crib." She tucks her straight brown hair behind her ear. "Ms. Moore, it appeared Ben was trying to get to his sister in her crib. Nicky's fine. I got Ben out of there immediately, but this isn't the first time this has happened."

"I'm sorry?" I crease my brow. "What do you mean? What else has happened?"

"Last week," Chelsea continues, "Ben had his hands over Nicky's mouth. I asked him what he was doing, and he said he had to keep her quiet."

My heart drops because I now know where this is going.

"Of course, Nicky was fine, and it was only for a moment," Chelsea says. "I honestly didn't believe it required a conversation with you until now. Until he acted out again."

"Evelyn," Brenda cuts in, trying to inject informality into the conversation. "What seems particularly odd is that he insists Nicky is not his sister. So, we have a few things going on here that we see as problems."

6

This is exactly what I had feared. Ben has been plagued by nightmares of what happened to him and to us. He and Nicky have only been enrolled here a few weeks, and I thought being around other children would occupy his mind, keeping him engaged. But I see my son is dealing with the trauma the only way he knows how. And now, I've put us all at risk. "As you know, my children have been through a lot recently . . . with the loss of their father, the move. It's been a lot."

"Sure, of course," Chelsea continues, "but this was unusual. Ben has mentioned in the past that Nicky wasn't his sister, and I took that to mean he was still adjusting to having her in the family — being a baby, that made sense to me—"

"He's in therapy," I cut in, knowing that's a lie. "We're working through some things. I'll talk to him. I'll remind him that he's safe. Nicky's safe. And that we're all one family, despite the loss of his father."

The women trade uncomfortable glances, and I sense they want to unburden themselves with this problem. "Please, I was just hired at a law firm in town. This is my best shot at getting a fresh start with my children. I need this place. Ben loves it here. Nicky does, too. Can we please go on as we are, knowing I will continue to get Ben the help he needs?"

"Yes, of course," Brenda concedes. "We just needed to make you aware of the situation, and I'm certain you and Ben's doctors will get a handle on things." She looks at Chelsea. "I'll remind the staff to take a few extra precautions where Ben is concerned until he gets through this rough patch."

That's putting it mildly, but I don't press my luck. "Thank you, Brenda. Thank you so much. And Chelsea. I couldn't do this without you. Ben just adores you."

She smiles. "He's a great kid. And I hope your family continues to heal."

CHAPTER 2

I remind myself every day that I made the right choice. Even months after it all occurred, the decision haunts me. The constant feeling of having to look over my shoulder . . . It's all worth it. Nicky would have been left to the state. I couldn't let my husband's daughter grow up without knowing she had a brother. And I can't deny that a part of me, who has always wanted a baby girl, also wanted a piece of my late husband, no matter what he'd done.

"Mommy, it's time to leave."

I turn away from the coffee maker to find Ben with his backpack slung over his shoulder. "You're right, kiddo. I'll get Nicky, and we'll load up the car."

Ben is still in preschool. It lets out at midday, and a bus takes him to the daycare center, where Nicky gets dropped off every morning. Now that I've got a full-time job, that's where they'll stay for the foreseeable future.

It seems I've mitigated Brenda's concerns about Ben. Nothing has happened in the past two weeks since our talk. No doubt, part of that is due to their hypervigilance. I know my son needs help, and I'm ashamed to admit I haven't gotten him any. Not because of money, but because I don't know

8

what he'll say. Probably something similar to what he told Chelsea. But she's not a doctor who might see through my lies as I attempt to explain away my son's insistence about Nicky or what happened to them.

Her bedroom is down the hall from mine. I walk inside to find her standing in her crib, gripping the handrail and smiling at me. She's developing early, standing with some assistance at just six months. I'm certain Ben was seven or even eight months before he did that. She's the most perfect baby I've seen since Ben. Happy. Laughing all the time. I love her as if she were my own. I need it to stay that way.

"Good morning, sweetheart." I lift her out and get her dressed. Soon, we return to the living room, where Ben awaits us. "All right. Let's go." I snatch my laptop bag, tossing it over my shoulder, before grabbing the diaper bag. With full hands, I walk outside.

It's another warm day. The sun shines on us, a reminder of all we have to be grateful for. I look out over our street — a humble neighborhood with friendly people who don't ask a lot of questions. A far cry from Beaufort.

The neighbors offer polite nods when we cross paths, saying good morning or good night, as the case may be. No lurkers. No judging gazes. I suppose they're all too busy with their own lives to care much about anyone else's. It's the perfect place for us.

We load up and head out in the direction of the daycare. After I drop off the kids, I continue toward the office. Downtown Asheboro consists of about four blocks. All mom-and-pop stores, boutiques, flower shops. And then the Goddard Law Firm.

Tom doesn't have any partners and prefers it that way. I'm an associate, along with Renee and Brandon, who've been with Tom for a few years. Both are younger than me, and I admit, it's humbling. They're smart. Smarter than I remember being at their age. Then again, I didn't have much of a chance to advance my career before having Ben.

I've been with the firm for a few weeks now. This morning, I have a new client coming in. When I enter our small office, Lily offers a pleasant smile.

"Good morning, Evelyn. How are you?" she asks, her tone just as fresh as her face. With light blond hair worn stick-straight, and big brown eyes, she can't be more than twenty-three. I almost envy her youth. What I might have done at her age instead of what I did — hindsight being twenty-twenty and all that.

"Doing well, Lily. And you?" I walk through the lobby.

"Good, thanks for asking." She glances at her monitor. "Don't forget, you have that appointment in thirty minutes. Mrs. Crenshaw."

"Yep. I'm on it." I nod and continue through the hallway until I reach my office. The other doors are closed, so I assume Brandon and Renee have appointments as well. But I imagine Tom will pop in to ask me about this prospective new client.

I haven't made much effort to connect with my new co-workers. We won't have much in common, but I need to work at making a life here, and that means making friends. Even acquaintances.

For now, I am preparing for Mrs. Judy Crenshaw. I happened across her at the county clerk's office last week, overhearing her conversation. When she was leaving, I followed her out and asked if she'd like some new representation. Yes, it was a little underhanded, but lawyers are out for blood. It doesn't matter whose.

I settle in and prepare my files when Lily buzzes into my office.

"Ms. Moore, Mrs. Crenshaw is here to see you." Lily keeps it formal when in the presence of clients, which I can appreciate.

"Thank you. I'll come up." I get to my feet, tugging on my gray suit jacket as I walk back into the lobby.

I pass by a wall mirror on the way and double-check my hair. I recently cut it to my shoulders, and I'm still not sure I like it. I thought it would make me look more professional.

Instead, it makes me look a little dowdy. Derek used to love my long dark hair. He always told me the way it lightly covered my cheeks turned him on. I don't know about that because, well, I know others kept his motor running much more than I did.

I see a middle-aged woman sitting on one of the chairs as I enter the lobby. She's well-dressed, and her short blond hair is dyed but elegantly styled. In fact, given her Chanel suit, I'm inclined to believe she comes from money. Whether it's hers or her ex-husband's, I'll soon find out. "Mrs. Crenshaw," I say, hand extended. "It's so nice to see you again. Thank you for coming."

She rises and accepts my hand. "Well, Ms. Moore, you made a compelling argument. I do hope that wasn't the only tool in your shed."

"I assure you, I have plenty from which to choose. Why don't you follow me so we can talk in my office?" I start on, glancing at Lily. "Would you bring in a couple of bottles of water?"

"Of course," she replies.

I peer over my shoulder at my new client. "Mrs. Crenshaw, would you like a coffee?"

"No, thank you. Water is fine."

We arrive at my office, and I show her inside, closing the door behind me. "Take a seat, and we'll get started."

I return to my desk. "So, when we talked, you mentioned your divorce last year. And your current situation pertaining to the custody of your son and daughter."

With her perfect posture, she regards me. "That's right. It has been finalized. However, given present circumstances, I'd like to look at my options regarding obtaining sole custody."

"I see." I begin jotting down notes. "How old are your children?"

"My daughter is twelve. My son is ten."

I lay down my pen and fix my gaze on her. "As you know, I approached you last week after it seemed you were less

11

than pleased with the attorney who'd represented you in the divorce. So, the first thing I'll want to do is get the files from that firm and take a look at the current custody agreement. See what kind of wiggle room we have. And from there, we can meet up again and discuss your options."

"Well, that sounds like a solid plan, Evelyn. Thank you," she replies.

I sense there's more she wants to say, but I know when not to push. After a few moments of silence, I close my notebook. "For now, we'll draft the retainer agreement and get you scheduled for a follow-up appointment. The timing will depend on how quickly your previous attorney can send over your files. We'll go from there."

"I sincerely appreciate it." Mrs. Crenshaw gets to her feet. "I should've done this from the beginning, but I was trying to be cordial." She slings her bag over her shoulder. "It seems my ex-husband had other plans."

"I'm sorry to hear that, Mrs. Crenshaw," I say, showing her to the door.

"Please, call me Judy. Are you married, Evelyn?"

"Um, no. Not anymore." I open the door.

She winks and aims a finger gun at me on the way out. "Smart woman. I like you already."

I return to my desk, feeling confident Tom will be happy to take Judy Crenshaw's money when a notification appears on my laptop. It's a reminder to check the database for any changes or new information. This is how I control the narrative of my past.

The first few weeks after it all happened, I'd battled with Derek's family. They'd wanted custody of Ben, but I was never going to let that happen. Eventually, we'd agreed upon visits over holidays, when possible. 'When possible' being the key. They don't know about Nicole. If I'd told them, they would've insisted on full custody of her. After all, she's not my child, but she is Derek's. And a day will come when Ben tells them about her. I don't know what I'll do when that happens, and I try not to think about it.

See, the thing is, no one here knows Nicole isn't mine. Only three other people know the truth at all, and two of them are dead. The third? Josie Brewer would never say anything. She and I have an understanding, and neither of us wishes to change that.

Nicole's birth mother, and I hate to even mention her, had been living under an assumed name. Her family had disowned her. There will come a time, if it hasn't already, when Beaufort PD Detective Langston will uncover her true identity. DNA is a bitch. When that happens, her family will be notified. Will they care? Did they know about the baby? I have no idea. It's a Pandora's Box that has yet to open. A clock that ticks in the back of my mind, ready to detonate the bomb that could destroy my life.

CHAPTER 3

The scream startles me awake. "Ben." I jump out of bed and run to his bedroom. Flinging open the door, I see only the shape of him writhing beneath his covers.

"Mommy, Mommy!" he screams, eyes shut tight.

"It's okay, Benny. I'm here. I'm here." I rush to his bed, gripping his shoulders to offer comfort and to calm his body. Sweat clings to him. "Honey, you're safe. Mommy's here, and you're safe."

His screams turn into frightened moans. He clutches me, burying his head in my chest, sobbing.

"I know, baby. Everything's okay. It was just a dream, sweetheart. I promise it was just a dream." I smooth his dark hair that matches Derek's, pulling loose strands that cling to his face. His breathing begins to steady. His heartbeat returns to normal. "There you go. That's it. The bad dream is all gone now."

He pushes away, taking in my appearance, turning over my hands. I know what he's looking for. Blood. The blood he saw on me the night his father died.

"See? All okay."

"Can I sleep in your bed?" he asks.

"Of course, baby. Come on." I help him out of bed and take his hand. We walk into the hall. "Let me just check on Nicky, okay?"

He nods but refuses to let go of me, so we walk into her room together. Moonlight spills in through the window, scattering hazy light over her crib. I can't believe she slept through all that noise.

"Is she okay, Mommy?" Ben asks.

I turn to him and whisper, "She's okay. All right, baby, let's get you into bed, and we can both go back to sleep."

We continue toward my bedroom and climb under the covers. He pushes up next to me. "Get some sleep, baby. I love you."

"I love you too, Mommy."

I caress his hair while he closes his eyes. This isn't the first time he's had this nightmare, and I doubt it will be the last. What he remembers, I can't be sure. The blood on my hands — yes. The fact that his father died? Yes.

But he never mentions her name — Summer. Not once since that night. The way she'd used him as a shield, covering his mouth so he wouldn't scream.

I try not to think about it, but the images worm through my brain. And now tears prick my eyes. Ben needs help — the kind of help I can't give him. I'd hoped the nightmares would subside, yet they grow in frequency and intensity. And with the incidents at the daycare, I wonder, if it happens again, will they call me, or will they call the authorities and have him taken away?

He's mostly a happy, friendly boy, but if I don't get him help, the bad dreams will eat away at that wonderful personality, turning him into someone I won't recognize. Someone I may even fear, who will give away all our secrets.

So, whose future am I willing to sacrifice? My son's or my daughter's?

* * *

15

I've taken precautions. Every day, I search for new information. Missing persons' reports. News articles. I take nothing for granted, and I prepare for the worst. It's all I can do. I don't want to move again, dragging the kids away from friends and schools, but I will if I have to. I won't lose my family.

My phone buzzes, startling me out of my thoughts. I answer the call. "Evelyn Moore, how may I help you?"

"Ms. Moore, this is Wes Parker, Judy Crenshaw's divorce attorney, returning your call."

"Oh, yes, hello." I need to stay focused. I can't afford to lose this job for many reasons. "Thank you for calling me back."

"Of course. I do have the files you requested, but I'm afraid you'll have to come and collect them. I'd send a courier, but as Mrs. Crenshaw is no longer a client, I have no one to bill for the delivery costs."

"I understand. Yes, of course, I can pick them up. If you text me your address, I'll run out this morning."

"Sending it to you now. Have a good day, Ms. Moore. And, uh . . . good luck."

The line goes dead. "Good luck? I don't like the sound of that."

Never mind. I need to get some billable hours of my own, so I prepare to head out. As I enter the lobby, I set my sights on Lily. "I'm running out to pick up my new client's files if anyone's looking."

"Okay. See you later," she says with a smile.

As I step outside, I notice a nip in the morning air. It's cooler than it's been lately, and I can tell it's spring because my allergies are kicking into high gear. I climb behind the wheel of my car and retrieve directions for the address the lawyer texted. The map says it'll take twenty minutes to get to his office. Lucky for me, he's in the next town over. I don't need the other two firms in Asheboro knowing I'm poaching clients, even if I'm not — technically.

The smell of coffee seeps into the car — a delicious aroma, which I noticed outside too. I gaze up at the café a few doors down. "I wouldn't mind a cup for the road." I step out again and head over, opening the door to a blast of warm air.

The smiling barista greets me. "Good morning. We'll be right with you."

"Good morning." I get in line behind three others. As I gaze at the menu above, wondering whether also to get a bite to eat, the glass door opens with a woosh, and a man enters. I glance over my shoulder.

He stands in line behind me. I keep my eyes ahead, ignoring his woodsy fragrance that conjures an image of a remote cabin and a handsome lodger motioning me inside. As I try to keep from smiling at my overactive imagination, I do my best to decide what to order.

"Hmm, I wonder what's good here," he asks no one in particular.

But since I'm standing in front of him, I should probably reply. "I come here all the time. Everything's great. You can't go wrong." I only casually glance back at him.

"Thanks. I appreciate it."

The line moves along at a snail's pace. No one in this town ever seems to be in a hurry. The man moves in close behind me, his scent growing more fragrant.

I glance back at him again. He's still peering at the menu, arms folded, brow creased, as though focusing all his efforts on making a decision. I lean back and whisper. "If you're still undecided, I'd stick with the basics. Plain ol' coffee. Always a safe bet."

His smile is disarming. "Black coffee it is."

We lock eyes for a moment too long, and my heart flutters. Yes, flutters, like a twenty-year-old girl. I'm no novice when it comes to men, but I can't remember the last time that happened to me.

He leans forward, almost too close, but I don't flinch. "What's your name?"

"Evelyn." Never mind how he's making me feel at this moment, I remain guarded, as always.

"Evelyn." He smiles. "It's nice to meet you. I'm Tyler."

"Ma'am? Would you like to order?" The woman behind the counter pulls me from his gaze. "Ma'am?" she asks again.

"Oh, sorry. Yes, I'd like a Grande half-caf latte with skim milk, please."

She keys in my order and then puts her pen to my paper cup. "And your name?"

"Evelyn," Tyler cuts in. "I'll have the same." He reaches for his wallet.

I raise a preemptive hand. "It's fine. You don't have to . . ."

He's already handing over his credit card. "I know I don't have to, Evelyn. I want to."

We step away from the counter and stand beside each other. I don't know what to say, and an awkward silence settles between us.

"Evelyn?" The server holds out two paper cups.

Tyler collects them and hands one to me. "Here you go."

"Thank you again, really. That was very sweet." I thumb back. "I — uh — should head out. I have an appointment."

He tips his head. "Sure thing. Maybe I'll see you around?"

I'm already at the door. "Yeah, maybe."

CHAPTER 4

I'm late again. It's the second time this week. Fourth this month. I don't know how many more times the daycare will overlook my tardiness. It's not like they don't already have enough cause to kick out my kids. A client meeting took longer than expected, and so here I am, racing through town to pick them up before the daycare closes.

No one tells you how hard it is being a mother — working or staying at home. Let alone a single mother. All prove difficult in their own ways. But now I've experienced all of the above, the stress of a working single parent can be overwhelming at times.

I make the turn into the parking lot as the sun drops behind the building. It's past dinnertime, and both kids will be starving. Nicky is on solid foods now, and I can hardly keep up with her appetite. Ben, well, he's a growing boy and devours everything I put in front of him.

There she is. Brenda Hall. She's standing just behind the double glass doors, Nicky on her hip, Ben next to her. She doesn't look happy. I park in front of the building and rush inside.

"Hi, Brenda, I'm so, so sorry I'm late again." I immediately take Nicky from her.

"Evelyn, I understand the demands of your job, but I can't keep allowing this to happen. I have a family, too. They demand as much of me as your family does of you."

"Yes, I know. It won't happen again, I promise you." I probably shouldn't have promised, knowing I can't be sure I'll keep it.

She purses her lips, and the look on her face reminds me of my mother. It's a look I'm sure I'll find useful when my two are teenagers. Nevertheless, I understand her frustration, especially considering the extra care they've taken with Ben. "Please, Brenda, I have no place else for them to go."

"Then please work on timely pickups, Evelyn. If you can't, then you will have to find other arrangements."

"Yes, of course. Thank you again." I reach down for Ben's hand. "Let's go home, buddy." As we step outside and head to the car, she calls out to me.

"Oh, there was something I wanted to mention."

"I stop to look back. "Yes?"

"I'd like to discuss your progress with Ben's doctors. It seems we had a minor incident today. Nothing critical, but in light of our previous discussions, it bears following up."

I freeze, blinking hard, searching my mind for how to respond. How many more times can I repeat the lie? How much longer before they stop believing me? "Yes, I understand. I'm happy to bring you up to speed." I look down at Ben. He's not paying me any attention. Instead, he keeps tugging on the door handle, asking to be let inside.

"We'll schedule it for next week, as your work allows," Brenda replies. "Goodnight, Evelyn."

"Goodnight, Brenda. And thank you, again, for your understanding." I finish loading the kids inside and climb behind the wheel. Brenda is turning off the lights in the lobby, preparing to leave. I've dodged a bullet, or rather, postponed it.

As we head home, I peer at Ben through the rearview mirror. "How was your day, buddy?"

"Fine," he says.

"What did you do at school?"

"Nothing."

Something is definitely off with him. I want to ask him what happened today, but I'm afraid. I know I'm not handling this the right way, but it's the best I can do for now, or so I tell myself. "Well, how about, when we get home, we make some pizza for dinner?"

His eyes light up. "We're going to make it?"

"Sure. That'll be fun, won't it?"

"Yeah, that sounds fun."

I peer at the road ahead. The dusky light makes it difficult to see where the landscape ends and the road begins. Streetlights flicker on as I turn into our neighborhood, and then our home comes into view at the end of the cul-de-sac.

I get the kids inside, feeling guilty that they'll be eating dinner late tonight. But who am I kidding? It's not the first time and probably won't be the last. However, the more pressing concern is Ben.

As I see it, I can leave it alone and hope for the best. Hope he doesn't remember all the horrors of that night and how Nicky came into our lives. Or I can plant my version of events in his mind and pray that, in time, they become his version, too. Because if they don't, I could lose them both.

CHAPTER 5

We had fun last night, Ben and me — making pizzas, dancing in the kitchen, and playing with Nicky. We behaved like a normal family, and it reminded me of just how important it is to do everything in my power to keep it that way.

I take nothing for granted, and as I sit at my desk this morning, I again check for any news about Riley Dittrich. I have to assume her family has been found and contacted. And maybe that's a good thing because no one has contacted me, meaning they don't know about Nicky. That's the notion I'll cling to for as long as I can.

It's been more than three months. With each passing day, I grow more relieved, safe in the knowledge that no one has yet come for her. But as I said, I take nothing for granted.

I hear a knock on my office door. "Come in." Lily walks inside. "Hi."

"Sorry to bother you, Evelyn," she says.

"It's no bother. What's up?" I ask, always pleasant, always appearing as though I have nothing to hide.

"There's a gentleman out front asking for you."

I tilt my head. "A client?"

"No, he says he met you at the coffee shop yesterday. His name is—"

"Tyler," I say, cutting her off.

"That's right. So you know him?" she asks.

"I do. Sort of." I rise from behind the desk. "Did he say what he wanted?"

"Just that he wants to talk to you." Lily glances over her shoulder. "Should I tell him to go pound sand?"

I chuckle, surprised Lily is familiar with that particular idiom. "No, no, it's fine. I'll come up."

"Okay." She walks away, leaving my door open.

I don't know whether to be flattered or frightened, though my pragmatic side warns me to stay alert. To be fair, the café is only two doors down. He could've used the process of elimination to find me. Still, we'll see.

As I arrive in the lobby, he's standing near the window, peering out. "Tyler?" I ask as if I don't know it's him.

He turns around, and his face lights up. "Evelyn. So you do work here." He shrugs. "I took a shot in the dark."

"You have pretty good aim." I glance at Lily, who appears glued to our conversation, blinking and smiling as if watching a romantic comedy, and this is the meet-cute. "Can I help you with something?" I ask him.

"Uh, well, not exactly." He moves toward me, hands in the pockets of his dark jeans, glancing sideways at Lily.

"Why don't we talk in my office?" I say, quickly realizing this isn't a conversation to be had out in the open. I turn to Lily. "Would you mind holding my calls for a few minutes?"

"Of course." She flicks her gaze between us, still smiling.

"Great, thank you." I turn back to him. "Right this way." He walks beside me, but we say nothing. I'm still not sure what to make of this, but after our exchange yesterday, I have an idea of where this is headed. "Come on in. Have a seat."

He walks inside. "Thanks. I didn't come at a bad time, did I?"

"Not at all." I close the door and walk around to my desk. "Can I get you some water or coffee?"

"Uh, no, thanks." He sits down. "Listen, I'm sure you didn't expect to see me here—"

"No, I didn't," I reply, smiling but with a furrowed brow.

"I promise you, I'm not a stalker," he says, raising his hands in surrender. "I'm looking at leasing the building across the street, which was why I was in the area yesterday. And then this morning, I came back and happened to see your car out front. I assumed this was where you worked."

It takes a moment to run through yesterday's encounter. How does he know my car? Then I remember that he watched me get inside it. "A building lease?" I ask. "What kind of work do you do?"

"I'm an accountant."

He doesn't look like an accountant. In fact, he looks more like a home improvement show host — rugged and charming, who knows how to swing a hammer.

"I'm looking to move my office. Right now, it's too far outside of the downtown district," he adds. "I think that if I move locations, it could open the doors for new clients."

"Seems like a good idea," I reply. "So you noticed my car outside?"

He lowers his gaze, but a crooked smile appears on his face. "I did. I hope it's okay that I'm here." He returns his attention to me. "I don't know, but I sort of felt a connection to you yesterday. I got the feeling it wasn't one-sided."

Now, I'm red-faced. "Well, I guess it wasn't." I know better. This is not the time to explore anything even remotely resembling a relationship.

"You think maybe we could get dinner sometime?" His gaze now locks onto mine for a moment before briefly sliding down to my ring finger.

It's just a glance, but it reminds me of my past. The betrayal I'd suffered. I want to be happy again, maybe even find love again — one day. But how can I let the past go so quickly? The answer is, I can't.

So I'm condemned to a life alone? Is that it?

His brow creases a little, like he's wondering why I'm not answering him. He sees nothing of my inner turmoil. If he did, he'd run away — fast.

It's just dinner. It's *just* dinner.

"I'd like that." *Damn it.* "Fair warning, though, that my schedule can be hectic. I have a family."

"But you're not, uh—"

"Married?" I interrupt. "No. I do have children."

"I love kids," he says before seeming to realize the over-zealous response. "I mean, I understand the responsibilities involved with having kids, even though I have none of my own."

"Great. Okay, well, how about we exchange numbers and see what happens?" Exactly. We just see what happens. No pressure. No big deal.

He nods and flashes a smile that sends my pulse racing. "Perfect."

CHAPTER 6

It's been twelve years since I've been on a date. And I'm still second-guessing my decision. I've been so wrapped up in the past and protecting the future that I haven't thought about opening my heart to anyone. But at some point, there must again be trust. Will it be with Tyler? It's much too early to tell. And I remind myself yet again — this is just dinner.

Getting a sitter was the easy part. A few of the younger women who work at the daycare also babysit as a side hustle. And I trust them. I've seen how good they are with Ben and Nicky. It's a huge load off my mind. Chelsea accepted my request, and I couldn't be happier. It's no coincidence. She's already familiar with Ben's issues, so I thought she was the safest bet.

As I put on my makeup, that little voice in my head keeps telling me this is a mistake. That it's too soon. It's only been three months. It'll end badly. But I can't deny the instant attraction Tyler and I both felt.

I shake out of my thoughts, focusing instead on getting ready for tonight. It's just dinner — a notion I repeat *ad nauseam*. I'm putting too much pressure on myself over this. Besides, Tyler might turn out to be a jerk, and all this worry will have been over nothing.

A knock echoes from the front door. Chelsea's here. I head downstairs to find Ben playing with Nicki as she sways gently in the motorized swing. I'd gotten rid of all Ben's baby things after it became clear more kids weren't in the cards for Derek and me. So, I had to buy it all again.

As I open the door, Chelsea is standing on the other side. At just twenty and a little on the plain side, she is also putting herself through college, which she attends at night. "Hey, Chelsea, thanks for coming over."

"Of course. Happy to. Your kids are amazing. We'll have a lot of fun."

She walks in, and before I get a chance to close the door, Ben wraps his arms around Chelsea's slim waist.

"Yay. Hi, Miss Chelsea," he says.

"Hey, Ben." She pats his head. "Are we going to have fun tonight?"

"Yeah."

I check the time. "Why don't you go and get settled in? Nicky's in her swing in the living room. I'm just touching up my hair and will be leaving soon."

"Great, thanks." Chelsea and Ben head off while I return upstairs to finish getting ready.

My phone rests on the bathroom vanity, and I see it light up. It's a message from Tyler. He'll be arriving a little early at the restaurant. "Well, guess I'd better hurry." I text him back that I'm heading out the door, even though I won't be leaving for another few minutes.

He'd offered to come here and pick me up, but that's a step too far. I won't risk him knowing where I live or meeting my children. Too much is at stake for me to repeat old patterns.

I rush downstairs and grab a light sweater. The evening air still has a chill to it. "I'm heading out." As I enter the living room, Ben smiles at me while they all play a game. "Everything good? You have what you need, Chelsea?"

"Yes, ma'am. Go and have a good time. Don't worry about us. We'll be fine."

"All right." I lean down to kiss Ben's head. "Night, buddy. Be good for Chelsea."

"I will."

I kiss Nicky on her soft little cheek. "Night, sweetheart." As I start away, I turn back to Chelsea. "I won't be late."

"Don't worry. Have fun tonight," she replies.

"I'll try."

CHAPTER 7

Chelsea

I volunteered to babysit Ben — not for the extra cash, but because I needed to understand why he says that Nicky isn't his sister, why he insists on trying to keep her quiet. Something about the way he says it freaks me out. So, I'm here to get to the bottom of it.

Evelyn trusts me. If there is something in this house that points to the truth, she won't have bothered hiding it because she thinks I'm just some college kid, too selfish to care about anything other than myself. Maybe part of that is true, but this feels different. This feels — darker.

The kids are finally settled. Nicky is asleep in her crib. Ben is in his bed, covers pulled up to his chin.

We played games and I fed them dinner. He interacted with me as he always does, happy and engaged. But parents are great at projecting shit onto their kids. And I've seen a side to him that forces me to dig deeper.

Once I'm sure both kids are down for the night, I start my search. It's not snooping, I tell myself. It's . . . concerned babysitting. Some people should never become parents. They ruin their kids with lies about who they are and what the world is. Some are cruel and selfish, only having kids to satisfy their egos. What I intend to find out is whether Evelyn is hiding some horrific truth about Nicky, a truth Ben seems to at least be partially aware of.

Evelyn's bedroom is my first stop. The room is immaculate to a fault. The bed is neatly made, and the nightstands are practically bare. I open the drawers carefully, expecting . . . I don't know what. A hidden diary containing a confession? A stack of disturbing Polaroids? I know how this seems. Still, something pricks the back of my mind, telling me to keep looking.

But all I find are neatly folded clothes and a lavender pouch that smells like her perfume. I close the drawers and move on, checking the closet and even peeking under the bed. If she has something to hide, she's not keeping it there.

I search the rest of the house. The living room, the hall closet — it all screams, "I've got nothing to hide." No signs of dysfunction or hidden family secrets. Standing inside the kitchen, I notice the door that leads to the garage. I open it, and a light flickers on. I walk down the steps, the cold of the concrete seeping through my socked feet.

Along the side wall are several boxes. As I approach them, it becomes clear what they contain. Written in black marker in capital letters is the name "Derek." I already know he is Ben and Nicky's father, who recently passed. The boxes are taped shut.

I stare at them, wondering how he died. After all, he was probably around Evelyn's age. He probably didn't die of natural causes. Ben must have some knowledge, but do I have it in me to ask? To put him through that?

What I want is to find paperwork, specifically about Nicky. How the hell do I do that, though? There must be something here among these boxes. "Where did you come from?" I know they're new here. Maybe I can work with that.

I return inside and walk upstairs again, checking in on Ben to see that he's asleep. When I peek into his room, I notice his eyes open, even in the darkness. "Hey, Ben. How about I tuck you in?" I say, trying to comfort him.

As I walk to his bed, I see a sweater hanging over one of the bedposts. I pick it up and walk to the closet to hang it. Inside, I notice a stuffed tiger on the shelf. This will make him feel better and help him sleep. What kid doesn't want to cuddle up with a soft plush tiger? I pull it down and walk back to him. "Is this yours?"

The moment he sees it, Ben bolts upright in bed. His face twists into something that looks like fear . . . "No! No, put it back!" he shouts, his voice breaking.

I freeze, the tiger dangling in my hand. "Ben, it's just a stuffed animal. What's wrong, buddy?"

"Put it back!" he screams again, his voice full of panic.

I step closer, holding it out for him to get a better look. "Ben, it's okay. Look, it's just a toy—"

"It's not!" He cuts me off. "It has blood on it."

"What?" I rock back on my heels. Blood? On a stuffed animal? I look at the tiger. Its faded fur and glassy eyes seem perfectly normal. "Ben, honey, there's no blood on this."

He shakes his head violently, pulling the covers up over his face. "I don't want it. Mommy was supposed to throw it away."

"Okay," I whisper. "I'll put it back." I back away from the bed, the tiger still clutched in my hand. The fear in Ben's eyes is real, and it's terrifying. I place the tiger back on the shelf. Ben's body relaxes, but his eyes stay fixed on me, watching my every move.

I return to him, pulling up the covers as he lies back down. "It's okay, Ben. Nothing's going to hurt you. You're safe. I promise," I whisper.

As I turn off the light and step into the hallway, I can feel his gaze burning into the back of my head. Maybe I don't want to know what's really going on in this house.

But who am I kidding? This just tells me I have to look harder.

31

CHAPTER 8

Evelyn

We've been waiting for our table for almost an hour. Soft amber lighting shimmers off the elegant chandeliers. Voices murmur. Glasses clink. For a moment, I forget who I am and what I've done.

Tyler sips on his glass of wine. "I'm so sorry about this. I made a reservation."

"It's okay," I reply. "I don't mind sitting at the bar, enjoying a drink." That is true, except I have a babysitter who I'm paying handsomely for.

His gaze roams over me. "Have I told you yet how great you look?"

"You have." I laugh. "But it's always nice to hear."

He glances back at the hostess station. "They keep telling me it'll only be a few more minutes."

"I'm sure it will. Like I said, I don't mind waiting." It's a nice restaurant, expensive. So are the people here. "I'm in no rush."

"How about I order another one?" Tyler asks, leaning on the sleek, polished stone bar top.

"That'd be great," I reply.

"Okay." He turns to the bartender. "We'll have another round here, please." He sets his sights on me again. "So, you managed to get a sitter without too much trouble?"

"I did, yes. The kids go to a daycare center, and some of the workers moonlight as babysitters."

"Oh, that's nice. So you already know and trust them," he replies.

"I do." He hands me the glass of wine. "Thank you." The chatter around us fills the emptiness of our conversation. I'd forgotten how awkward these things can be — dates, if I dare call it that. "How long have you been an accountant?"

"Since college," he replies. "Graduated. Got my CPA license, and here I am."

I raise the glass to my lips, peering over the rim. "And you enjoy it?"

A smirk spreads on his lips. "Does that surprise you?"

I shrug. "A little. Then again, I'm a lawyer."

"Excuse me, but that sounds far more exciting than crunching numbers." He swirls the golden-brown whiskey in his glass.

"You'd be surprised."

We continue making idle chit-chat when the hostess finally garners Tyler's attention. "Sir, your table is ready."

We follow her back and take a seat at the table for two. It's draped in white linen with a single rose floating in a small vase with two tea lights on either side of it.

My guard remains high, no matter how he looks at me. I'm careful not to reveal too much as we continue our surface-level conversation. And I'm careful not to ask personal questions of him that could require a mirrored response from me. Navigating this dinner date is harder than I expected.

"How long have you been with your firm?" he asks.

Definitive timelines are something I try to avoid, so I answer as vaguely as possible. "Just a few weeks. I only recently passed the bar exam here in Pennsylvania, so I'm a relative newbie."

"I see." He shakes out his white linen napkin and lays it across his lap. "Did you practice somewhere else before?"

"No. Not since my son was born," I reply, wading into waters I don't want to drown in, so I think a change of topic is in order. "What about you? Sounds like your business is expanding with this prospective new lease. That's exciting."

He grunts. "Not really. Don't get me wrong, I'm happy for the work, but I prefer crunching other people's numbers, not my own. It's a big investment and I'm still a little leery."

"I can understand that." He hasn't asked me where I'm from, and I hope to keep the question off his tongue. The best way to do that is to keep the conversation focused on him.

"Is your children's father in the picture?" he asks, raising a hand. "Forgive me if that's too personal. I guess, since we're out together, I assume your separation or divorce is behind you."

I spoke too soon. "My husband passed away a while ago."

"Oh . . . Oh, I'm so sorry. You — you don't have to go into it."

"Good. I hadn't planned to," I say, following it up with a smile that I'm sure he sees through. But he doesn't press.

The evening winds down, and when the bill arrives, I take out a credit card from my wallet. As I'm about to set it on the table, he places his hand over mine.

"Please . . . I'd like to take care of this. After all, I asked you out."

"I don't know." I glance away. "I'd feel better—"

"I'll tell you what. If you agree to go out with me again, I'll insist you pay. In fact, I'll be sure to leave my wallet at home so I don't change my mind. How's that?"

I smile despite my best efforts. "Okay. I guess that would be all right. Thank you."

He leads us out and ushers me to my car. The air has turned colder, and I rub my arms for warmth. "I enjoyed tonight. Very much."

"Me, too, Evelyn." He places his arm around me, and my breath catches in my throat.

"You okay?"

"Yeah, of course." I carry on, uncomfortable yet undeniably stirred by our proximity. His cologne lingers, and his breath is laced with a hint of whiskey and wine.

"You'll be okay to drive?" he asks, glossing over my initial hesitation.

"Oh, yeah, I'll be fine," I reply. "I don't take unnecessary risks when I have children who depend on me."

We arrive at my car, and I press the remote to unlock it.

"I don't doubt that you're an amazing mother." He gently turns my shoulders until we're square in each other's gaze before he leans in, placing a light kiss on my cheek. "I had a great time tonight. Good night, Evelyn."

"I had fun, too. Good night." I watch him walk to his car parked down a few spaces. He turns back and waves. I'm a little embarrassed he caught me still looking, but I wave back. Finally, I climb inside and press the ignition.

I still feel his touch, the peck on the cheek, sweet and gentle. Undemanding of anything. But I won't be fooled as I have been in the past. I know better now, and I will take precautions.

CHAPTER 9

Far-off cries rip me from my sleep, and I bolt up in bed. I'm thrust back to that night, back to the terror, but I shake out of it, taking in my surroundings. "You're home. You're safe." A sentiment I often have to remind myself of. So, what is the source of this wailing? Is it Nicky? No. No, it's Ben. "Not again, please."

I rise to my feet, woozy from the brutal awakening as blood rushes from my head. He screams again, a gut-wrenching, horrific sound that raises goosebumps on my arms. "I'm coming, baby. I'm coming." I hurry to his room and find him flailing around in bed. "Benny, sweetheart. You're okay."

At his side, I grip his shoulders to steady him. I've learned from the first few times that he can easily hurt himself. A bump on his head. A bruise on his arm. "Honey, wake up. It's just a dream. Mommy's here." These are words I have spoken many times before.

It seems to dawn on him as he captures my gaze with wild eyes, searching for whether I am who I say. "It's me, baby. It was just another bad dream." I place my hand on his chest to help slow his breathing. Taking breaths with him. In and out. In and out. "That's good, sweetheart. You're okay."

He grabs my hands, examining them as he has before. And then I know for certain what he dreamed — the same nightmare that tortures his sleep. God knows what other havoc it inflicts on him during the day.

Again, he buries his head in my chest, sobbing. My heart breaks. Tears fill my eyes. I don't know how much longer I can let him suffer like this. I thought they'd go away, and maybe they still will, but when? When he no longer recognizes dreams from reality? When he looks at me and only sees his father's blood on my hands? When he realizes Nicky is not his sister at all but the child of a woman I murdered?

I gently push him back a moment. "I'm going to get a washcloth, okay? I'll be right back." His grip on me remains tight. "I promise. I'm coming right back." It slowly loosens, and I slip away to the bathroom.

I close the door and turn on the light, barely able to contain my emotions. Tears fall freely as guilt slices through my chest. Turning on the faucet, I dampen a washcloth with warm water and press it against my cheeks to settle my emotions. He can't see me rattled. Rinsing it off, I run the cloth under cool water and return to Ben's room.

"Okay, baby. Let's get you settled back in, okay?" I crawl in beside him, placing the cloth over his forehead. "There. Doesn't that feel better?"

He nods almost imperceptibly.

I do my best to soothe his heated face and damp skin. "How about I stay in here with you? Do you want Mommy to stay?"

"Yes." His tiny voice stammers.

"Okay, baby. I'll stay." I lie down, pulling the covers over both of us, squeezed together on his tiny single bed. But I don't care. He needs me. Even if I don't get another wink of sleep for the rest of the night, I won't leave his side.

I can do at least that much for him. The rest? Getting him the help he needs? It's a decision that must be made, or my little boy will disappear into himself, and he'll be lost to me forever.

* * *

This delicate balance is tilting too far in one direction. That direction is the undoing of my son. When I left him at school this morning and he looked back at me, what I saw in his eyes was nothing short of dread. Will it pass as he plays with his friends and forgets all about his dream? Maybe. But it doesn't change the fact that when it happens again — and it will happen again — he may not recover as quickly.

The tug of war in my mind continues as I arrive at the office. Something will have to be done. I just have to figure out how to do it so as not to destroy all our lives.

"Morning, Lily," I say as I enter the lobby.

"Good morning." Her gaze narrows as it follows me. "You're not going to say how the date went?"

I'd told her only because she dragged it out of me. I stop in my tracks and face her. "It went well. Thanks for asking. He's a very nice man."

"How nice?" she asks, her tone laced with interest. "Did you two . . . you know . . ."

"What?" I squint and pull back. "No, of course not."

She raises her hands. "All right. All right. I was just asking." A moment later, she props her chin on her hands. "Are you at least going out again?"

The conversation, while incredibly intrusive, feels light and fun. It helps pull me out of my own head for a moment. "I think so. No pressure, though."

"Well, he might think differently," she adds.

"What do you mean?"

Lily tosses a casual gaze toward the hall. "You should go to your office."

"And what will I find in there?"

She shrugs while her lips curl into a smile. "Guess you'll have to wait and see."

"All right." I walk into the hall and arrive at my office at the end. The light is already on, and when I enter, a dozen red roses in a beautiful vase wait for me on my desk. "Oh, boy." A card lies nestled between the stems, wedged on a plastic stick.

Last night was amazing. You're amazing. I want to see you again and the sooner the better.

I lean into the fragrant roses, inhaling their sweet aroma. "See?"

Spinning around, I see Lily. "These were delivered this morning?"

"He dropped them off, actually," she replies. "I'd only just arrived to open the office. Enjoy." Lily winks at me before heading back to her desk.

Renee appears at my door. The bright, young attorney could probably work circles around me. And she's gorgeous. Long brown hair, slim, a face that belongs in magazines. It makes me wonder what she's doing here in this small town, at this even smaller law firm.

"Oh." She crosses her arms and leans against my door. "What's with the flowers?"

I grin, eyeing the floor in mild embarrassment. "I had a date last night. No big deal."

She raises her thick brows. "Looks like he feels differently, huh?"

"Maybe."

Renee clicks her tongue. "See you later, lucky girl."

I admit the flowers are beautiful, but I remind myself not to get carried away by his kind gestures. So I dive into my work. I have a new client — Judy Crenshaw. A new custody case. Focusing on this life I'm building for my family is the only thing that matters.

"Evelyn?" Lily's voice crackles through my desk phone. "Yes?"

"Mrs. Crenshaw is here for your appointment."

"Yes, of course." I glance at the time, not realizing it had gone by so quickly. "Can you go ahead and send her in, please?"

"Sure can." The line goes quiet.

I move the flowers to the top of my file cabinet on the far wall. "I'll deal with you later." As I return to my desk, the door opens, and Lily shows in my client. "Good morning, Mrs. Crenshaw."

"Now, Evelyn, I think you know to call me Judy."

"Absolutely." I gesture to the guest chair. "Please take a seat, Judy." Lily has already made her exit. I sit down again and open her file. "As you know, your former attorney has been cooperative, and I now have your previous case files."

"So, what do you think?" Judy asks. "Do I have a leg to stand on, or is that son of a bitch going to get to keep his kids three nights a week?"

I want to ask her why she wouldn't want her husband to share custody and be part of his children's lives, but after reading the divorce proceedings, I have some understanding of her actions. Regardless, understanding does nothing to help. I need proof I can take to a judge that shows her ex-husband's involvement in their kids' lives is harmful to them. It's a tough row to hoe.

"Can you give me some ammunition?" I ask. "Something I can take to the judge to bolster your case?"

She crosses her long legs draped in flowy ivory pants and rests her arms on the chair. "How much time you got?"

I hear her out and take my notes. She might have some legal standing, but not as much as I'd hoped. "Well, Judy, I think this will help me build your case. I'll file the paperwork tomorrow and see what we can do about a custody hearing date." I rise, offering my hand. "I'll do what I can for you."

"I know you will, Evelyn, I really do." She shakes my hand and eyes me. "If this was you and your kids, would you be going about this the same way?"

I raise the corner of my lips into a smile. "Judy, if I were you, I'd be doing exactly the same thing. Trust me, there's nothing I won't do for my kids."

CHAPTER 10

Chelsea

I sit with Ben in the lobby behind the front desk, bouncing Nicky on my knee. Brenda is closing down the center. The other kids have already gone home, leaving me to keep them both entertained. Evelyn texted that she was running late once again. Brenda isn't happy. As for me? It only raises my suspicions further.

"Ben, can I ask you something?"

He doesn't look at me. He just keeps drawing on a piece of paper I gave him. "Okay."

"Where did you live before you moved here?"

His crayon stops mid-spiral, and for a moment, I think I've lost him. Then he shrugs. "A house."

"Did you like it there?" I press. "Were you happy?"

He shrugs again, his movements appearing forced. "I guess."

"What about Nicky? Was she there too?"

This time, his hand tightens on the crayon, his knuckles turning white. He stares at the paper for a long moment before finally looking up at me. "We didn't have her then."

I think back to the timing. Nicky is six months old. I know they haven't lived in Asheboro for very long, so where was Nicky in this other house? "What do you mean, Ben? She wasn't born yet?"

He shakes his head, his little face twisting. "She's not. She's just . . . she's not."

"Ben, is there something I should know? You can tell me anything. Anything at all about your mommy or daddy . . ."

He doesn't answer. Instead, he drops the crayon and folds his arms on the table, burying his face in them. "I don't want to talk," he mumbles.

"I'm very sorry your daddy isn't here anymore," I say, knowing I've crossed a line, but I can't stop myself.

"Daddy got hurt and died," he says. "Mommy saved us."

Saved us. What does he mean by that? I'm terrified to push him, but I have to know. "What was your daddy's name?"

"Daddy," he replies.

I nod, the corner of my lips raising into a smile. Of course, that's the answer I should expect from a five-year-old. "Your mommy says you sometimes go talk to a doctor and tell them how much you miss your daddy. Does that help you?"

He looks at me, furrowing his brow in confusion. "I don't have a doctor. And Mommy says I should only talk to *her* about Daddy when I'm feeling bad."

"Oh." I sit back, swallowing hard. So, Evelyn's lying to Brenda. Why? Why would she do that? I look at the computer in front of me. It would only take a minute to look up her file. Maybe Ben's records are there . . . preschool, medical. I know for a fact we require the name of the primary care doctor. No way they'd tell me anything. But . . . at least I'd have some background, and that could be enough.

CHAPTER 11

Evelyn

Once again, I barely managed to pick up the kids on time today. When I arrived with two minutes to spare before closing, the stern look on Brenda's face suggested she'd had about enough. Well, with respect, so have I. Unfortunately, I have no high ground in this particular situation, and I suspect Brenda knows that. In the legal world, that's called having one's balls in a vice — not to put too fine a point on it. I chuckle.

"What's funny, Mommy?" Ben asks from the back seat.

"Nothing, sweetie. Just thinking." I glance at Nicky as she chats to herself in her carrier. She's getting more vocal with each passing day. Ben seems better than he was this morning. I hope that's a good sign.

My phone rings, and I glance at the name on the screen. I'm hesitant to answer with the kids in the car, but he did send me flowers, which I have yet to thank him for. I press the button on my steering wheel. "Hello?"

"Hi there, Evelyn. How are you?" Tyler asks.

"Doing well. I'm so sorry I didn't call you today. I-I want to thank you for the flowers, though. They were gorgeous."

"I'm glad you liked them. And it's no problem. I understand all too well how the day can get away from you."

The headlights from an approaching car shine in my rearview. I squint. "Jeez."

"Everything all right?" he asks.

"Yeah, sorry. Some guy behind me has his brights on or something." I shift the mirror to reduce the glare. "So listen, I've got my kids with me at the moment—"

"Oh, man. I'm so sorry. I should've asked. Of course you do."

My attention is drawn again to the rearview mirror. "What in the world?" The lights are coming up on me quickly. I check my speed, wondering if I'm driving too slowly, but I'm going just over the speed limit. Then, I check to see if I can change lanes. It's probably best to get out of this idiot's way.

"Evelyn, are you all right?"

I flip on my turn signal and prepare to move over. "Yeah, I'm fine. It's this person behind me. I'm changing lanes." As I enter the slower lane, the vehicle moves behind me again. "Uh, Tyler, I'll have to call you back." I want him off the line in the event I need to call the police.

"You sure you're okay? You sound worried," he replies.

"I'm fine. I'll talk to you later." I end the call, keeping an eye on my rearview. I glance back at the kids. They don't seem to notice my rising alarm. I'm sure it's nothing. Everything's fine. No need to get worked up. Just go home.

I press on the gas to gain some distance between us. I don't know what this person's problem is, but he needs to back off.

Finally, he falls back. "Okay. Good. What a jerk."

"Are you okay, Mommy?" Ben asks.

"Yep. Just fine. We're almost home." I take the next exit — not my usual route home. I have to know if this guy's going to follow. Driving down the ramp, I keep an eye on the rearview. "Oh my God." There he is. He's following me. *Us.*

I can't go home, so I drive faster in search of the nearest store, getting my bearings on a location. Once I feel like I might have outrun him, there, ahead — it's a grocery store. That'll do. I pull into the parking lot, finding a space as near to the front of the well-lit building as I can get.

My gaze is fixed on the sideview mirror as I wait to see if he'll catch up.

"Why are we at the store, Mommy?"

"Just sit tight, Benny, okay? We'll go home in a minute."

The kids grow restless. Nicky is beginning to whine. Soon, that'll turn into a cry if I don't do something.

There it is. I think. My breath catches as I wait to see if it'll turn in. It's just a black rectangle from here with beams of light at the front. But when it drives past me, I exhale. "Thank God."

"Mommy?" Ben asks. "Can we leave now? Nicky's getting squirmy again."

"Yes, honey. We can leave." I shift into Drive and head home again. That familiar feeling settles in my bones — fear and paranoia. Yet, it wasn't my imagination. Someone was following me.

We arrive home, and I get the kids out of the car. My neighbor waves at me as he pulls in his garbage can from the curb. I don't bother saying hello, only offering a hurried wave in return. I don't know any of these people, and that's how I intend for it to be — for a while, anyway.

I get the kids into the house, securing the deadbolt behind me. "Let's get dinner ready, huh, buddy? Why don't you go wash your hands, and you can help me?"

"Okay." Ben drops his backpack and runs into the hall bathroom.

Nicky looks up at me from her car carrier. "All right, sweetheart. Let's get you out of there and get you changed."

I go about my routine tasks, doing my best to forget about what just happened. I don't know who or what it was about, but maybe it was nothing. Instead, I feed and bathe the kids, then put them to bed.

My mind continues to process the event. Can I even call it that? Still, should I be afraid someone found me? Even now, while I sit curled up on my sofa, surrounded by the quiet, I run through plans of escape.

It would be easy to find me if one was determined enough. But that someone would have to know everything that happened in Beaufort. Maybe Medford, too.

My phone lights up with an incoming message. As I pick it up, Tyler's name appears on the screen.

Just checking in to see that you're okay.

It's comforting — having someone to check on you, to care about you. I type my reply.

All okay here. Thanks for checking.

I hit send, and his reply is almost instantaneous.

Want company? :-)

The emoji's a nice touch, but if nothing else, what happened earlier reminded me to keep up my guard. And that includes him.

Sweet. But I'm good. Speak soon.

I almost hate to send it because it sounds so cold. But I realize now that going to dinner with him last night was a mistake. I knew it was too soon. I guess I just needed a reminder that the kids and I aren't free from our past. Not yet.

* * *

Nothing like getting the pants scared off you to put yourself back on course. Last night did just that. My imagination could've been running in overdrive, but I don't discount incidents like that anymore. I've been that route and learned my lesson.

So, while I won't let it derail our lives, it serves as a reminder that I'm the only one these kids have. It's up to me to protect them. I've become complacent. I see that now, and it ends today.

It's a beautiful Saturday morning. The sun shines, the skies are clear, and the air carries a hint of the warmer weather to come.

The kids and I walk to the neighborhood park, arriving to find several other families who had the same idea. I don't mind, though. In fact, it's nice to be surrounded by parents and kids doing normal things on a normal Saturday.

Ben tugs on my shirt. "Can I go to the playground?"

I peer out over the grounds, surrounded by trees and open grassy areas. Two playgrounds in the distance draw my gaze. "We'll go to that one, there. It's for kids your age."

Nicky seems happy as I push her stroller along the path. Ben's gaze wanders to the other children. He wants to make friends. I'm all for that. Anything to help take his mind off the nightmares. But it's the parents of those friends who I'll have to keep at arm's length, reminding myself that there could be people out there waiting to hurt us.

As we reach the playground, Ben rushes toward the swings. I find the nearest bench and sit with Nicky by my side. For a moment, I'm lost in the contentment of it all. However, in the back of my mind, I'm plotting a way to keep us safe. A way to ensure our truth never sees daylight. I must get a new birth certificate for Nicky. One that will pass the scrutiny of law enforcement or anyone else. With my new position, I think I can find the right people to do that.

Mired in the details, it takes a moment for the wailing to reach me. I whip my head toward the swing set. "Oh my God." Jumping to my feet, I sprint toward Ben, who is lying on the ground. "Benny! Benny, are you okay?"

He clutches his arm, screaming so hard and loud that other parents run toward him to help. I reach down to pick him up.

"No, don't!" a man yells at me. "I'm a paramedic. Let me see him. Please."

Stunned, I step back, and that's when I realize I've left Nicky alone. I spin around, losing my bearings, forgetting where I was sitting, but only for a moment. There she is, her stroller, still next to the bench. I can't leave her, but I can't leave Ben either.

"My daughter. She's over there in the stroller."

"Go," the man says. "I've got your son."

I have to trust him. Other parents gather around us. He won't take Ben. He won't harm him, not in front of so many others. So, I take my chances and hurry back to Nicky. "Are you okay, baby?" I peer into the stroller.

She smiles at me, and relief swells in my chest. "All right. We're going to go see Ben and make sure he's okay." I push her down the path to the playground. It's covered in wood-chips, making it harder to push the stroller, but I won't leave her again.

"Ben?" He's sitting up, still clutching his arm, whimpering.

The man looks at me. "It appears he might've suffered a fracture in his left arm, ma'am. You'll want to get him to the hospital."

"Yes, of course. Thank you so much."

"I can help get him to your car," he adds.

The rest of the parents begin to disperse, and I'm more at ease. "Thank you. I'm grateful for the help."

We arrive at the car, and the paramedic gently places Ben in his car seat. "It'll be a tough ride, buddy, but your mom will get you taken care of, all right?"

Ben nods, tears still streaming down his cheeks.

"You're very kind," I say to him as he returns upright.

"No problem. Uh, I didn't catch your name."

I hesitate, glancing down for a moment too long."

"Ma'am?" he asks.

"Evelyn. I'm Evelyn Moore. And you know Ben. Over there is my daughter, Nicky. And you are?"

"Mark Engels." He offers his hand. "Nice to meet you, Evelyn. Your boy will be fine. If you want, I can follow you down there and talk to the doctor."

"Oh, no. That's very kind of you to offer, but you've done so much already. I can take it from here."

"Sure. Then, I'll leave you to it." He peeks inside again. "Take care, buddy. You're a trooper."

When he leaves, I get inside and start the car. "We were lucky that man was there, huh, Benny?" Glancing into the rearview, I see him nodding. "I know it hurts, but we'll get it taken care of. Mommy will always take care of you."

CHAPTER 12

It's just a sprain. The nurse puts Ben's arm in a sling, and he winces, though he's been given a mild painkiller to dull the worst of it.

We've been here for four hours and are now awaiting the doctor's discharge order. So much for our family day out. Ben has never had something like this happen to him before. It scared me as much as it did him.

The doctor enters, holding papers. "Here you go, Ms. Moore. Ben's free to leave." He looks at him. "Just do your best to keep your arm in that sling, okay, son?" His smile deepens the lines on his face. "In a week or so, you can take it off, and you'll feel much better. Okay?"

"Okay," Ben replies.

"Thank you, Doctor."

"Any time."

He leaves, and I gather our things. Nicky's been so good in her stroller, even dozing off for a while. But now, she's fully awake and it's best we get out of here quickly. "Ben, honey, are you ready to go?"

The nurse helps him off the bed. "Take care, kiddo," she says with a gentle tousle of his hair. She looks over at me. "You can continue to give him the ibuprofen as directed on your discharge orders. But if you notice additional swelling—"

"I'll bring him back."

"Please do." She plants her hands on her slim hips. "All right, Ben. You're set to go."

We carry on through the waiting room and head outside, walking back to the car. I get them loaded inside, taking extra care with Ben's injury.

As I buckle him into his car seat, my thoughts drift to Derek — what he would've done in this situation. Despite his shortcomings and the way he disregarded our marriage, he'd always been a good father. I wonder, if he'd lived, would he have wanted Nicky? Taken care of her like his own flesh and blood?

Then again, he turned out to be someone I didn't recognize at the end of it all. So maybe we are all better off this way. But the question remains . . . when Ben gets older, when Nicky gets older, what will I tell them about their father?

"Okay, buddy. Let's go home."

* * *

I'd taken off a few days while Ben recovered from the worst of the pain. He's been doing well and doesn't need the medication any longer. So, today, we are back to our usual schedule.

Arriving at work, I glimpse Tyler's SUV parked in front of the building he said he would be leasing. I haven't heard from him since he texted the other day. Then again, the tone of my reply pretty much said it all.

I'd been frightened by what I thought was someone following me. Maybe I was wrong. Nevertheless, I'd taken out my fear on Tyler, pushing him away.

Sitting at my desk, I notice Brandon enter. "Hi."

"Hi," he says. "How's your son doing?"

"Better. Thanks for asking."

"That's good to hear. Listen, I know we haven't had much chance to get to know each other, but maybe you, me, and Renee should go out to lunch soon."

I smile, feeling like maybe not everyone is after me. From the moment I met Brandon, I liked him. He's young and single. No kids. And he has a good head on his shoulders. I could do worse than having him and Renee as colleagues. "I'd like that very much. Thank you."

He nods. "Anytime. I'll set something up." He walks away, a slight swagger in his step. Nothing I wouldn't expect from an attractive man who has the world at his feet. I'm not sure Tom realizes how lucky he is to have these two working for him, though I suspect they won't be for too long.

I peer through my window, thoughts of Tyler running through my mind as I stare at his car. I'm beginning to feel safe, and I don't know if I should. The people around me have proven to be kind and caring. Even strangers in a park.

I head into the lobby. "Hey, Lily, I'm going to walk across the street. I'll just be a few minutes."

She glances at the door, and a smile curls up on her lips like she knows exactly what I'm about to do. "Okay."

Lily's smart for a younger woman who may not have as much experience with men as I do. Then again, my knowledge of men hasn't done me any favors.

I step outside, squinting in the low morning sun. Shielding my eyes from the glare, I peer across the street as I walk over. The glass front offers a clear view of the lobby, but it appears empty. I'm already here, so I might as well try the door. It's unlocked.

Pulling it open, I lean in. "Hello?" It doesn't look like it's open yet. A few chairs. A main reception desk, but no computer.

Tyler appears from around the corner. "Well, hello."

I step inside and let the door close behind me. "Hey, I saw your car outside. Thought I'd pop in. Hope that's okay."

"Of course it is. I couldn't be happier to see you." He continues toward me, narrowing his gaze. "You haven't been around much. Is everything going okay?"

"Yeah, uh, I had a little family trouble, but it's all good now," I reply.

"Oh? Were you sick?"

"No, it was my son. He had a playground accident. Turns out, he sprained his arm." I raise my hand. "He's okay. In fact, he's doing well, and I got him back in school today."

"Oh, that's good news. Sorry to hear he was hurt, though."

"Thanks." I look around. "So this is the place, huh? Your new office?"

"Yep." He gestures out. "This is it. Signed the lease and everything. As you can see, we're not quite open just yet. Still waiting on furniture, the internet guys. Stuff like that."

"Sure. Sure." I'm out of things to say, and now I don't know what I'm here to do. "Listen, uh, the other night—"

"Don't worry about it, Evelyn. I can take a hint. No harm done," he replies.

"It's just, well, I was — I was just getting in my own way, as usual."

He walks toward me, looking into my eyes. "Listen, I can see you've been hurt before. It doesn't take a genius to notice. But I want you to know that I'm your friend, first and foremost. Anything beyond that?" He shrugs. "Is your call."

The closer he gets, the more nervous I become. "I'm glad to hear you say that. So, uh, maybe you'd like to join me for lunch today?"

He looks around as if assessing the work that still needs to be done. My resolve wavers and I'm already planning my escape from this mortifying situation.

"Sure, I can swing that. If we stick to someplace close by, I can break away for an hour or so."

"Great, okay," I reply a little too eagerly. "So, noon? We can hit that bistro down the block. I hear they have a nice lunch menu."

"Perfect. I'll pick you up."

"From across the street?" I laugh. "Sure. Sounds good. See you then."

CHAPTER 13

Chelsea

I called in sick for this. I knew Ben was going back today after his injury over the weekend, which meant that Evelyn would be returning to work. I decided that pressing him any more would only result in harming him, and I couldn't do that. So, I've found another way to get the information I need — to finally learn the truth about the Moore family and whether those kids are in danger.

My first stop is the public records office downtown. I enter the three-story building, surrounded by red brick and ornate wood carvings, walking into the lobby. Three workers sit behind a long desk, partitioned off, where visitors are called up.

I notice a ticket machine and grab a number. Apparently, there are five people ahead of me, so I sit and wait. Still, it's not as bad as the DMV.

It takes about twenty minutes before my number is called. I approach the woman behind the counter and hand over my ticket. "Hi."

She looks about thirty-five. Straight brown hair and a button-up blouse. "Good morning. How can I help you?" she asks, her tone light and friendly.

"I'm looking for some public records — maybe a marriage certificate or property deeds for a woman named Evelyn Moore."

The woman glances up at me, her expression neutral but vaguely bored. "Evelyn Moore, you said? Do you have an approximate year for the marriage or property purchase?"

I hesitate, trying not to look as clueless as I feel. "Um, not exactly. Maybe sometime in the last ten years?"

She sighs and starts typing. "This might take a minute. Hold on."

I hear the tearing of another ticket off the machine, which is only feet from me. A man in a well-tailored suit takes it and sits down in the rows of chairs behind me. I admit he's handsome, but I'm here for information.

"Okay," the clerk says, snapping my attention back to her. "I've got a property deed for a house on Montrose Avenue, purchased a few months ago. No marriage certificate in this county, but I can check neighboring counties if you want."

What I really want is Ben's birth certificate or even Nicky's, but that's not public information. "Anything under the name Derek Moore?" I remember the boxes in the garage, Derek's name printed in large letters across the tops of them. Could be something there.

"Let me take a look," she replies.

It takes several more minutes, and I notice other customers have come and gone. Then I see the man in the suit approach the window next to me. I glance at him, offering a tight-lipped smile. He nods in return.

He sounds like some kind of lawyer, the way he's talking, using legal jargon I hear on TV sometimes.

"I'm sorry, miss," the woman says. "I didn't find anything under the name Derek Moore. But I do have Evelyn Moore's deed for the house on Montrose."

"Oh, okay. Thank you. This will do."

"Of course." She looks past me. "Number 239."

Disappointed but not entirely surprised, I walk out. I know Evelyn moved here recently, so the house deed makes sense, but anything else would've been from the public records office of wherever she used to live. Still, at least I didn't walk away empty-handed.

As I reach my car, I hear someone calling out.

"Excuse me," he shouts.

I stop and turn toward the building, where the man in the suit jogs toward me. For a moment, I don't know whether to get in my car for safety or whether he might ask me out on a date. I feel it's safe to consider the latter.

"Me?" I ask.

"Yes, you." He stops a few feet away. "Did I hear you right back there? Were you asking about Evelyn Moore?"

Fear races up my spine. Who is this guy? "Uh, yeah. Why?"

"I work with her. She's a colleague." He offers his hand. "Brandon Lytle."

"So you are a lawyer," I reply, accepting his greeting.

"I am." He tilts his head. "How do you know Evelyn, and why were you asking about the deed to her house?"

The words stick in my throat. I can't tell him. Evelyn will have me fired. "Um, sorry, but I really need to go." I climb behind the wheel of my car and shut the door, leaving the man standing there with confusion on his face.

I press the ignition and give him a little wave. He steps aside, and I pull out of that spot as quickly as I can without running him over.

As I drive away, I glance into the rearview mirror. He's still looking at me.

CHAPTER 14

Evelyn

Tyler arrives minutes before noon. Lily, wasting no time, calls me up to the front. As I reach the lobby, I notice the two are engaged in conversation. He stops and looks at me. "There you are. Are you ready to go?"

"Sure am." I smile at Lily, and she smiles back, only it's the kind of knowing look I've come to expect from her. A young romantic, Lily hasn't yet seen the darker side of love. Certainly not the kind I have. And when you've seen that, it's hard not to let it color everything in your world.

We step outside into a cooler day with gray skies, though more and more leaves have appeared on the trees. I admit that I'm still conflicted, but Tyler has tapped into feelings I haven't experienced in a long time. The kind of feelings I wasn't sure I still possessed.

"So, how's your day going so far?" I ask him, trying to keep the conversation light.

"I've hit a few bumps in the road, but nothing I can't overcome." He looks at me. "And you?"

"Going well, thanks. I have a meeting with a client this afternoon. She's in the middle of a heated custody battle. It's not fun."

"No, I don't suppose it would be."

As we arrive, he opens the door. "After you."

"Thanks." I walk inside, smoothing down strands of my hair blown around by the light wind. A sign at the front indicates we can seat ourselves, so I turn back to him. "Where do you want to sit?"

He aims his index finger ahead. "That booth there at the back."

The place isn't that busy and there are plenty of booths, so I wonder why he wants to sit all the way back there. Then I remember, I'm overthinking things again. Getting in my own way.

"Sure."

We take our seats, and the server immediately takes our order. While we wait, she brings two glasses of water and an iced tea for me. Coke for Tyler.

"So, how's your boy doing?" he asks, sipping on his drink.

"Much better, thanks. Yeah, it was one of those things. Kids get hurt all the time, right?"

"So I hear," he replies.

I study him a moment, wondering whether to ask my next question or if I'm opening myself up to too much in return. "You mentioned you don't have kids, but were you ever married?"

"Uh, no," he replies, almost embarrassed. "And at my age, I know many women consider that a big red flag."

"They do? Why?" I ask.

He raises his gaze, a smile pushing up his cheeks. "Because I'm thirty-two. Never been married. No kids. Apparently, I'm terrified of commitment, or so I've been told."

"Commitment is overrated." I laugh.

He shakes his head. "Ouch."

I raise my hand. "I did lose my husband, but if I'm honest, he wasn't the best husband a wife could ask for, so, it's — really, it's okay."

"Must've been hard on your kids, huh? How old are they?"

That voice in my head warns me to keep my mouth shut. "Young," I reply. "They're both young enough that I don't think either will remember much about him."

"Well, I suppose that's a blessing in disguise, then." He raises his glass to his lips. "Sorry if I overstepped. It wasn't my intention."

"No, not at all," I reply. "It's a chapter in my life I'd rather put in the rearview, you know?"

"All too well, Evelyn." He takes a sip. "All too well."

CHAPTER 15

Chelsea

The door to my apartment creaks as I push it open, the sound grating and sharp in the silence. I step inside, and something feels . . . wrong. An unfamiliar smell hangs in the air. Cologne or perfume? It's not mine.

I set my keys on the counter. Everything looks the same as I left it — my jacket still draped over the back of the couch, the stack of mail I didn't bother to sort last night. Maybe that run-in with Evelyn's co-worker has put me on edge.

Should I consider it a coincidence that he was at the public records office at exactly the same time as me? Then, he confronts me, wanting to know why I'd asked for her records?

Did he follow me there? Does he know where I live? But why would Evelyn send someone to follow me? No. It can't be. Can it?

I double-check my door is locked, and then I stand there, listening. The fridge rattles a little. The clock on my shelf ticks, but that's it. Nothing else, just the feeling that I'm not alone.

I'm suddenly aware of my breathing. I look around. The blinds in the living room are tilted slightly, and the slats open just enough to let in some sunlight. "Did I leave them like that?"

I move toward the kitchen, every step careful and focused. I'm sure it's just me. No one's here. No one's been here. I'm freaking myself out because I got caught doing something I shouldn't have been doing. That's all this is.

The floorboards pop beneath me, and I flinch. I'm on the second floor of this old building, and every sound echoes around me. I peer into the kitchen. The cabinet doors are all closed, and the dishes are still in the drying rack, exactly where I left them.

"Hello?" My voice cracks. It feels ridiculous, but I wait for a response as if I plan on becoming this intruder's friend instead of running the hell out of here.

I check the bedroom next, flipping on the light and scanning every corner. My bed is still unmade, my pillow still dented in the shape of my head. But the closet door is cracked open. I *never* leave it open.

For the first time in my life, I'm actually scared. My heart pounds so hard I feel it in my throat. My fingers grip the edge of the door, and with one swift motion, I yank it open, letting out a shaky breath. It's just my clothes — hanging there, judging me on how stupid I must look right now.

I rush to the window, parting the blinds enough to peer outside. The parking lot is mostly empty. It is, after all, the middle of the day. But I do see something out of place — a car I don't recognize. It's a dark sedan parked near the corner, looking shady as hell.

I stare at it, my pulse racing, waiting to see if someone steps out or if I can glimpse a shadowed face behind the windshield. Is someone inside watching me? My fingers tighten on the edge of the blinds, and I suddenly feel exposed, standing here like this.

"Screw it." I grab my keys and march outside. The parking lot is sprawled out before me.

A man in a hoodie walks his dog along the sidewalk. He glances at me as I step out, and for a second, I wonder — is that him? Was he inside my apartment?

I shake my head, but then I see a woman in a long sweater vaping near the building's entrance. She looks up as I pass, and her gaze lingers on me for too long. My nerves are shredded, and my mind spins. It feels like everyone is watching me.

I scan the parking lot again, my gaze landing on the dark sedan. I'm crazy for doing this. I take a step toward it, then another, but before I can get close, the engine roars to life. The car backs out and drives away from me.

The license plate has a tinted cover on it, and I can't read it. I can barely make out the model, just the color. Did she send someone after me? Evelyn? Did that guy follow me here? What did he say his name was? Brandon? Jesus. Maybe I am getting close to something.

CHAPTER 16

Evelyn

While Judy Crenshaw continues to draw out our meeting, I eye the time, knowing I only have a few minutes before I have to leave if I hope to make it to the daycare before they close. If I don't, there's no telling what Brenda will do. And with Ben still recovering from his injury, I've already pushed my luck. She would've preferred I keep him home for several more days, but of course, that wasn't a choice I had.

I thought I'd built in enough time for my client, but her case includes an intricate web of correspondence, receipts, judges' rulings, and I simply didn't factor it all in. Not to mention, she's a talker.

"I hate to do this to you, Judy, but I need to leave so I can be sure to pick up my kids on time tonight."

"Oh, oh yes, of course. I'm so sorry. Here I am blathering on and, of course, you have a life outside this office."

"It's my fault. I should've scheduled enough time for us to thoroughly review everything. Please forgive me. I can type it all up this evening and send you an email. You can review it and let me know if I've missed anything."

"Well, that sounds just fine, Evelyn. I know how it goes. I'm not so far removed from those early mothering days that I can't sympathize." She gathers her things.

"I do appreciate it," I reply. "Being a single parent is tough."

"Yes, ma'am, it is." She stands, slinging her Louis Vuitton purse over her shoulder. "I'll show myself out. You go on and get yourself out of here. Send me what you can tonight."

"Will do, Judy. Thanks again." I wait until she leaves before scurrying around, cleaning up the files, and packing my things. I look at the time on my phone. "Shit. I'm not going to make it if there's traffic."

I head out the door and into the lobby. "I gotta go, Lily. Good night."

"Night, Evelyn."

I rush out to my car and hear my name. I stop to look back toward the office. "Brandon."

"Hey, you have a minute?" he asks, standing half in and half out the door.

"I'm so sorry, but I don't. If I don't leave now, I'll be late picking up my kids."

"Oh, yeah, sure. But, uh, come see me when you get in tomorrow."

"Will do. Night." I climb behind the wheel. He watches me reverse out of the spot, and I offer a wave. He appears concerned before he dons a smile and waves back at me. I don't have time to ponder his reaction. Instead, I speed through downtown.

"I might just make it," I tell myself, checking the time once again.

With no snarled traffic, I race up to the building and see that they've closed. "No." My heart sinks. But I'm only a few minutes late. Surely, Brenda will understand. I hope.

I reach the entrance, which is already locked, so I knock on the glass door. A moment later, Brenda appears in the reception area and glares at me with what seem to be daggers shooting out of her eyes. I swear, I can almost see the exasperation radiating from her.

"Sorry. I'm here. I'm here," I plead, still standing outside.

She walks toward the door, unlocks it, and finally pushes it open. "You're late, Evelyn. Again."

"I know. But not by much." I check the time. "Six minutes. That's all."

"And then you bring in Ben, who's still recovering and requires extra care from our staff."

"He can't be the only kid who's come here hurt before. Brenda, please. I have to work. It's just me. You know that."

"It's not just you, Evelyn. Many of our parents are single parents, yet they manage to arrive on time to pick up their children." She sighs. "Look, I'm sorry, but I think you need to find another facility."

"What? No, please. This one's perfect. The school brings Ben here, and I drop off Nicky in the mornings. It's perfect. I-I won't be late again."

"That's what you said last time," Brenda replies. "I do feel as though I've given you plenty of chances, Evelyn. I'm sorry, but after the end of this week, you'll need to find another facility that can take your children. There's plenty around here. I don't think you'll have any trouble. Someplace that'll be more flexible than I can be."

She turns around. "I'll go get the kids for you."

I close my eyes, dropping my head into my hands. "Goddam it."

CHAPTER 17

After getting Ben to sleep, I walk to Nicky's room and check that she's still out. Tiptoeing toward her crib, I peer inside. There she is, just as perfect as ever. I aim the baby monitor down a little more and return to the hall.

I didn't tell Ben he wouldn't be going back to see his friends at daycare after this week. I'm not sure how much more this kid can take with change after change to his life and routines. Is it any wonder the nightmares he has?

I pour a glass of red wine and carry it into the living room. Nestling on the sofa, I turn on the television and stream one of the latest shows. I don't know what it is because I'm not focused on it. All I can think about is how the hell I'm going to find another daycare by the end of the week.

I liked this one. The staff were all so kind and friendly. Chelsea even babysat for me the other night. So I'm supposed to start over? Build trust with a whole new set of people? I take a long drink from my glass, setting it on the side table. What more do I have to do to maintain a sense of normalcy for my children?

My phone lights up with an incoming message. I swipe open the screen and smile.

Thanks again for buying lunch today. My treat next time?

Tyler asks the question, assuming I'll agree to see him again. I admit that it was nice today.

Sure, but let's make it dinner next time. However, I'm not sure I can use the same sitter, so it could be a while.

Oh? What happened?

I don't really want to go into the whole thing, but as the wine is hitting me, I feel a little like venting my frustration. And I admit that I'm comforted by the notion he's interested. So, I fill him in as briefly as I can on what happened. And his reply is quick.

I'm so sorry to hear this. I'm sure it's the last thing you need right now.

He has no idea, I think. But I type my response.

Don't suppose you know a nanny who might be available? With my hours, I'm not sure I can do another daycare center. Will probably end the same way.

I wait for his reply, but it doesn't come. He probably got called away, so I finish my wine and watch television. I glance at my phone every few minutes, but still nothing. "Strange."

And just as I'm about to give up, his reply appears.

As a matter of fact, I do happen to know of someone who's looking for a new gig. She's the sister of one of my accountants. I can put you in touch with her if you'd like.

Oh my God. He's a lifesaver. I reply to him again.

Yes, please do. That'd be wonderful. Thank you so much. I owe you!

This time, his reply is immediate.

I'll keep that in mind.

CHAPTER 18

Chelsea

I lie in bed, terrified to close my eyes. What have I gotten myself into? Who is Evelyn Moore and what is she hiding? Tomorrow, I'll risk it. I'll log in to the system at work and look at her file. There must be more information there. The kids' birth certificates or Social Security numbers. Previous addresses. References, even. Maybe.

I need to know where they came from. Where they lived before. Still, I can't help but wonder if the man I saw at the records office today could be the one who followed me home. He probably didn't need to follow; he just pulled up my license plate and got my registration details, which, of course, lists my current address. But why would he? Who is he to Evelyn?

The more I think about it, the wider awake I become. I should tell Brenda. She needs to know that Ben and Nicky could be in danger. We'll have to report this. There's no other way.

I hear a groan, and my thoughts halt while I strain to listen. A window opening? It's not the front door. The deadbolt is locked. I made sure of that. The windows are locked, too, but that noise came from something opening.

I search for something to use as a weapon inside my dark room. I have no gun, no knife. Not even a bat. The best I've got is a stiletto shoe. It's better than nothing. I quietly pull off my covers and step out of bed. My pulse beats in my ears, and my hands shake. "Calm the fuck down, Chels," I whisper.

This is my first apartment, my first time living away from my parents, but right now, I want nothing more than to run into their bedroom and tell my dad to take care of this — whatever this is.

I tiptoe to my closet and quietly slide open the door. It rolls along the metal runners, squeaking with each inch I pull it. Inside, my shoes lie on the floor. There they are . . . black stilettos with a four-inch heel, sharp like an icepick.

I wait a moment, listening for movement inside my apartment, but I can't hear anything more than the beating of my heart. I've never known what it's like to fear for my life, but I know now. I want to call my parents and tell them I love them because I'm afraid I won't get out of here alive.

Tears well, and I try to blink them away. I can't lose my shit now. But as I stand by my door, listening for more sounds, I hear nothing. Are they gone, or are they waiting for me to come out?

Clutching my shoe, I wrap my other hand around the handle. I can barely control the tremors running through me, but I have to keep it together. I can't be that girl who falls apart.

I turn the handle and wince. As I edge it open, I see no light in the hall. No light anywhere. If they're here, they're hidden in the darkness. Great. My worst fucking fear.

Slipping through the narrow opening, I stand in the hallway. My breaths are loud, bouncing off the walls that feel like they're closing in on me. I hear nothing, so I take a step, then another. The shoe, raised high in my hand, is ready to come down at a moment's notice.

As I near the end of the hall, I see a faint light in the living room. The silence scares me more than anything, and I scan the room with wild eyes. If I take another step . . . out into the open . . . they could get me.

"Who are you?" I say, my words coming out fractured and weak. "What do you want?"

I get no response. I hear nothing more. My hand feels along the wall for the switch, and I turn on the light. The living room illuminates, burning my eyes. I squint, searching for anyone, but I see nothing. I see no one.

I drop the shoe and collapse at the end of my hall in a heap of tears. It takes me a minute to gather my wits again. "No one's here, Chels. You're okay." Maybe no one was ever here, and it was a trick my mind played on me.

The adrenaline wanes, and I exhale a long breath. I walk to the kitchen and turn on the light. Nothing looks out of place. I return to the living room, and as I make my way to the sofa, I freeze in my tracks.

"Oh God." My hand clamps down over my mouth. Tears spill uncontrollably. "No. No. No. How did you get here?"

With a shaky hand, I reach for it — the stuffed tiger from Ben's closet, sitting right here on my couch. Only it doesn't look the same. It's dirty, grimy. As I raise it for a closer look, I notice words scrawled in permanent marker over its belly.

She's not yours.

CHAPTER 19

Evelyn

For the first time in months, I don't feel so alone. I have a friend who, in time, may become more than that. It's too early to tell, but I'm grateful he's putting me in touch with this woman, Marissa Warren. In fact, the three of us are due to meet for lunch today.

I arrive at the same spot, near work, and walk inside. Tyler waves at me from a nearby table, and I see a woman with him. I expected someone younger, but she appears to be in her thirties.

I head over and Tyler stands. "Hi, Evelyn. I'd like to introduce you to Marissa Warren. Marissa, this is Evelyn Moore."

We exchange a greeting.

"Nice to meet you, Marissa." I take my seat across from them.

"You too, Evelyn. I'm excited to talk about the possibility of working for you."

"Great. Me, too." I take in her appearance. Auburn hair, just past her shoulders, full and thick. Hazel eyes. Freckles that dot her cheeks and the bridge of her nose. Her face is thin, her shoulders narrow. By the look of her, she keeps fit.

"So, why don't you tell me a little about your experience?" I ask.

"Well, as you know, my brother works for Tyler, which is how I've come to be here today," Marissa begins. "I understand you're on the lookout for a new option for the care of your kids."

"That's right," I reply.

She launches into her background. Education, special training, CPR, and all that.

"Sounds great. Do you happen to have your references handy?"

"Of course." She hands them to me. "Feel free to reach out to any or all of them."

Tyler sets his gaze on me. "So, what do you think? She's perfect, right?"

His enthusiasm is genuine, which I appreciate. However, this deal is long from being sealed. "She sure seems like it. I can't thank you enough for making the introduction." I turn back to her. "You may know that I'm looking for someone to start next week. The hours would be seven thirty to about six but could go past that and probably will. Because of that, I'd consider a live-in situation if it helps. I'll be honest . . . I'm a single-income parent, and including accommodation allows me to offer a little less pay."

She glances at Tyler. "I understand completely. And I would consider that."

"Fantastic. So if you'll give me today and tomorrow to check references, I'll get back to you."

"Well, now that's settled," Tyler begins. "We should eat."

* * *

When I return to the office, I feel lighter with this weight off my shoulders. I stop at Brandon's office, but his door is closed. He wanted to talk to me this morning, but I didn't see him

73

come in. It'll have to be another time, then. I need to make some calls and check out Marissa's references.

It doesn't take long to learn that she'd been an excellent employee for all of them. The only reason she left was because the kids had gone to school, or the parents divorced. Still, I couldn't be happier — and relieved.

But there's one last step I must take, so I pick up the phone to call a trusted friend. "Chuck, it's Evelyn Moore."

"Well, would you look at that? How you been, Evie? Haven't heard from you in months."

I knew Chuck back when I practiced law the first, albeit brief, time. It's always good to have a private investigator on speed dial, even as a family lawyer. "Yeah, I know. A lot's happened. I'll tell you about it someday."

"All right. Then what can I do for you today?"

"I've joined a new firm and—"

"Well, congratulations. That's wonderful to hear. Where you at?"

"Just a small family law firm with one owner. I'm one of three associates. It's early yet, but things are going well so far. Anyway, I was wondering if you could run a background check for me on someone I'm looking to hire as a nanny?"

"Oh, well, sure. What's the name?"

Marissa Warren. I can text you her social and address," I reply.

"Sounds simple enough. Just the basics?"

"Yes, don't bother with credit. I don't need that. Just criminal."

"I'm on it. Should be pretty straightforward. I can get you something by tomorrow morning if that suits you."

I smile. "It does, Chuck. Thank you."

"Anytime. Glad to hear you're back on the job, kid. You're damn good at it."

He ends the call, and I lay my phone on my desk. I peer through my window and notice Tyler's office across the street. Just a small glimpse of it, but I don't see his car.

But the more I think about it, the less excited I am about the prospect of Marissa living with me. I'm not sure I'm ready for that, especially with Ben's nightmares. I might have to rethink that offer and hope she'll still consider the job. I might have to ask Tom for a raise, which I think I can get — if the Crenshaw custody case goes our way.

As the end of the day arrives, I know I'd better leave on time. Never mind that Brenda kicked my kids out of her daycare, they're still going for the remainder of the week, and I can't afford to piss her off again.

I shut down my laptop and pack my things, including the Crenshaw file, which I need to review. I plan on submitting the formal complaint to the circuit court tomorrow. After turning off my light, I head into the corridor, where Brandon pops out. "Hey."

"Hey, you have a minute?" he asks.

I glance at the time on my phone, knowing I really don't, but Brenda's decision has been made. What difference will being a few minutes late make now? "Sure. You wanted to talk to me? I stopped by your office after lunch, but your door was closed. I thought you had a client in there."

"I did, yeah, sorry. But listen . . ." He folds his arms and leans against the door jamb, darting his gaze back and forth. "Something strange happened yesterday while I was at the records office."

"Oh?" I ask, a lump rising in my throat.

"Yeah, a woman was there." He shakes his head, narrowing his gaze as if confused. "She was—"

"Brandon? There's a call for you on line two," Lily calls out from the front. "It's Ed Silva."

"Damn it," he says. "Okay. Put him through, please." He looks at me. "Sorry, I have to take this. You'll be here in the morning?"

"I will."

"Okay. See you then." He returns to his office.

Relief fills my chest. But it could be fleeting. Did he find out something about me? What does he know? I check the time again and I have to leave, but I stare at his door a moment longer. "Shit."

I head into the lobby and wave to Lily. "Good night. See you tomorrow."

"Have a good night, Evelyn," she replies.

I step outside as the sun lowers behind the building, casting an orange and purple hue across the sky. As I reach my car, I see Tyler driving down the street, parking in front of his building. I stop a moment, waiting for him to step out. "Tyler," I call out to him.

He smiles, checks the street for cars, then crosses over to see me. "Well, hello, there. Are you heading home?"

"Just about. Gotta swing by the daycare and pick up the kids."

"Ah, right." He thrusts his hands in his pockets.

"Listen, I can't thank you enough for introducing me to Marissa. Honestly, I don't know what I'd do if I didn't have a personal recommendation from you. It'd take longer to find someone than what I have."

"Hey, I'm glad I could help. And it helps her, too. Don't let her fool you," he replies. "She needs the job, and you need the help. Perfect fit."

"I think so, too. And maybe once she's onboard, you and I can go out for dinner again?"

He tilts his head, stepping just a little closer to me. "I'd like that very much."

For a moment, I feel like he might kiss me, and I might let him. So, I lean into him, our mouths inches apart.

"Uh, I should probably let you get going," he says, taking a step back. "Don't want you to be late again."

I try to hide my disappointment. "Yeah, you're right. I should go. So, I'll see you later."

"Definitely. Good night, Evelyn."

"Good night." I step into my car and peer through the rear-view as he walks back to his side of the street. I'm embarrassed.

"Never mind," I tell myself, pressing the ignition. "He just didn't want you to be late. That's all."

I start to drive away and catch sight of him standing by his car, talking on his phone. He's looking at me, watching me leave. "Maybe I misread his intention."

CHAPTER 20

Today's the day. Marissa's impeccable references and clean background check mean I can bring her to meet the kids. We agreed to see how things went for a while before we decided on living arrangements. No point in putting the kids through that if this ends up not working out for either or both of us. And I'm not ready to risk Ben's nightmares coming to the surface. Too many questions would be raised.

The knock on the door comes, and I turn to Ben as he sits in the living room. "She's here, bud. You want to come meet her?"

"Yeah." He jumps down from the couch and joins me.

Nicky is in her playpen, looking at us with interest. "You'll get your chance too, baby."

I open the door. "Marissa, hi. Thanks for coming over."

"Are you kidding? I've been looking forward to this all day," she says, stepping inside.

Ben clutches my leg, turning shy. "Ben, don't you want to say hi to Marissa?"

She walks closer, squatting low to meet him. "Hi, Ben." She offers her hand. "I'm Marissa. It's so nice to meet you."

He stares at her hand, seemingly unsure of what to do.

"It's okay, buddy," I say with a gentle nudge.

He finally lets go of my leg and takes her hand. "Hi. I'm five years old."

"You are?" she asks, displaying exaggerated surprise. "Such a big boy."

"Yeah." He turns to the living room, darting away toward Nicky. "Come meet my sister."

I shrug. "Right this way, Marissa." We carry on through to the living room. "This is my daughter, Nicole. We call her Nicky."

"Oh my gosh. She's just beautiful." Marissa squats again, peering through the playpen's mesh surrounding. "Nicole. Nicky. What a beautiful name for a beautiful girl." She looks back at me. "How old did you say she was?"

"Almost seven months now." I had to give her a birth date, so I'm not entirely sure how old she is. I only went by what Riley told me.

"She's big for seven months," Marissa replies with a laugh. Finally returning to her feet, she looks at me. "Well, Evelyn, you are very lucky to have two such gorgeous children."

"Thank you. I am lucky." I take in a breath, feeling confident we're all going to get along well. "So, is anybody hungry? I've got pizza."

* * *

Tonight is our first test run. Marissa is scheduled to start Monday, so we thought letting her have the kids for a few hours while I go out for dinner was a solid plan. I'm not nervous at all. That's what I keep telling myself.

I've done my best to avoid Brandon today, pretending I had meetings and visits to the clerk's office. I didn't want to discuss whatever it was he'd found out. However, I'm relieved because, had it been serious, I imagine he would've informed Tom. So, there's hope I'm in the clear.

I'm on my way to pick up the kids from daycare for the final time. And I am right on time. Stepping out of my car, I enter the lobby, which is still full of other parents picking up their children. I admit that I'm a little sad. Everyone here was kind to the kids and me. I adore Chelsea, and I should say goodbye to her.

As I approach the front desk, I smile. "Hi. I'm here for Ben and Nicky Moore." I don't recognize the girl. She must be new.

"I'll have them brought up," she replies.

"Thanks." I look around, searching for Brenda or Chelsea, but see neither. So I turn back to the girl. "Excuse me, is Chelsea around? I'd like to say goodbye to her. It's the last day my kids will be here."

"Oh, you know, she's been sick, I guess. Hasn't been in for a few days."

My shoulders drop. "That's too bad. Well, if you wouldn't mind, could you tell her I was asking for her and that I wanted to thank her for taking such good care of the kids?"

"Yes, of course. I can do that."

A moment later, Ben and Nicky appear in the lobby, brought up by another member of the staff.

"Here you go, Mom," she says, handing Nicky to me.

"Thank you." I look down at Ben. "You ready to go home, kiddo?"

He nods.

"Both of them were great today," she says. "Have a nice weekend."

She smiles and walks away. That's it. No 'it was great getting to know them,' or 'we'll miss these guys.' Now, maybe I don't feel so bad not saying goodbye to Brenda.

* * *

"It's a test run, right?" Tyler asks as he sits across from me in the busy restaurant.

80

"Yep. A test run to see how they all get along. For a few hours anyway," I reply.

"You seem nervous. You shouldn't be. Marissa's great."

I shrug. "Yeah, I know. It's just me. But I'm so glad you wanted to do this — meeting up again."

"Of course. Why wouldn't I?" He raises his glass of wine. "I enjoy spending time with you, Evelyn."

"Thanks, it's just . . . well, the other night, when I was leaving work . . . I don't know. I guess it felt like you didn't . . ."

He reaches across the table, taking my hand in his. "If I made you think anything other than that I enjoy spending time with you, then I'm a jerk. This whole moving thing . . . it's been crazy. And I knew you needed to leave in a hurry. I didn't want to start something that couldn't be finished."

"Yeah, you're right. Bad timing was all it was." He holds my hand a moment longer, rubbing his thumb over it, and then finally lets go.

I try not to let myself fantasize about a life with a good man like Tyler. I'd let myself get swept away before. Danger could still await my children and me, so I need to have the strength to keep him at arm's length until I'm certain we're safe.

* * *

He walks me to my car as the evening ends. The food was amazing, the company even more so. I'm drunk off his presence. "Thank you for dinner, but again, you didn't have to pay."

"Why do you keep saying that?" he asks. "I already told you I know I don't have to. I want to." He pulls me close as we stand by the driver's side door. "How about you just leave it at 'thanks for dinner?'"

"I guess I can do that," I reply, feeling the heat rising between us. Will he kiss me? Do I kiss him? No. No, I can't do this. "I should get going."

"Sure, yeah, of course." He retrieves his keys from his pocket. "I'll see you again soon?"

"I hope so. Good night, Tyler."

He kisses my cheek. "Good night."

Climbing behind the wheel, I watch him return to his car. I don't want our night to end, but I'm anxious to get home and see how things went with Marissa and the kids. There will be other opportunities with Tyler.

Arriving home, I walk inside. "I'm back."

Marissa greets me in the foyer. "Hey, hi." She glances up the staircase. "The kids are in bed. They went down just fine."

"Oh, that's great to hear." I set down my purse on the foyer table. "So, how'd it go?"

"Great," she says with a smile. "They're both really amazing kids. You're very lucky."

"I think so, too." I regard her a moment, raising my brow. "So, are we good for next week?"

"Yes. We're good. I'm happy to work for you, Evelyn. In fact, I can't wait."

I help her with her things. "Perfect. I'll pick up two extra car seats for you this weekend, and we'll see you here Monday morning." I lean in for a gentle embrace. "You're a lifesaver, Marissa. I can't thank you enough."

"It's me who should be thanking you." She opens the door. "The kids and me? We'll get along great."

I stand at my door, waiting for her to get into her car and drive away. For the first time since I left Beaufort, I'm beginning to feel like this is home. For me and the kids, this is our shot at a new life.

Slipping off my shoes, I walk upstairs in bare feet, wanting to be as quiet as possible. As I reach the landing, I continue down the hall and come to Ben's room. I hear a light snore, and inside, I see his frame outlined beneath the covers. Sound asleep. A smile tugs at my lips as I pull the door closed again, praying for a night without nightmares.

I make my way to Nicky's room and head inside. She hasn't wanted to go to bed on time for me lately, so I'm pleased Marissa got her down at a decent hour.

When I reach her crib, I look inside. My perfect little girl. Her tiny hand rests next to her head. The other, down at her side. She's an angel. My gaze drifts over to the monitor I placed next to her crib. The camera is facing down, away from the bed. Did I bump it by mistake earlier today? It would've taken quite a bump to move it down that far. Nicky can be a handful at times, so I suppose it's possible since I was in a rush to get ready earlier. Could've been bumped by Marissa when she put her down as well.

I reposition it, ensuring it's locked in place. With a gentle brush of her fine blond hair, I leave her to rest and head to my bedroom.

A weight has been lifted from my shoulders — a chain, more like. Dragging behind me, reminding me of the pain and loss. The violence and damage done by two people who thought of no one but themselves. But now that chain has snapped. The weight — gone.

I change into pajamas and climb into bed. My phone lights up just as I'm ready to close my eyes, and on the screen is a message from Tyler.

I heard things went well. So happy for you. I had fun tonight.

I don't want to admit that I feel a little like a schoolgirl, but what can I say? My heart flutters at the thought of him. I type my reply.

All went great. And I had fun, too.

I press 'send.'

Maybe next time I can meet your kids since I feel like I already know them.

I stiffen for a minute, rereading his words. Am I ready for that? Then again, he led me to Marissa, so my resolve wavers.

I'd like that. We'll set it up soon.

CHAPTER 21

She's here. The knock on the door confirms it. "Time to go, Ben," I shout as I stand at the bottom of the staircase. Glancing into the living room, Nicky seems content in her playpen, so I answer the door. "Marissa. Right on time."

"I try to be." She walks inside.

"I have the car seats ready for you. Do you need help putting them in your car?" I ask.

"No, I can do it."

"Are you sure?" I narrow my gaze. "They can be tricky, and they need to be in just right."

She places her hand on my shoulder. "I've done it before. I got it, Evelyn. We're good."

"Okay," I reply, relief in my tone. "I'll drop off Ben on my way to work. Just remember that school lets out at noon. You have to be right on time to pick him up."

"I will. I know where I'm going, and you've already given the school my name. We should be good to go," she assures me again.

"Right. Okay." Ben's footfalls echo lightly on the stairs. He reaches the bottom. "I'm ready, Mommy."

"Great. Let's head out then." I glance at Nicky and then to Marissa. "This will give you two a chance to start bonding."

"Exactly." She looks at Ben. "I'll see you soon, Ben. Remember, I'm picking you up today."

"I know," he replies, already heading out the door.

"Guess we're leaving." I look around one more time, assessing everything is up to snuff. "Well, have fun today. Oh . . ." I dash over to Nicky. "Bye-bye, sweetheart. Be good." I kiss her head and hurry toward the door again. "See you tonight."

"Have a good day, and don't worry . . . I've got everything under control."

Relief washes over me. "Thank you, Marissa." I march toward the car where Ben stands at the rear passenger door. "All right, baby. Let's head out."

I drop him off at preschool and continue driving to work. As I park, I can't help but glance over my shoulder to see if Tyler's car is across the street. It isn't, and I'm a little disappointed.

Today's a big day, regardless. I have to file the complaint on behalf of Judy Crenshaw to begin the custody proceedings. It'll be months before a hearing is set, so I need to make sure to temper her expectations.

It's amazing how not worrying about my kids allows me to focus on work. The relief is quick and unexpected yet welcome.

My phone buzzes on my desk. It's Judy, so I quickly answer. "Evelyn Moore."

"Evelyn, hi, it's Judy Crenshaw. Listen, we have a problem."

I lean back in my chair. "I'm listening."

"My piece of shit ex-husband says if I go through with this custody battle, his lawyer will file a countersuit to cut my alimony in half, claiming he'll have to fork over more cash if I take full custody of the kids. I can't afford that, Evelyn. I need your help here."

I rub my forehead. "Okay, listen, let me make a call to his lawyer and get the specifics. Let's make sure this isn't an empty threat first."

"And if it's not? Do we have standing?" she asks.

"I don't know. I'll work on it and get back to you as soon as I can."

"Please do, Evelyn. I need answers, and I trust you'll get them for me."

"I will," I reply. "We'll talk soon. Don't worry, Judy. I'll get it handled."

"See that you do." She ends the call.

I lean back in my chair. "Shit."

* * *

Papers are strewn on my desk. The day's gone by in a blur, dealing with this new development in the Crenshaw custody case. It's time to head out, but by the look of things, I'll be bringing work home with me tonight.

I quickly pack up and head toward the lobby, where Brandon stops me. "Oh, hey."

"I do need to talk to you, Evelyn. Do you have just a minute or two?" he asks. "It seems we keep missing each other."

I glance back to see Renee heading out. "Good night," I say.

"Good night, guys. See you tomorrow," she replies.

I wait until she walks outside and glance at Lily, who seems as concerned as I am about what Brandon has to say. "I, yeah, sure," I tell him. "I've got a minute."

He pulls me into the hall, toward his office. "Listen, I don't know if this will be a concern to you or not, but last week, at the public records office, a woman who looked to be twenty-one or twenty-two . . . she was asking for records about you."

"Me?" I say, my hand on my chest.

"Yeah. I thought it was strange, too. I couldn't hear the entire conversation, and she finished before I did, but I managed to catch her outside," he continues. "I asked her if she knew you, and she didn't answer. In fact, I didn't get her name."

"No? Huh," I reply, trying not to look bothered by this news but wondering who the hell was asking about me.

"She practically jumped into her car and took off." He tilts his head, his blue eyes showing real concern. "I got her plate, and I considered checking it out, but I really wanted to talk to you first." He raises a preemptive hand. "I don't want to get into something personal, you know?"

"Yeah, no, I appreciate that." My mind scrambles to think of who could've been asking about me. The age range . . . could've been a friend of Riley's. Could've been anyone. "Would you mind texting the plate number to me? Maybe I should check it out."

"Yeah, of course." He takes out his phone from his back pocket. "I'll text you the picture I got."

I hear the ding on my phone and look at it. "Great. Thank you, Brandon. I appreciate you letting me know."

He shrugs. "Hey, there's a lot of crazies out there. Especially ones looking for revenge against an attorney they think screwed them over."

"Yes, I'm sure," I reply, knowing that's not the problem, but I almost wish it was. "Thanks again. I'd better get going."

"Okay. See you tomorrow," he says, returning to his office.

I head back into the lobby. "Night, Lily. Gotta run."

"Okay. Have a good night," she replies.

As I walk to my car, I glance across the street, only to be disappointed that Tyler's car still isn't there. He hasn't called or texted, and now I feel insecure, but at the moment, I'm more concerned about this woman looking for me.

I'll feel better once I get home and see my kids. I didn't hear anything from Marissa, so I have my fingers crossed that the day went well.

I slow down as I near my house. "Where's her car?" A surge of panic rises in me when I pull onto the driveway. Marissa's car isn't here. I shift into Park and pick up my phone, opening the screen to messages. No texts. No phone calls. But

I do see the text from Brandon. I open the image and immediately recognize the car. "What?" I breathe out. "Chelsea?" As I stare at the photo, I know it's hers — Chelsea's. Was she the one looking into me? How . . . why?

I shake my head clear, realizing I'm losing sight of the problem at hand. Cutting the engine, I jump out, leaving behind my bag, taking only my keys and phone. When I reach the door, I see that it's locked. I fumble with the keys for a moment until the deadbolt disengages. Thrusting it open into the darkened foyer, I call out, "Marissa? Ben?" No reply comes, and now, I'm in full-on panic mode.

I hurry through the house, flipping on every light. "Marissa? Ben?" I jog upstairs and head into Nicky's room. Her crib is empty. "Ben!" I spin around, screaming. "Benny!"

My heart is beating so hard, I'm growing dizzy. In the hallway, I open my phone and press Marissa's number. The phone rings. "Come on. Come on. Answer, goddam it."

Then I hear something downstairs. I run to the staircase, and Marissa walks into the foyer. "Jesus." Ben is at her side, and she's holding Nicky's car carrier. "Oh my God. Where have you been?" I run downstairs. "Where were you? Why didn't you answer?" I lean down and pull Ben into a tight embrace. "Are you okay, sweetheart?"

"Yeah," he replies, sounding frightened. I'm sure it's because I'm panicked. I stand up again. "Marissa, what the hell is going on?"

"I'm so sorry. I took the kids out to the park earlier, and then we went for ice cream. I-I texted you."

"No, you didn't." Still holding my phone, I look at it again. "There's nothing here from you."

"Evelyn, I swear, I sent you a message." She sets down the baby and checks her phone. Her hand covers her mouth. "Oh no. It didn't go through. I didn't realize it." Her eyes glisten with tears. "I'm so, so, sorry. I must not have had a signal."

I catch my breath, trying to calm myself down, knowing part of my reaction is because of the image Brandon sent me.

"And when I didn't reply, you went ahead and took them anyway?"

"I assumed it meant you were okay with it. You've mentioned how busy you get at work, and I didn't want to bother you." She reaches for my arm. "Please, Evelyn, it was a misunderstanding. It won't happen again. I promise."

If she knew of my trust issues, she would understand my anger. But the kids are here, and they're safe. Am I overreacting? I don't think I am, but I'm so rattled that I can only feel the effects of adrenaline coursing through my veins.

Her references were excellent. Nothing turned up in her background. I have to let go of my fear. Not everyone is out to hurt me or my children. *Chelsea*. "Okay," I whisper. "Next time, please just make sure you get a response from me before doing anything like this again."

"Yes, of course, I will," she replies.

"Then — uh — I guess you can head home."

Ben's already in the kitchen, having snatched a juice box from the fridge. Nicky still lies in her car carrier on the floor.

"I'll see you tomorrow?" she asks tentatively.

I cross my arms and walk her out. "Yeah. See you tomorrow."

CHAPTER 22

The television is off. Only the lamp on my side table burns. The house is quiet, with the kids now asleep. That familiar fear I'd felt those months ago returned today — with a vengeance. I don't want to go back to feeling that way after making so much progress. But will that be possible now with what I know about Chelsea? Did she find something here? Is that why she hasn't been to work? Was she the one who followed me that night?

Then there's Marissa. I believed her despite nearly ripping out her throat for putting me through that kind of panic. She has no idea what my family has suffered, so how can I be mad at her? The kids went to the park and had ice cream. Can I be angry with this woman for taking care of my children while I worked?

My phone rests on the table, so I pick it up. I want to call him. I want to see him. Though I could never tell him why I'm desperate for him to be next to me right now. Despite that inner voice warning me once again, I call him. Putting the phone to my ear, I wait for an answer. He picks up and tears sting my eyes. "Hi."

"Hey. How was your day?"

His tone is light and refreshing, as though he hasn't a care in the world. "Good, yeah. Busy but good. I — I didn't see you at your new office today." I do my best to steady my voice.

"No, I was slammed trying to close out the old one. So, you missed me, huh?"

"Yeah, I guess I did." I smile, but hesitate for a moment, knowing that if I ask this of him, it will change everything. Even with the kids asleep, he'll see me here, in the place where I feel the safest. I'll be opening myself up to him. But right now, I need that. More than I could ever say.

"Listen, this is kind of last-minute, but would you want to pop over for a drink?" The line goes quiet. I chew on my lower lip, praying he'll say something soon because I feel completely vulnerable right now.

"Uh, yeah. I can do that. Send me your address, and I'll be on my way. But what about the kids?"

"They're asleep," I reply.

"Oh, okay," he stammers. "Then I guess we'll have to be quiet."

"I'm sure we'll manage." I laugh. "See you soon."

I text my address and wait. My glass of wine is still half full, so I drink it down the rest of the way. I have to relax. I have to get my mind right. This is a mistake. I'm sober enough to realize that much. I'm not ready for him to know more about my life. But the kids are asleep. He won't be meeting them tonight. I feel like I'm about to crawl out of my skin, and I can't be alone right now.

Several minutes pass, and I walk into the kitchen to grab another bottle of wine and another glass. I open the red and inhale its fragrant notes of chocolate and black cherries. The aroma is soothing. The first glass of wine has smoothed the edges. I know what I'm faced with, but for the moment, I can push it to the back of my mind.

As I return to the living room, setting down the wine and glasses, I hear a soft knock on the door, and I know it's him.

In socked feet, I enter the foyer and press an eye against the security lens, then unlock the door and open it. "Hi."

"Hi." He shrugs. "I wasn't sure you heard me, but I didn't want to ring the doorbell."

"I heard. Come in." I step aside, and he walks in. "Thanks for coming over."

He takes off his light jacket, draping it over his arm. "It seemed like you needed a friend tonight."

I close my eyes, holding back the tears because it feels like he can see right through me. "Let me take that for you." I drape his jacket over the banister and show him into the living room.

"Your home is beautiful," he says.

"Thanks. It's getting there." I gesture to the sofa. "Have a seat. Can I pour you a glass?"

"Please." He sits down, appearing laid back.

I join him, handing him the glass. "Cheers." We clink. "Cheers."

We settle in, and the conversation flows more freely than I expected. He's so easy to talk to. Genuine and kind.

"Listen," he begins. "Not to bring you down or anything, but you seem a little glum. I didn't want to ask over the phone, but I wonder — your husband. You said the relationship wasn't great, but I imagine his death must still hurt. And I take it, it hasn't been all that long since he passed."

"No," I whisper, not wanting the conversation to head down this road. But I don't think I can stop it now.

"Is his loss the reason you're not feeling like yourself?" he asks.

The baby monitor that sits on the side table crackles to life. A light *coo* from Nicky comes through. Tyler turns and takes hold of it. "Oh, wow. This is your little girl?"

"Yep. That's her." I couldn't be more grateful for her interruption than I am at this moment.

"And she's how old again?" he asks.

"Almost seven months," I reply.

He smiles at the monitor as she shifts in her crib. "She's gorgeous."

"Thanks. I think so, too." I watch him looking at her. He seems mesmerized, and I see he must want children of his own someday. I take the monitor from him and place it on the table.

My heart pounds and my head feels light from the wine. I can't remember the last time I wanted any man this much. Though I've only had one man for many years who didn't seem to want me in return. My lips part, and I close my eyes as I draw closer to him.

"Uh, I should probably let you get some rest," he whispers.

I stop in my tracks, flicking open my eyes again. "What?"

"Evelyn, I'm sorry. I can't take advantage of this situation. You're clearly not yourself right now. You're going through something I can't possibly understand. And I don't want to confuse you."

"Confuse me?" I pull back, now on the verge of tears.

He takes my hand. "We can go slowly, okay? There's no rush here. I'm not going anywhere. I think we should get to know each other better and just be sure this is what you want."

"Yeah," I whisper. "Sure." I get to my feet, doing everything in my power not to let him see me falter. "Thanks for coming over. I enjoyed talking to you." I lead him to the door and hold it open for him. "Drive safely."

He slips on his jacket. "Are we okay? I'd hate to think you were upset with me."

"No, I'm not upset. I promise. Good night, Tyler."

He presses his lips into a thin white line and walks out. I close the door, securing the deadbolt. And then the tears come.

CHAPTER 23

With a clearer head this morning, I did my best to smooth things over with Marissa. I was in the wrong, having lost control and panicking unnecessarily. She couldn't have known why. And that *why* is something I still have to understand myself.

I'd all but forgotten about Tyler's hasty departure last night, accepting the idea that he was actually being a good and decent man, seeing that I wasn't myself.

So, this morning offered a fresh start. Marissa arrived right on time. I apologized for my behavior and received an apology in return. If I'm to move on, then that means trusting in others. I'm working very hard at doing just that.

Now, as I sit in my office, I realize I've put off the inevitable, so I grab my phone. I have to talk to her . . . Chelsea. I have to know what it is she thinks she knows. So, I press her contact and the line rings.

I wait for her to answer, but the call goes to voicemail. "Damn it." When the tone sounds, I hang up. She's part of that generation that doesn't leave voicemails, preferring text messages instead. So that's what I'll do.

It's Evelyn. Can we talk soon, please? There are some things I need you to know. The sooner, the better.

94

I press send and wait, but no reply comes. Is she avoiding me? Probably. I'll give her a little time and pray that she reaches out. Otherwise, I'll have to go to her place. I know I can't ignore this, and I won't.

* * *

I didn't bother reaching out to Tyler today. I'll let him come to me and try not to seem so goddam desperate. Who wants a needy woman with two young kids? Probably not him. Probably not any man.

I arrive home and see Marissa's car in the driveway. I admit that I'm relieved not to have a repeat of yesterday's disastrous events.

As I enter, the house is filled with the sounds of my kids laughing and playing. I couldn't ask for anything better. "Marissa, I'm back." And on time, I might add. Though I've again brought work home with me.

She emerges from the kitchen with Nicky on her hip. "Hi there. How was your day?"

"Good, thank you. And yours? The kids do all right for you?"

"Of course." She bounces Nicky a little. "Just gave her a tiny snack. Hope that's okay."

"Absolutely," I reply, extending my arms to take my girl. "I'll take her so you can get your stuff together."

"Here you go." She hands Nicky to me. "I'll just say goodbye to Ben."

"Okay." I follow her to the living room, where Ben is watching cartoons. "Hey, buddy. Marissa's leaving if you want to say goodbye."

He pulls his attention from the screen and raises his hand. "Bye, Rissa." He can't say her name just yet, but the nickname is pretty cute.

"Bye, Ben. I'll see you tomorrow after school." She hoists her bag over her shoulder and heads toward the door. "Have a good night, Evelyn."

"Same to you." I close the door behind her. "Okay, guess I should think about getting dinner ready." That's when I notice the smell. "Uh, oh." I lift Nicky to check her diaper, and that is definitely the source of the odor. "Looks like you need to be changed. Come on, sweetheart." I carry her upstairs and lay her on the changing table.

Unsnapping her onesie, I realize she's soiled it, too. "Well, it looks like I'll have to put you in something else until your bath tonight." I put on a fresh diaper and place her into the crib, having taken off the dirty clothes.

I open her dresser drawer and stop for a moment. "I did laundry already. Where's the rest of her stuff?" I know something's missing. I walk to her hamper and see only a handful of items inside, and not the ones I was expecting.

"Okay. Are they in the wash? Did Marissa do a load of laundry?" I glance at Nicky and see she's entranced by her own feet, so I feel comfortable leaving her for a moment to check the laundry room. The dryer's empty, and so is the washer. "What the hell?"

I return to Nicky's room and pick out a set of pajamas that will have to do until her bath later. "All right. Guess we'll put you in these." I pick her up again and return her to the table. She smiles at me, giggling. "I know. Mommy's funny, isn't she?"

I get her dressed, and holding her beneath her arms, I tilt my gaze. "What?" I lean toward her head. She doesn't have much hair, but something doesn't seem right. "Oh my gosh, what happened? Did — did she cut your hair?" It doesn't look like a full-on haircut, but a section of it, right behind the ear, appears shorter.

My mind spins through various scenarios, landing on the only one that makes sense. "Did you get something stuck in your hair today, sweetie? Did Marissa have to cut it out? Well, I'll have to ask her about that tomorrow."

I place her on my hip and head toward the door but stop to look at the closet. I don't like where my mind is going, but

I have to check. I open the bifold doors, flicking through the hangers. "Okay, what is happening here? Nicky, more of your clothes are gone. I don't understand." She doesn't answer but does offer a high-pitched squeal in my ear.

I'm sure there's a reasonable explanation, but then why didn't Marissa tell me tonight before she left?

* * *

I've let myself be controlled by paranoia to the point that it ended in the death of my husband. I won't let myself succumb to it again. This morning, I'll ask her — straight out — no hesitation. No thinking she's out to get me or my family. It was a few articles of clothing and a swatch of hair. That's it. Don't freak out over this, Evelyn. You're better than that.

Never mind that Chelsea hasn't answered me yet.

When Marissa arrives, I'm ready to take Ben to school. Nicky's been changed, dressed, and fed. She walks inside, and I grab my laptop bag. "Ben, let's go, honey. Time to go to school." I smile at Marissa. "Morning."

"Good morning," she replies, setting down her things.

"Listen, uh, last night, I was looking for a few of Nicky's outfits," I begin. "I was wondering if maybe you'd put them somewhere else? Maybe intended to wash them?"

"Uh, actually . . ." She trails off a moment. "This is my fault. Yesterday, I got a little ambitious, and Nicky and I were playing with paints. Not the washable kind, either. I must've picked up the wrong brand by mistake. Anyway, she got some on her clothes, so I changed her. And then she did it again. Needless to say, we stopped playing with the paints."

"So where are these clothes?" I ask.

"I'm sorry, Evelyn, I ended up throwing them away. They were pretty ruined. I was embarrassed to tell you last night."

There it is. A perfectly reasonable explanation. "And I noticed, well, it looked like you might've had to cut something out of her hair?" On the left side, behind her ear—"

"Gosh," she interrupts. "That was the paints again. I bathed her, but this one part was really bad. It wasn't much. An inch, maybe? So, I cut it out." She scrunches her face. "Are you mad?"

"No, no. I just wish you'd have said something last night, so I didn't have to wonder about it."

"You're absolutely right." She cast down her gaze. "I should've come clean. Honestly, I didn't think too much about it. You know how kids get."

"I do. But maybe next time, give me a heads-up?" I ask.

"Of course. You got it."

"Great. Well, we should go." Ben's at my side, and I place my arm over his shoulder. "All set?"

He nods.

"Okay." I look at Marissa again. "Have fun today." Nicky's in her playpen, and I call out to her. "Bye, sweetheart." I walk out to the car and load Ben into the back seat. As I slip behind the wheel and press the ignition, I feel better for having cleared the air. "See? Perfectly reasonable explanations."

* * *

I walk into the office. I didn't bother looking out for Tyler across the street. After the other night, I'm embarrassed, and it's best if I don't see him right now. Not to mention, I've been preoccupied with Chelsea. She hasn't called me back, and now I'm wondering what she found out. If she doesn't respond, I'll be left with no choice but to go see her. This isn't over, and I won't have loose ends.

Lily is at her desk, but her expression appears solemn as the door closes behind me. An unexpected welcome. "Good morning. Is everything all right?"

She glances toward the hall. "Tom wants to see you."

"Okay," I reply with concern. "Should I be worried?"

Her lips press into a thin smile, and she shrugs. "I don't know."

It's a less-than-certain answer, which raises the hair on my neck. "All right. I'll drop off my things and head straight to his office." As I enter the hall, passing by Brandon's office, I see that he's wearing the same expression as Lily. "Good morning."

"Morning," he replies in a hushed tone.

Now, I'm nervous. I continue down the corridor and glance into Renee's office. She's on the phone and sees me but quickly looks away.

The office feels colder now, and uncertainty creeps into my head. I reach my office and turn on the light, stepping inside. While I set down my things and turn on my computer, I rack my brain thinking of what I could've done to piss off the boss. I've been doing my job. Working hard. Yes, I've been leaving on time, but can he be angry about that? Maybe. Law firms are cutthroat operations. You stay so you can be seen, never mind that you have a family to care for. I just didn't think Tom was that way. Maybe I was wrong.

The only way to find out what's going on is to see the man himself, so I walk to Tom's office and stand in his doorway. "Hi. You wanted to see me?"

"Evelyn, come in. Take a seat. And, uh, close the door behind you."

My throat dries in an instant. I feel as though I'm about to be fired. But I sit down, doing my best to appear stoic. Forcing a smile on my face, I wait for him to speak.

Tom, dressed in a tailored suit, rubs his temples as if staving off a headache. "Explain to me," he begins, his voice low and measured, "explain how you managed to file a complaint in the circuit court with *that* many errors. Do you have any idea how badly this reflects on the firm?"

My stomach churns. My brain scrambles to think of what I'd done wrong. I'd gone over the complaint several times, and I don't recall a single mistake. Every page, every paragraph, every damn footnote had been meticulously checked — hadn't it?

"I double-checked everything," I say, steadying my voice. "I don't understand what you mean—"

Tom slams his hand down on the desk, and I flinch. "Then you must need glasses, Evelyn, because the court denied it outright. Mrs. Crenshaw called me, telling me she'd been copied on an email sent by the clerk. That email went to you as well."

"I'm sorry. I haven't checked my emails yet," I reply. My cheeks burn, embarrassment and anger twisting in my gut.

"She claims your incompetence has cost her the custody of her children." His tone drips with contempt.

Incompetence. The word slices through me, ripping my insides. "There must be some kind of mistake," I insist. "I followed procedure. Every signature, every attachment—"

"And yet it was denied," Tom snaps back. He leans in his chair, steepling his fingers. "So, Evelyn, enlighten me. How exactly would that have happened if you followed procedure?"

The words stick in my throat. I don't know. I don't have an answer, and Tom knows it. He's staring at me like I'm just a stupid woman who has no business practicing law.

"I'll look into it," I reply with as much confidence as I can muster. If I lose it now, I might as well pack up my things. "I'm sure there's an explanation. I'll contact the clerk's office."

"I suggest you do." His voice is sharp. He stands, signaling the end of the conversation, and waves a dismissive hand toward the door. "Fix this. Now."

I'm numb. My legs carry me out of his office, but I can't feel them. I pass by my co-workers' offices, my gaze straight ahead because, if I look at them, they'll see my humiliation.

My thoughts spin, and my pulse echoes in my ears. I reach my office and close the door softly so as not to confirm everyone's suspicions that something has gone terribly wrong. I collapse onto my desk chair and bury my face in my hands.

Churning through the process in my head, I recall every step. The client's documents — intake forms, affidavits, the complaint itself. I filed it correctly, didn't I?

What's done is done, and now I have to fix it. Pulling my laptop closer, I key in the password to open the case file. My hands shake as I scroll through the documents, scanning for anything I might have missed. A signature? A date? An attachment?

Nothing. Everything is there.

My only option is to drive over to the clerk's office to try to figure out what happened. I need to see what they have compared to my copies. Do I call Judy Crenshaw first? Explain that this is nothing more than a clerical error, and I won't let her lose her kids. I can't. Not until I'm certain I didn't screw this up.

CHAPTER 24

If I hadn't seen it with my own eyes, I wouldn't have believed it. The complaint filed with the court didn't match the documents I had. In fact, it wasn't even related to the Crenshaw case. The clerk denied it was their error, but how could it not have been? I refiled, having taken my own copies of the complaint.

While I'm relieved to have cleared up the incident and relieved Tom didn't fire me after I explained, I can't help but be concerned by it. Clerks don't make those kinds of mistakes. I didn't practice for that long before Ben was born, but I had enough experience and knowledge to understand that they have their own checks and balances, and such an egregious error would've been flagged by someone along the line. *Then what happened?*

Driving home, I feel paranoia and fear snaking their way through me. With my senses heightened, I glance at every car that passes me. I peer at every person walking along the sidewalk. Then I recall being followed last week, and I haven't forgotten about Chelsea looking into me. Did she do this? "What the hell is going on?" I whisper, alone in my car.

I arrive home, and as I see Marissa's car in the driveway, I begin to feel like myself again. A bad day at work. That's all it was. The problem's been solved. When I walk inside, I see the usual goings-on. "Hey, Marissa."

She's walking out of the hall, holding a dirty diaper. "You're early. How was your day?"

"Fine. Thanks." I'm not about to tell her what happened. "Where are the kids?"

"Ben's putting away his toys in his room, and as you can see, I just changed Nicky."

"Great." I place my bag on the foyer table. "Looks like you can knock off a little early today. I'm sure that'll be a nice change of pace for you since I've kept you late a few times this week."

Marissa swats her hand. "Oh, I don't mind. I have no one at home waiting for me." She carries on into the kitchen to dispose of the diaper.

I walk toward the staircase and grip the banister. "Ben? Mommy's home. Come say hi."

He appears at the landing. "Mommy!" Taking a step at a time, clinging to the handrail, he descends.

I pick him up and pull him close. "Hi, baby. How was your day?"

"Good," he replies. "I'm glad you're home." Ben wraps his arms around my neck.

"Me, too, sweetheart. Me, too." I turn back to see Marissa pulling on her sweater. "Are you heading out?"

"Yep. I'll see you tomorrow."

"Sounds great. Thanks, Marissa."

"See you, later, Ben," she says to him.

He whips his head around. "Bye, Rissa!"

I lower him down and walk upstairs. "Let me get Nicky, and then I'll start dinner. What would you like tonight?"

"Pizza!" he shouts.

I place my hands on my hips. "Besides pizza."

"Chicken nuggets and French fries."

After the day I've had, I don't mind the easy meal, despite feeling a little guilty. "All right. We can do that for tonight.

Only because Mommy's tired." I continue upstairs and find Nicky in her crib. "Hi, sweetheart." I pick her up. "Look at that face. Happy and smiling."

She lets out a laugh and my heart melts. "I'm glad to see you too, baby. Come on. Let's go downstairs."

* * *

The kids are settled in for the night. I'm on my sofa, sitting in silence as I do my best to put the day's events at the back of my mind. It's over. It's fixed, and I need to let it go. But my mind won't let me. I pick up my phone and try Chelsea again.

"I swear to God if this is your doing . . ." The line goes straight to voicemail. "Great." I toss the phone onto the cushion next to me.

I'm grateful to have Marissa working for me. It's one less concern among many that seem to be piling up. Then my thoughts drift to Tyler, but I quickly squash them. I can't be sidetracked. Besides, he's made it clear that he wants to remain friends. I can accept that. In fact, it's probably for the best, all things considered.

A flicker catches my gaze. The side table lamp sputters for a moment before it stops. Then the television. The signal drops, the screen turns black, but only for a moment, and it's on again.

But when I hear a low hum that seems to shudder through the house, the power cuts out. I'm plunged into darkness. Peering into the kitchen, I notice the glow of the microwave clock in the kitchen disappear, along with the soft whir of the refrigerator and the distant hum of the baby monitor. All are silent.

I stay still for a moment, gripping the edge of the couch and waiting for the power to come back on. It has been a long day — a draining, high-adrenaline kind of day at work. One of those days when the universe seemed determined to test just how much I could take. And now, this.

"For God's sake. What now?"

My phone is next to me, and as I reach for it, the screen lights up the immediate area with a dim bluish glow. Five per cent battery. "Of course. Why not?"

With a sigh, I stand up and fumble my way toward the kitchen. My footsteps sound hollow on the hardwood floor. It's fine. These things happen. Power outages are perfectly normal occurrences, especially in this old neighborhood with its overhead powerlines. But the nagging feeling in my gut refuses to relent. It's the same feeling I've had all day, like my world is unraveling one small thread at a time, and I'm powerless to stop it. But why? Why now, when things are finally going well for me and the kids?

When I reach the garage door, I hesitate. The breaker box is out there in the cold black space. I don't park in there because it's full of boxes — all the things that belonged to Derek. I hate even stepping foot inside it. The garage makes my stomach twist, but I have no choice, so I grab a flashlight from the kitchen junk drawer. The beam sputters, flickering in and out as I aim it ahead of me.

"Figures," I say. "Do I even have more batteries?" I open the door to the chilly air trapped inside the garage. In socked feet, I walk on the cold and dirty concrete floor, aiming the light toward the wall where the electrical panel is located.

The breaker box looms in the corner, a metal rectangle that intimidates me. I've never been handy at do-it-yourself tasks. Derek wasn't either. We hired people for those sorts of things.

I reach for the door on the panel, pulling it open. With the flashlight aimed inside, I see the switches, all labeled. One by one, I flip them off and back on. Nothing. I repeat the process. Still nothing. The air around me feels colder, heavier. My skin tingles with the distinct sensation of being watched. That's ridiculous, of course. It's just my imagination. I have to do these things on my own now. I have children who depend on me and me alone.

But then comes the noise.

A low creak, barely audible, coming from somewhere above me. The hair on the back of my neck stands on end. I halt, straining to listen. Maybe it's the house settling. Old wood and shifting foundations. But then it comes again — a deliberate sound, like footsteps.

"Ben? Nicky?" I call, my voice unsteady, knowing they can't hear me out here.

My pulse rushes in my ears as I return inside, leaving behind my useless attempts at resetting the breakers. The flashlight's beam trembles across the walls, distorting everything it touches. The refrigerator looks like a towering monster. The staircase disappears into darkness.

The house feels dangerous, like I don't belong here, and it's telling me to leave.

Another noise. A faint tapping, this time coming from the living room. My breath catches. It's not the wind. It's not an old house settling. I grip the flashlight tighter, its beam flickering again. "Hello?" I call out, having no idea what to do if I get an answer.

The tapping stops.

For a moment, there's nothing. Just my ragged breathing and the terrifying stillness of the house. And then, from upstairs, a new sound. The creak of a door hinge, slow and deliberate.

"The kids."

CHAPTER 25

I hurry upstairs, careful not to tumble in the darkness. The flashlight dims as its battery drains, but there's just enough light to see a figure in the hallway. "Ben?"

"Mommy?" he replies in a tired, small voice. "It's so dark in my room. I got scared."

"Oh, honey." I walk toward him, meeting his gaze. "The power went out. That's all. That's why it got dark in your room. Your nightlight shut off. I'm sure it'll come back on soon." It occurs to me that the noise I'd heard was him, and I couldn't be more relieved.

A hint of light emerges from my bedroom as I stand up again. "Take my hand, sweetie." He grabs hold, and we walk inside. The window that faces the street lets in the light. I move toward it and peer outside. "What in the world?"

"Mommy?" Ben asks.

Craning to see in each direction, the situation becomes clearer. "It's okay, honey. Looks like it's just our power that's out. Must be something wrong with the electrical."

"What does that mean?"

I turn to him. "It means I need to call out an electrician." Will I be able to get anyone out this late? If I do, it won't be cheap. Nevertheless, two young kids and no electricity? Not a good combination. "Okay, sweetheart. I'm going downstairs for a minute. Do you want to come with me or try to go back to sleep?"

"I'm tired," he replies.

"All right then." I help him back to his bed, tucking him in. "I'll make sure we get the lights on again soon, okay?"

"Okay."

I kiss his cheek and step out of the room. Returning downstairs, I use the flashlight to shine into my computer bag and reach inside for the portable charger. Plugging it into my phone, I let it charge.

The glow of headlights catches my eye through the curtain's opening, stopping me in my tracks. I lean closer to the window, hiding behind the panel, and cast a wary eye outward.

A car is parked along the curb, fronting my house. "Who the hell is that?" It sits between the streetlights, cast in shadow. I can't make out what it is other than possibly a dark-colored sedan. Its headlights flick off, and it sits there in the shadows, waiting. Waiting for what? I've had enough happen tonight that I don't dare chance a confrontation. Now, I'm frightened.

A moment later, the headlights flare again, and the engine rumbles to life. The car takes off, not in a cloud of smoke and squealing tires; it simply rolls away, unafraid of anything I might do.

I throw open the front door and run outside, feeling like a coward for waiting until it left. In socked feet, the cold concrete porch seeps through to my skin. I run down the steps and toward the end of the yard. By the time I reach the curb, the car is already halfway down the street, its tail-lights glowing red against the dark.

I squint into the distance, trying to catch anything — a license plate, the make or model of the car. But it's moving too fast, disappearing into the black, leaving nothing behind but the faint whiff of exhaust.

The night air presses around me, and I stand still, shivering. Who the hell was that? And when I look back, my house lights up. "The power's back." As I turn to head inside again, something on the ground near the curb captures my eye. I survey the street. No neighbors are outside. No one else is around. With a deep breath, I decide to investigate.

As I make my way to the curb, I see a stuffed animal in the gutter — a tiger. My lips part, and I stifle a gasp. Fear edges up my spine as I bend down to pick it up. "No. It can't be." I turn it over and read the words scrawled in black marker across its stomach.

She's not yours.

I can't breathe. My gaze is transfixed, reading the words over and over as if they might take on new meaning. But I know exactly what they mean. This is Ben's tiger or a close replica. I can only confirm that by looking in his closet. I was going to throw it away, but I thought, maybe one day, he would understand.

Whoever left this — they knew that. I turn it over in search of any other clues, but I see nothing. Just those three words. The car is long gone. The neighborhood is dark. I'm left alone with this reminder of that night.

"Nicky." I run inside, my front door still ajar, and dash up the staircase. Nicky's bedroom door is open, and I can't get to her crib fast enough. When I reach her, she's fast asleep, and I nearly collapse. "Thank God. Thank God." I put the tiger on the dresser and begin to inspect every inch of the room. Was the car a distraction? A way to get me outside and away from my children? How did they cut the power? But it's the one final thought from which there is no escape.

Someone knows what I've done.

CHAPTER 26

I couldn't comfort Ben in the night, his nightmares rising to the surface again. No doubt because of the fear of having lost power. After everything that's happened, I couldn't bear to be apart from either of the kids, so I kept them with me in my room.

Ben's stuffed tiger was still there — lying on a shelf in his closet. Is it a coincidence that Chelsea hasn't called me back? I'm certain it wasn't her car out there last night, so could it have been a friend or accomplice? Why would she do this? If she intends to blackmail me, she's out of luck.

I hear a car pull onto my driveway. Marissa's here. As I stand in the kitchen, Ben eating his breakfast and me sipping on my coffee, I don't know if it's safe to leave.

Marissa knocks on the door, and then I hear her key push into the lock. The deadbolt disengages, and she opens it. "Hello? It's just me."

"In the kitchen," I call out.

She appears around the corner, a smile on her face. "Good morning, Moore family. How is everyone today?"

"Was it you?" I blurt out, surprising myself.

Marissa tilts her head. "What?" She continues into the kitchen, setting down her bag. "Evelyn, are you feeling okay?"

"In the car . . . last night . . . was it you?" I press, terrified of her response but desperate to know.

"I'm not sure what you're talking about. I went straight home after I left here." She peers at Ben, who's just finished his cereal. "Hey, Ben."

"All the lights went out last night," he replies.

Marissa looks at me. "What does he mean?"

I set down my mug. "It means we lost power. Then all this weird stuff started happening. Noises. A car was outside, but it took off before I could see who was in it."

"Oh, my God. Evelyn, I'm so sorry. That must've been terrifying. But I don't understand. Why would you think it was me? Why would I do such a thing? Did you call the police?"

"No." I look away. "The power came back on, and that was it. Nothing else happened."

"Well, thank God for that," she replies. "But I promise you, Evelyn, first of all, I'd never do such a thing. Secondly, I can show you that I was at home. The GPS on my phone will show my location." She takes out her phone and sets it on the kitchen counter. "If it makes you feel better, please . . . take a look. I don't like the idea of you not trusting me."

My emotions rise to the surface, and my lips quiver, knowing how much my accusations must sting. She's been working for me only a matter of days, and it seems all I've done is point fingers at her. Could I blame her if she just up and quit right now? "I'm sorry, Marissa. I didn't sleep much last night. I was scared. I hate being alone in this house." I regard her. "I don't know who it was. Maybe just someone parked in front of the wrong house." I say nothing of the stuffed tiger, or the message scrawled on it. "Please forgive me. It was a lot to deal with."

"I'm sure it was," she replies, walking closer to me. "It's okay, Evelyn. I know you recently lost your husband. I can't imagine what you must feel every day knowing you're the one these kids depend on. It would stress out anyone."

I can't stop the tears from falling as I cover my eyes. I don't need Ben seeing me this way. "I'm sorry. Please don't quit. I promise I'm not usually like this." I grab a paper towel from the holder and dab my eyes. "I should get Ben to school."

Marissa reaches out for my arm. "I have no intention of quitting. You sure you'll be okay?"

I nod. "Yes. I have to be. I can't afford to miss work. There's too much going on there right now and I have to handle it too." I clear the emotion from my throat and look at Ben. "Okay, kiddo. Are you ready to leave for school?"

"Yeah." He jumps down from the barstool and grabs his backpack from the hook in the foyer.

"Is there anything you need me to do today?" Marissa asks. "I'm happy to run to the grocery store or if you want me to throw in a load of laundry."

I smile, wiping away the last remnants of tears. "I appreciate the offer, but no. I — I don't need anything. Besides, it's not your job to run my errands for me."

She shrugs. "I'm happy to help any way I can, Evelyn. I want you to know that."

"Thank you." I walk into the living room and kiss Nicky on the head as she bounces in her swing. "Bye, baby. Love you." Returning to the foyer, I open the door. "All right, Ben, let's head out."

* * *

I feel myself unraveling one strand at a time. Last night. The problems with my court submittals. Now, I have to consider the notion that Chelsea knows everything. She asked about me at the records office. She was in my house. Ben could've said something. She might've seen the tiger and asked him about it. Any number of things could've led to her discovery of our previous life. It's my own fault. I let her in. And now, I'll have to find a way to stop her.

How do I do that? How do I protect the kids?

As I arrive at the firm, troubling thoughts raging through my mind, I step out of my car. I hear another vehicle rolling

112

up and glance back. The morning sun reflects off its hood, and I can't see the driver, but I don't like that it's crawling along toward me.

Without letting my thoughts run rampant with theories, I keep my gaze fixed on it, determined not to let last night cloud reality. Anticipation clutches my chest as it seems my assumptions are unavoidable. *It's you, isn't it? How do you know where I work?*

The driver sees me, yet I can't make out the face that is hiding behind a cap and sunglasses. The car accelerates. Seeing me standing here is unexpected. Whoever it is seemed to only want to confirm my whereabouts, and now . . . here I am. I don't waver. It's daylight and I'm surrounded by people inside office buildings and shops.

The make of the car comes into focus. A dark Ford sedan. I note the specifics, almost certain it was the car from last night. But I need to see the license plate.

It speeds by in a whoosh, kicking up leaves and debris from the road in its wake. "Goddam it. Who are you?" I jump back into my car and throw the gearshift into reverse. I have to find out who this is. Someone knows who I am, and where I work. This game ends now.

I follow the car from a distance, having no idea if the driver sees me trailing, but I keep another vehicle between us. I grip the wheel with steely resolve. I won't let you destroy our lives.

The dark gray Ford is moving just fast enough to keep me guessing, weaving through traffic like it knows I'm following. Maybe it does.

My chest feels tight, my breath shallow, but I don't let up. That stuffed tiger . . . Seeing it on the curb like that had left me reeling.

I'm terrified, but I press the gas enough to keep the dark sedan in view. I have to know who it is. I have to know why they're doing this.

The car takes a sudden left turn. I'm too far back to follow without running a red light. *Damn it.* I slow to a stop at the intersection, my heart hammering. It's already pulling farther away, disappearing down the road.

Defeated, I pull into a nearby gas station parking lot and cut the engine. I need a minute to think, to compose myself again before heading back to the firm. *What the hell is happening?* I can't afford to get fired. I have to stay on top of my game. Yet my thoughts are on the driver of that car. I'm certain they're connected to Chelsea.

"Okay. Okay," I tell myself after a few minutes. "You need to go back now."

I press the ignition and head out onto the road. Soon, I return to the firm, and I step out of my car. From the corner of my eye, I see Tyler heading toward me. I'm not in the mood to deal with him right now.

"Good morning," he says, a wide smile on his face. "Early meeting this morning?" He checks the time on his phone as if I'm late and he's my boss. "Figured you would've been here already."

"Yeah, hi, good morning." I wave a dismissive hand. "It was nothing. I-I left late and had to get gas, so I was running behind schedule." I don't even believe what I'm saying.

"Oh, okay." He thumbs back. "I was getting the last few things moved over. I haven't heard from you in a couple of days."

"Sorry, yeah, it's just — it's just been busy." I'm drained of energy, of desire to pursue anything with this man right now.

"Oh sure, yeah," he replies. "So, listen, I don't suppose you're up for some lunch today?"

"You know, I'm actually pretty swamped—"

"Oh." He shoves his hands in his pockets, nodding.

He's disappointed, and now I feel guilty. Maybe there's a way I can attempt to salvage this while benefiting the kids and me. I don't want to be alone again tonight. If they come back, if they lure me out of the house again . . . "Why don't you come over for dinner tonight? You wanted to meet the kids."

114

"Dinner would be great," he replies, his face lighting up. "I'd love that. Well, okay. So, I guess I'll see you around seven?"

"Make it six thirty," I say. "The kids go down pretty early."

"Sure. Perfect. Six thirty it is." He leans in and kisses my cheek. "I'll see you then. I should let you get to work, huh?"

"Yeah, thanks. I'll see you later." I wave as he heads across the street once again. I should be happy about this. Instead, it's a temporary solution to a problem I've yet to determine how best to handle. I won't let Chelsea terrify me like this. I will put an end to it.

CHAPTER 27

Things were smoothed over with Judy Crenshaw. She understood that the court had made the error, and not me or the firm. But in light of recent events, I suspect what happened could have been intentional. God knows how, but I'm not so naive to think it was a coincidence, which frightens me more if Chelsea has that kind of reach. If she does, I have to think she's not in this alone.

I arrive home to find my kids happy and fed, and Marissa reading to them. Seeing them together now, guilt weighs on me for launching such a horrible accusation at her. "Hi, everyone." I walk into the living room.

"Mommy!" Ben runs to me, practically jumping into my arms.

"Hey, buddy. How was your day?"

"Good." He kisses my cheek.

Marissa walks toward us carrying Nicky on her hip. "You seem better this afternoon."

"I am better. Thank you. And — I'm so sorry for earlier."

She raises a pre-emptive hand. "Don't be. I understand. Well, I can't possibly understand, but I can sympathize. So, listen, the kids were great. No issues. Ben had his afternoon snack. Nicky's been changed and had a jar of carrots about two hours ago. I think you're all good."

"Perfect. Thank you — again." She hands Nicky to me.

"Guess I'll head out. See you guys tomorrow," Marissa adds.

"Night." I open the door for her and wait until she gets into her car. When I close it again, I look at Ben. "We have a guest coming over for dinner tonight, okay?" It occurs to me whether I should've said something to Marissa about my guest. Then again, if things don't work out between Tyler and me, I wouldn't want any awkwardness with Marissa. In all honesty, I need her much more than I need him.

"Okay." He shrugs, dashing off into the living room.

I place Nicky in her swing. "Just sit tight here for a little bit, all right, sweetheart? I'm gonna make us all some dinner."

* * *

The doorbell rings, and I smooth my hands over my blouse and check my reflection in the hallway mirror. I open the door, and Tyler stands before me, holding a bottle of wine and wearing that easy, crooked smile of his. He looks good in a casual button-up, the sleeves rolled enough to show his forearms.

"Hope I'm not too early," he says, his tone deep and soothing.

"Right on time." I step aside, letting him in. "Come in, make yourself at home."

The house smells like roasted chicken and rosemary, an aroma I hoped would remind him of home. A good home-cooked meal is the best way to a man's heart — or so I've been told. Derek didn't care what I made for dinner when he did come home to enjoy it.

Ben and Nicky are in the living room — Ben sprawled on the couch with some cartoon humming in the background, Nicky, playing in her playpen.

"So, I'd like to introduce you to the kiddos," I say, gesturing toward them. "This is my son, Ben."

"Well, hello, Ben," Tyler says, squatting in front of him. "It's very nice to meet you."

"Nice to meet you," Ben replies. "I'm five."

"You are? Wow. I bet you look after your mommy, too, don't you?"

"Uh-huh."

Tyler stands again.

"And this is my daughter, Nicky." I gesture toward her.

"Well, she looks even more perfect in person," he says, walking toward her playpen. "Hey, Nicky." He reaches in and gently takes her hand. "So nice to meet you."

"She can't shake hands." Ben laughs.

"Well, she's doing a fine job of it now," Tyler replies, glancing at me. "How old did you say she was again?"

"Seven months," I reply.

"Gorgeous." He stands and looks at me. "Just like her mom."

"Thank you," I reply, peering back into the kitchen. "Uh, dinner's just about ready."

"Great."

He follows me into the kitchen, and I pour him a glass of wine. The table is set, and I take the dish out of the oven.

"Wow, that smells amazing." Tyler rubs his hands together. "I've been so busy moving offices, I feel like I've been living on fast food. This is fantastic."

"Well, wait until you taste it before saying anything," I reply.

"Oh, no doubt it'll be great."

Dinner goes better than I could have hoped. Tyler talks to Ben like he's an actual person, not some bothersome child meant to be seen and not heard. He even helps feed Nicky.

By the time dessert rolls around, Tyler is playing with Nicky, who is sitting in his lap, and Ben is asking if he knows anything about a cartoon on Nickelodeon.

"I don't think I've seen that, buddy. But I guess I'll have to watch."

"Okay, Ben," I cut in. "I think it's time to get ready for bed. What do you think?"

"No," he whines. "I want to stay up with Tyler."

"Well, you have school tomorrow, and I'll let you skip your bath tonight because it's already getting late, but you do need to go upstairs and brush your teeth. I'll come up when I put Nicky down and say good night."

"Fine," he says, dragging his feet toward the stairs.

"Say good night to Tyler, please."

"Good night, Tyler."

"Night, buddy. I had fun tonight."

I finish putting the dishes in the sink and return to him as he continues to play with Nicky. "She seems to be taken with you."

"Ah, well, what woman isn't?" He smiles at me.

"And humble, too," I say, tilting my head. "What a great combination. Let me go put her down, and then we can sit in the living room and talk for a bit. Unless you need to leave?"

"Nope. I'm all yours tonight."

My heart skips a beat at his words. However, the pragmatic side of me finds comfort in knowing he's here and providing a deterrent to those hoping to scare me into submission. "Okay, Nicky." I take her from Tyler. Let's put you down, baby girl."

I get the kids settled in bed and return downstairs to find Tyler already in the living room, two glasses of wine sitting on the coffee table. "Perfect." As I walk ahead, I notice the kitchen. "Did you do the dishes, too?"

He shrugs, looking sheepish.

"Tyler, you're my guest. You didn't have to do that."

"You cooked. The least I could do was clean." He pats the sofa. "Come sit down."

"You're good with them, you know," I say, taking a seat.

"They're good kids. That Nicky is just a doll. And Ben? Funny kid you got there."

"I think so, too." I want to tell him what happened yesterday — last night. But I can't because then I'd have to tell him the truth. No matter how I feel about him, telling him would require trust I haven't yet developed.

Still, I feel safer with him here. I don't want him to leave. But I worry he'll stop again, pulling away from me as he did the other night. I admit that I'm in a fragile state, wavering between my desire for him and keeping my heart securely locked away.

He's already looking at me, his eyes soft. The playful edge, replaced with something deeper.

"I want you to know that I'm here for you, Evelyn. I feel like I've been sending you mixed signals, but that ends now."

I turn to him fully, my heart pounding in my chest, and before I can think of something to say, his hand brushes against mine. It's tentative at first like he's waiting for permission, but when I don't pull away, he leans closer.

His lips find mine, soft but sure, and the world shrinks around me to just him. The heat of him, the way his hand cups the back of my neck, the faint scent of wine on his breath.

I don't think about the awful, frightening things that happened last night. At least not at this moment.

* * *

I wake up from a noise downstairs. The door? I don't know. My eyes are full of sleep, and I squint to check the time on my phone. Tyler is in bed next to me, lightly breathing as he lies on his side. I can't let Ben see him in the morning. It'll be too confusing. But it's only 2 a.m. now, and the noise downstairs is my main concern.

Did I dream it — the gentle knock? My hackles rise, fear clutching me as it did last night. What if Chelsea's back, and she's not alone? What if seeing another car in the driveway wasn't the deterrent I'd hoped it would be?

I slip out of bed and pull on my robe as I walk downstairs. My heart is in my throat now as I approach the front door.

I don't chance looking through the front window. Instead, I press my eye against the door's security lens. The tiny, distorted opening skews my vision, but I think . . . yes, I see a car out front. It's not the same one. It's — Chelsea's. Why is she here? What is she trying to do?

I pull back, staring at the door, compelled to open it, yet terrified of doing so. "Just talk to her. This is your chance to end it."

Steeling myself, I open it, and my gaze is drawn to the welcome mat. A package lies before me, wrapped in brown paper, my name scrawled on top of it. I look out and see the car parked in the darkness. Do I confront her? I'm paralyzed by fear. "What the hell do you want?" I murmur under my breath.

Determined to put an end to this, my decision is made. Drawing back my shoulders, wrapped in my thick robe and walking in bare feet, I approach the car, fully prepared for it to drive off again as it had before. Instead, it sits there. No engine runs. No headlights on. As I draw near, terrified, I try to see through the tinted glass. Chelsea must be in there. Is she alone?

When I'm close enough, I glimpse through the passenger window. It's her. "Chelsea, goddam it. What do you want? What are you doing here?"

She doesn't move. Something's not right, so I walk around to the driver's side. Peering through her window, I see her head lolled to the right as though she's sleeping. I pound on the window. "Chelsea? Chelsea?" But she doesn't move.

I rock back, my breaths coming in short gasps, and then my gaze roams the street, searching for signs of someone else. "Oh my God," I whisper. "Oh my God, what is happening?"

I glance back at my front door, the package still lying there. Then I return to her. "Chelsea? Wake up. For God's sake, wake up."

I'm paralyzed with indecision, but I can't ignore the reality before me. She's dead. I can't hide this. I have to call the police. I march back to the house, snatching the package at the door, and head straight into the kitchen. I place it on the counter and search for my phone, but when I hear footsteps, I spin around toward the staircase. "Tyler?"

He shuffles toward me, appearing dazed and half asleep. "What are you doing up? Is everything okay?"

CHAPTER 28

Sirens wail in the distance, and I know they're coming here. Chelsea is still out there, sitting behind the wheel of her car, her body growing colder. The package still sits on the kitchen counter. I haven't been able to take my eyes off it.

Meanwhile, Tyler's been silent, seemingly absorbing his new reality. He sits at my kitchen table next to me, staring out the window, saying nothing more. Then again, I don't know what to say to him.

"And she was your babysitter?" he finally asks.

"Yes," I reply. "She worked at the daycare center."

"Did she . . . do that to herself?" he asks as if it couldn't possibly be true.

I shrug, staving off tears. "I don't know. I-I don't know how it happened."

He nods and sets his gaze on the package resting on the kitchen island. "What about that?"

If you wait for the cops to come, you might never see what's inside it. They'll probably take it as evidence," Tyler says. "It could give you some answers."

"I don't . . . I can't." I rest my chin in my hand, doing everything in my power to keep from falling apart. I have no idea what the package contains, but I'm certain it'll only bring up more questions than answers. Nevertheless, it's clear that Chelsea isn't the only one behind this. Maybe she was at first, but then something went wrong — very wrong.

"Then put it away," he says as if he's been in situations like this before.

Are we both keeping secrets?

Red and blue lights flash through my front window as darkness lingers. "They're here." I walk to the door, opening it before they have a chance to ring the bell.

A man in a suit approaches, and I get a sense of déjà vu. Another detective in another town. All because of my family.

"Mrs. Evelyn Moore?" he asks, a gruff, balding man with a slim figure and a brown suit that hangs loosely on him.

"Yes. I was the one who called." I point beyond him. "About her."

"Yes, ma'am." He retrieves a badge. "I'm Detective Damien Kent. Asheboro PD. May I come in?"

I step back to let him inside. "My children are sleeping."

"I'll do my best to keep from disturbing them."

I lead him into the kitchen where Tyler stands, propped against the center island, almost blocking the view of the package. "This is Tyler Mitchell. He's a . . . friend of mine."

The detective's gaze judges me, but I offer no further detail into my personal life. "Can I get you something to drink, Detective?"

"No, thank you." He glances through the window.

His officers have gotten inside Chelsea's car and look to be preparing to take her out.

"What happened to her?" I whisper.

"That's what I intend on finding out, Mrs. Moore. What can you tell me about her?"

I go into how we met. What she'd done for my kids, and how I don't take them to that daycare center anymore. "After that, we just didn't have any contact. Didn't need to." I leave

124

out the part where Brandon had seen her asking questions about me. I leave out the tiger.

"Why would she come here, of all places?" he presses.

Do I tell him that I'm certain it was her who'd followed me? Twice? I glance at Tyler, realizing he should leave now before my world unravels in his presence. "Um, could I get a minute?" I ask the detective.

He doesn't want to wait, but after a moment, he nods his approval. I step away, leading Tyler with me. "Look, it's probably best for you to go home. I don't want to risk Ben seeing you here. And with all this happening now, I gotta be honest, I'm not doing well."

He takes my shoulders. "I'm not surprised. I feel the same. A dead woman is sitting in her car in front of your house. And she left a package." He glances into the kitchen and then back at me. "I'll go, but let's make sure the detective is good with it."

"Yeah, you're right." I head back into the kitchen. "Detective Kent, would it be all right if Tyler leaves?"

He glances between us as if we've made some secret agreement. "I think it's best I speak to you both."

I take a step forward. "I have children upstairs. My son, Ben, is five. I don't want him coming down here and seeing . . ." I glance at Tyler. "He's been through enough already."

Kent takes out a voice recorder. "Let me just get a few things out of the way, and then I can have Mr. Mitchell come into the station later today to iron out the rest of his statement."

"Thank you," I reply.

He proceeds to ask Tyler his questions. "What time did you arrive here tonight?"

"About 6 p.m.," he answers.

"And where were you when Mrs. Moore discovered the vehicle and the body outside?"

Tyler glances at me and I nod for him to continue. "In Mrs. Moore's bed, sleeping. I heard her downstairs and came to see if she was all right. That's when she told me about the person outside."

Kent nods. "And do you recognize the woman or the vehicle? Have you ever seen her before?"

"No, sir. I had no idea who she was until Evelyn told me."

The detective clicks off the recorder. "All right. That'll do for now. If you wouldn't mind coming into the station later today at your convenience, we'll finish up."

"Yes, sir. I can do that." Tyler lays his hand on my shoulder. "Call me when you can. I want to know you're all right."

"Of course." I manage a smile, though I don't feel it. Many reasons come to mind as to why I need him gone. After I walk him out and return to the kitchen, I notice the detective studying his surroundings. "Thank you for that."

Kent folds his arms and tilts his head. "I'm going to need you to tell me everything you know about Chelsea. And why you think she would choose to come here."

CHAPTER 29

The package still sits on the counter. Detective Kent hasn't asked about it, and I haven't offered. I tell him about Chelsea. About how I was certain she'd followed me on my way home from the daycare center one night. And how I believed she'd been here only last night, though I fail to mention the stuffed animal she'd left behind. My reasoning? She is a stalker, plain and simple. However, that doesn't explain how she ended up dead in front of my house. A fact Kent reminds me of.

I wonder how long it'll take the detective to dig up my past. To learn that my husband was murdered and I killed his killer in self-defense. My guess is? About thirty seconds after he walks out my door.

Two officers appear in the kitchen. "Detective?" one of them says. He's a younger man who could be a rookie, for all I know.

"Yeah?" Kent replies.

"Coroner's ready to leave. We're getting a few too many looky-loo neighbors out there now."

Great. All I need is to have my neighbors turning against me, thinking I've brought crime to their perfect street. They'll ignore me. Whisper behind my back. Do all the same things everyone in Medford did. No matter how hard I try, I can't bury my past, even when I'm the one who carries the shovel.

Kent rises to his feet. "Let me talk to the coroner's people before they leave. Mrs. Moore, please stay right here."

"I will." I wait for them to step out, and I stare at the package once more. Could it contain answers? Now's my chance to find out.

I retrieve a pair of scissors from the junk drawer and walk to the kitchen island. I slice open the paper, and it falls away. And then I see it. "A music box." Small and square, the kind with a crank. Painted flowers on the lid.

I don't want to touch it; I shouldn't touch it, but my fingers move on their own as I examine it. Something shifts inside — a faint metallic rattle. A broken piece? Wedged under the lid is a folded piece of paper. I open it, and my heart sinks as I read the words:

This was meant for her.

Tears sting my eyes as I glance at the door, confirming I'm still in the clear. "Throw it away," I whisper. The longer I stare at it, the worse I feel. It contains no answers. No reason why Chelsea is dead or if she did it herself.

I don't know how long I've been standing here, staring at the music box, my mind racing with questions. Finally, I hear voices in the hall. I quickly put the box in the cabinet below me, getting rid of the packaging.

Within moments, Kent returns. I've already taken my seat again, holding a fresh cup of coffee. "Do you care for a cup?" I ask as if this is an everyday occurrence for me.

"No." He continues inside, glancing at the center island. "Where's the package?"

"Sorry?" I ask.

"The box wrapped in brown paper that was sitting on the island counter-top. Where is it, Mrs. Moore?"

My heart drops. "Oh, I put it away. It was delivered yesterday, and I'd forgotten to bring it inside." I keep my eyes fixed on him, wondering if he believes me.

"What did it contain?"

He's testing me, so I have to come up with something. "Just a music box I ordered for my baby's room." At least part of that is true. "Detective, do you know what happened to Chelsea?"

"Pills were found in one of her cup holders. It's too early to know, but given no other outward signs, the coroner will run a tox screen, and the car is being towed to our forensics department."

"So you think she overdosed on something and then drove here, or vice versa?"

"That's a good question, Mrs. Moore. Did you know Chelsea to be a drug addict?"

"I — no, I didn't," I reply. "Then again, I didn't know she was a stalker either."

He regards me with a narrow gaze. "You mentioned recently moving here. Where did you move from?"

This is it. This is where I lie.

CHAPTER 30

When daylight arrives and the cops leave, I know I can't keep the kids here today. Detective Kent couldn't offer assurances that we would be safe here, though he was fairly convinced Chelsea committed suicide and was likely stalking me.

Nevertheless, it's exactly the outcome I suspect these people wanted — whoever was helping Chelsea then turned against her. They wanted to frighten me and force me to leave, proving their hold over me.

Marissa arrives on time and lets herself in with her key. Now that she's here, I can try to explain what happened and do so without scaring her enough that she quits.

"Good morning," Marissa says, walking into the kitchen.

"Hi, good morning," I reply. "Listen, uh, is there a chance you can watch the kids at your house today?"

She tilts her head, concern masking her face. "Why?"

"We, uh, we had a break-in attempt last night."

"What?" Marissa takes a step back. "Oh my God. And this was just after that weird thing with the electricity and the car. Jeez."

"The police are involved now, and they tell me not to worry, that these things happen sometimes," I reply. "Though they suggest getting a security system and cameras." I wave my hand. "Anyway, I just feel like today, you know, maybe it's best to keep them at your place. I mean, if you have room."

Marissa seems to be considering my request. "Yeah, I guess that would be fine. I don't have all of Nicky's things there—"

"I know. In fact, I'll take Ben to school and pick him up today. I can drop him off at your house and then, to save you the effort, I'll pick them both up at the end of the day." I walk toward her. "I'm sorry. I know it's a hassle. And I realize, too, what a complete jerk I've been to you. None of what's been happening has anything to do with you and I'm just so very sorry."

She smiles, shrugging. "It's okay, Evelyn. And yeah, I think it's a good idea to hang around my house today. If you want . . . we can look at the option for the rest of the week. Until the police get some answers."

I smile, relief washing over me. "Thank you. I can't tell you how much I appreciate it." I head into the foyer, grabbing my bags. "Ben? Let's go, honey." I look back at her. "Do you want some help getting Nicky loaded into your car?"

"No," she replies. "I got it. And you have my address."

"I do."

Marissa smiles at Ben as he walks down the stairs. "Have a good day at school. Your mom's going to come get you, okay? And then you'll come over to my house for a little bit. Won't that be fun?"

"Uh-huh." He waves and starts toward the door. "Bye-bye."

"See you later," I say to Marissa. I look over at Nicky. "Bye, sweetheart." I blow her a kiss and head out the door.

The only good thing to come out of this is that I can make sure no one's been hanging around Ben's school. I feel like I have to play offense now because, while Chelsea is gone, I don't know if this is over. Not by any means.

* * *

When I arrive at work, I glance across the street. No sign of Tyler's car. What must he think of all this? That baggage I carry is too much for any man to want to contend with. I haven't called him like he asked, and he hasn't called me, which speaks volumes.

"Hey, Lily."

"Morning. Listen, Mrs. Crenshaw is in your office."

I stop on a dime. "She is? Why? We didn't have an appointment."

Lily shrugs. "She didn't say."

Dread settles around me yet again. I thought I'd fixed all that mess with the court, so why is she here? What else could've happened? "Okay. Please hold my calls."

"You got it."

I head into the hallway, nodding to Brandon and Renee, but I don't see Tom in his office, so I continue toward mine.

Walking in, I turn to greet her. "Good morning, Judy. What brings you by?" I head to my desk and I'm putting down my things when I notice a strange look on her face. "Judy, is everything all right?"

"I think it's best if we part ways, Evelyn."

Her perfunctory tone is a stark cry from our initial meeting when she seemed to put her faith in me. I slowly drop onto my chair. "Look, Judy, I know the whole filing issue was a concern, but that's all been cleared up. I don't understand—"

"Do you know what happened to me last night?" She tilts her head, her gaze boring into me with a seriousness I've never seen in her before.

"No. What happened?"

She aims her index finger at me, and her expression hardens. "Let me put it to you this way. As I took a walk with my kids down to our local ice cream store last night, some woman jumped out from behind a tree right at us. Frightened the bejesus out of my kids and me, if I'm being honest."

I lick my lips, feeling my world ready to crash around me.

"She asked if I knew what you'd done. How you'd murdered some young woman because she'd slept with your husband."

Just as I'm about to offer a defense, Judy shakes that finger at me.

"I'm not finished. I asked her what in the hell she was talking about, and she proceeded to tell me about your deceased husband. How he was murdered along with the woman he'd been with."

"You don't understand. It was self-defense," I plead. "Can you at least tell me what this woman looked like?"

You think I remember the finer details, do you? All I can tell you is that she freaked me the hell out, all right?" Judy rests her elbows on the chair and leans toward my desk. "Whatever happened, Evelyn, I honestly don't give a shit about. What I do care about is having some random person frighten my family. What I care about is risking losing custody of my kids when they tell their father I can't protect them." She takes a deep breath. "And finally, what I care about is not giving my ex-husband or his attorney a snowball's chance in hell of winning this case. And I'm afraid you have far too much going on that I simply cannot overlook." She gets to her feet, her poised and polished veneer, unwavering.

"Judy, please. I've overcome a lot to get here. Look, I can refer you to one of my colleagues if you don't wish to work with me any longer. But we are the firm that can help you navigate your custody battle."

"I'm sorry, Evelyn, truly I am. However, it's best I cut ties with your firm altogether. Good day. And best of luck to you."

Stunned into silence, I watch her leave. I'm being destroyed, piece by piece, my past unraveling into the present. Who was the woman who approached her? Given the timing, I suppose it could've been Chelsea. Hours before she died in her car at my house. At least I know it's a woman. But when

Tom finds out Judy Crenshaw just fired me, I'm out of a job. Then what?

* * *

That didn't take long. I'm in Tom's office. The door is closed, and he's staring at a file for an unusually long time.

"You know what this is about?" he asks.

"Yes, I do. The Crenshaw custody case."

"Then you know this is bad, Evelyn," he replies, his expression stern.

"I do know that. But if you can give me some time . . . a day or two . . . let me talk sense into her—"

"Oh, we're beyond that now, don't you think?" He eyes me. "She has a right to representation from whomever she chooses. And given what she's told me, frankly, I don't blame her for pulling her case."

"Tom, this is just—"

"What, Evelyn?" He leans back in his chair. "A misunderstanding? Sounds to me like you have personal issues that have spilled over into your work. Issues I, of course, knew nothing about."

My eyes well up as I struggle to contain my emotions. Without this job, we'll lose everything.

"I'm sorry, Evelyn," he continues. "I'm going to have to let you go."

There it is. "Tom, please . . . Someone's doing this to me. They're trying to . . . I don't know who or why, but I can figure this out."

He folds his hands together, resting them on his desk. "Then I suggest you do, Evelyn. For your sake and your children's. But your time here is done. I expect you gone within the hour."

The conversation's over. He's done with me. After barely a month here, I'm out. "I understand." I rise, tugging on my suit jacket, trying to maintain my composure. As I turn to leave, he calls out to me.

"I recommend you use what legal resources are available to you, Evelyn, in order to sort this out. To find this person who's supposedly out to get you. I am sorry for this, but I have to protect this firm."

CHAPTER 31

I left the office, saying goodbye to the co-workers I hardly knew at all. My sad little banker's box of personal belongings, I shoved into the back seat of my car. I didn't bother to see if Tyler was across the street, having no desire to face him right now. Too much has happened. I'll be forced to start over again, leaving behind yet another dead girl in my wake.

Feeling numb, I climb behind the wheel. Now, I have to pick up Ben, but instead of going to Marissa's, I'm going to see Brenda. I wonder if she knows about Chelsea or the secret she must've learned about me.

Fear propels me now. No job and soon no money. I'm forced to confront this situation head-on, and I'm terrified. Mainly because I don't know where to start. I should pack up and leave, I know that. But when will it end, or will it end at all? And I can't forget about Detective Kent. If I try to leave town, he'll come for me, convinced I'm somehow responsible for Chelsea's death. Then where will my children go?

I arrive at Ben's school. The bell rings inside, and the sound of children's laughter spills out. I head toward the entrance and wait for him, taking a moment to survey the grounds, searching for something out of the ordinary. I see no one lurking, no one driving by slowly as if waiting to catch a glimpse of him. No. It's just other parents and relatives — people who have no idea what haunts me now.

"Mommy!" Ben shouts, running toward me.

"Hi, sweetheart. Are you ready to go home?"

"Uh-huh," he replies.

I see his teacher ahead and wave to her. She waves back, acknowledging that I'm taking Ben home. As we walk to the car, I keep my eyes peeled, looking for Chelsea's accomplice. Is there one, or did she act alone? I'm not sure I'll get the answer to that question.

We get into the car, and I close the driver's door. I realize I'm supposed to take Ben to Marissa's house, but I want to stop at home first and drop off my files. "Are you hungry? How about I make you some lunch when we get home?"

"Rissa makes my lunch, Mommy."

"Oh, that's right. Of course she does. But we're going to go to her house today, remember? I thought you might want to eat first." Now, I'll have to let Marissa go when she's only just been hired, making me feel worse than I already do. On the other hand, how can I keep her after what's happened? I need to stick close to my kids until Kent finishes the investigation.

As I drive, I decide to take a detour to the daycare center rather than going home first. I want to know if Brenda's heard anything. Or if she even knows about Chelsea.

When we arrive, Ben recognizes the building. "Why are we here? Am I going inside to play? But what about Nicky?"

I peer over my shoulder. "We're not staying, sweetheart. Mommy has to go inside and talk to Miss Brenda for a minute. You can come in, too, and I'm sure they'll let you go back and say hello to your friends. Would you like that?"

He nods, wearing a big grin.

"Good." I step out, helping Ben from the back seat, and we walk inside. By the look on their faces, I don't think they know. It isn't until I see Brenda that I realize — she does.

"Brenda, hi."

She swallows hard, noticing Ben before addressing me. "What are you doing here?"

"You mind if Ben goes back and sees his friends for a minute while we talk?" I ask.

"Sure. That's fine." She turns to the front desk. "April, would you take Ben into the playroom? He wants to say hello to some friends."

"Of course." April rounds the desk and offers her hand. "Hi, Ben. Come on, I'll take you back."

"I'll only be a few minutes, honey," I say to him. "Be good." I return my attention to Brenda. "Can we go into your office?"

"Yes."

She leads the way and opens the door for me. I walk inside as she closes it again and shuts the blinds. "I take it, you've spoken to the Asheboro police?" I ask her.

"I have, but I've said nothing to the staff yet. Honestly, I don't know how to." Brenda takes a seat behind her desk. "Why was she at your house, Evelyn?"

I sit down across from her. "I don't know. I truly don't." I suspect, but I don't plan on telling her. "Does she have family in town?"

Brenda nods. "Her parents live here. God only knows how they're managing right now." She narrows her gaze. "But drugs? That just doesn't sound like her."

"That's what the detective said to me as well. There's a lot to this, and I know he's still searching for answers," I reply. "So, she didn't say anything to you? About me or Ben or Nicky?"

"Like what?"

"I don't know. But she didn't show up at my house at two in the morning and then die from a drug overdose without having a reason for coming. I mean, do you think she — wanted to take them from me?"

"What?" Brenda asks, her face masked in disbelief. "No. Where on earth is that coming from?"

138

I raise my hands. "Brenda, I think she followed me last week, too. And a friend of mine . . . he said he'd seen her at the public records office asking for information about me. Then this happens." I shake my head. "I just need to know if she said anything at all to you about my children."

"Like I said, she did not," Brenda replies, her tone hardened. "Listen, I'm very sorry this happened at your home. I am. But there's more to this than either of us knows. Chelsea was barely twenty, for Christ's sake."

"I know," I reply. "And I hope to God Detective Kent finds out what happened."

* * *

I text Marissa that we're stopping by the house before heading over. We drive home, and I'm almost in a hypnotic state. Ben is talking to me, but his words hardly register. I'll find a way out of this — I have no choice. I'm relieved Brenda doesn't know any more than what I initially told her, even if I'm sorry as hell that Chelsea is gone.

Arriving home with Ben at my side, I unlock the front door, pushing it open with my hip. "Come on, buddy. We'll grab a quick bite, then go see Rissa. Why don't you put down your stuff and grab a juice box? I'll get you some lunch."

He drops his backpack in the foyer and then slips off his shoes. He's already heading into the kitchen. The house is quiet. No hum of the television. No baby noises from Nicky. I usually enjoy the peace; instead, I feel even more alone.

I head to the kitchen and grab a loaf of bread from the pantry. As I set everything out, I see it — a folded piece of paper propped against the fruit bowl by the sink.

My name is written on the front in a rushed hand. Is this from the same person who left the music box? I peer around, now even more unsettled by the quiet. They were here. My stomach clenches as I unfold the note.

Did you really think you could keep her?

For a moment, I can't move. My brain stumbles over itself, trying to make sense of what I'm reading. The words swim before my eyes, my pulse pounding so loud it drowns out everything else.

"Nicky," I whisper, the word sticking in my throat, and I reach for my phone. I call Marissa, praying she has Nicky and they're both fine.

The phone rings. I close my eyes, willing her to answer. Instead, it goes to voicemail. "Please, Marissa. Come on." I text her and wait. I sent her a text when we were heading home, too, and it occurs to me that she hasn't responded. Now, she's not answering this one either. "Oh God."

I'm already moving, stumbling back toward the living room. It's empty, and an oppressive silence surrounds me. I bolt upstairs, heart slamming against my ribs as I burst into Nicky's nursery.

I swing open the closet and clamp my hand over my mouth. I shake my head, tears spilling down my cheeks. Everything inside is gone. "Please, God. No."

At her crib, I see the soft pink blanket folded neatly over the side. Inside, the stuffed bunny stares at me, accusing me of being a terrible mother. "No. No, no, no," I mutter, tearing through the room. I fling open the dresser drawers. Empty, too. No onesies. No burp cloths. Nothing.

Ben's small voice floats in from the hallway. "Mommy?"

I force myself to breathe, my hands trembling as I run them through my hair. Think. Think. "Hold on, baby." I run past him down the stairs once again. Nicky's toys are gone. The playpen. Jesus.

I grab my phone again and dial Marissa. The phone rings over and over. "Answer the goddam phone!" I scream. Then I hear Ben crying as he stands at the bottom of the stairs. "Shit."

I try to gather myself, try not to look like I'm on the verge of breaking down. "It's okay, honey. I'm sorry I yelled."

"Mommy?" Ben rubs his hands together as if he's nervous. "Are you okay?"

I swallow hard, forcing myself to calm down. "Yes, I'm okay," I whisper, though the words are a lie. "You know what? We're going to go ahead and go see Marissa now. All right? Can you wait a little while for lunch?"

"Are we going to see Nicky, too?"

My lips quiver. "Yes, sweetie. We'll see her too."

CHAPTER 32

Ben is buckled into his car seat, his knees pulled up to his chest, clutching his stuffed dinosaur like it's the only thing he trusts. Maybe it is. I glance at him in the rearview mirror as I pull out of the driveway, the tires screeching as I press too hard on the gas.

"It's okay, Ben," I say, my voice fracturing. "We'll be at Rissa's soon." I don't know if I'm saying it more for him or me.

I should call the police. Detective Kent. I know that. But my phone sits untouched on the passenger seat, its screen dark, because every time I reach for it, a voice in my head screams, *Not yet. Don't overreact. Marissa's home and you'll be there soon.*

Besides, if I call Kent, he'll almost certainly ask more questions. I've already lied to him. He'll have no reason to trust me or anything I say. He'll want to see Nicky's records. Those records won't stand up to that kind of scrutiny, and then what?

Who the hell is doing this to me? Who would be willing to murder Chelsea and then take my child? "Riley's family?"

She told me her parents wanted nothing to do with her, that they were ashamed of her because of the affair and getting pregnant. But was that another one of her lies to gain my sympathy?

Oh God. So many questions swirl with no resolution. I need to see my baby girl. I will see her. That's what I tell myself as I turn onto Marissa's street.

As I drive toward her house, I realize her car isn't in the driveway. Slowing down, I do my best to stay calm, but my heart plummets.

I pull up in front of her small single-level house. The curtains are drawn, and the driveway is empty. I cut the engine and sit there for a moment, the silence wrapping around me, my breaths echoing in my ears. "Stay here," I tell Ben, twisting around to look at him. "I'll be right back."

"Where's Nicky?" he whispers, his voice trembling.

I force a smile. "She's just inside with Rissa. I'll be right back." I step out into the warm air, the sun tingling my skin as I cross the lawn to Marissa's front door. I knock, hard and loud. "Marissa! It's me, Evelyn."

No answer.

I knock again, the sound echoing inside.

Still no answer, so I peer through the front window, cupping my hands around my face. The living room is dark, the furniture undisturbed. I try the door. Locked. "No. No. Don't do this to me." I step back and scan the yard as if a clue will suddenly present itself. I move around the house, testing the side gate and the back door. Everything is locked tight.

By the time I return to the car, my legs are trembling. Ben looks up at me, his wide eyes wondering why we haven't gone inside to see Marissa and Nicky.

"I don't know where she is," I whisper, sinking into the driver's seat. I press my forehead against the steering wheel, doing my best not to cry. Marissa's gone. Nicky's gone. And I have no idea what to do.

"Tyler." My head snaps up. She's the sister of one of his accountants. Maybe he knows where she is. Or maybe I'm in denial, and the person who's been after me came for her and my daughter.

My fingers fumble for my phone as I scroll through my contacts, pausing at his name. We haven't spoken since Chelsea. I stare at the screen, my thumb hovering over the call button.

"Mommy?" Ben's small voice pulls me out of my thoughts.

I glance back at him. "I'm going to make a call, sweetie. Just sit tight."

I hit the button, holding the phone to my ear as it rings. "Come on, Tyler," I whisper, my heart pounding. "Pick up."

"Hello?" he answers.

I burst into tears. "She's gone. She's gone."

"Evelyn? Hey, hey, it's okay. Slow down . . . Where are you, and who's gone?"

Ben looks at me through the rearview mirror. I have to get a hold of myself. I inhale through my nose, trying to calm down. "I'm . . . I'm outside Marissa's house. Tyler, she and Nicky . . . they're gone."

"What? No. No, that can't be right. She must've just gone out to run an errand. You're not at work?"

"No." I look up, peering out onto the quiet neighborhood street. "I don't know what to do. I tried calling her, texting her. She's not answering. And then . . . I found a note in my house."

"Hang on. What note?" he presses.

"It must all tie back to Chelsea. Whoever killed her . . . they came into my home. All of Nicky's things . . . they're gone."

"You said they left a note?"

I wince, knowing I shouldn't have told him about that. He's going to want to see it. How am I supposed to explain it? "It was just a note saying I couldn't have her — Nicky."

"Oh my God." I hear his hesitation. "Listen, I'm here for you, Evelyn, all right. Everything will be fine. I promise I'm going to help you. Did you call the police?"

"No, not yet. I thought they'd be here," I reply.

"Go home. I'll meet you there, okay? I'll help you figure this out."

"Yeah, okay."

"Good. I'll be there soon. We'll figure this out, Evelyn. I need you to trust me." He ends the call.

"Mommy?" Ben asks, the fear in his voice, palpable.

I clear my throat and peer over my shoulder. "I'm sorry, honey. I'm just a little anxious. I'll be okay. Sometimes we get big feelings that we don't know how to handle, right? Like when you get upset sometimes?"

"Yeah," he says.

"That's all this is," I add. But who am I kidding? He knows something's wrong. He knows Nicky isn't here and that I'm terrified.

I turn the engine, and I'm backing out of the driveway when I notice the mailbox. I stop hard, lurching both of us forward. "What the hell?" The name on the mailbox — it's not Marissa's last name.

CHAPTER 33

It wasn't her name. Maybe she lives with the owner? Maybe she's renting? I checked her out. She came back clean. I rationalize everything as I peer into the rearview mirror, noticing Ben has fallen asleep, only minutes from home.

By the time I pull onto the driveway, my body feels like a live wire, buzzing with panic and exhaustion. I carry Ben inside, careful not to wake him as I settle him on the couch. He stirs but doesn't open his eyes. I wish I could curl up beside him, let sleep take me, and forget about this nightmare. But Nicky's gone, and I have to find her.

I barely have the energy to pace the living room when I hear the knock at the door. My heart lurches, and I freeze. For a split second, I think it's Marissa — with Nicky — but I push the thought away, trying to keep myself grounded.

I force myself to move, unlocking the door with more effort than should be necessary. Tyler stands on the porch, his expression shadowed with concern. "Did you tell the man who works for you? Did he try to call Marissa?" My trust in him hinges on what he says in these next moments.

"Evelyn," he says softly, stepping inside without waiting for an invitation. "He knows and he's calling around."

"She's gone," I blurt out, my voice cracking. "Nicky. I-I don't know where they are, or if they're okay."

He closes the door, his movements calm and deliberate. "I'm here to help, okay? Let's just sit down and go through each step."

I fight the urge to break down in front of him. "I was going to call the police, but I—" I stop myself, looking away.

"But you didn't because you thought everything was fine," he finishes, his voice steady.

"Right," I whisper. "But now . . ."

He puts a hand on my shoulder. His touch is warm and grounding. "Let me try to get a handle on this first, okay?"

"Get a handle on it?" I repeat, stepping back. "How? Tyler, they're gone."

"Give me time," he says. "I'll go back to my employee and see if he's found out anything new."

"Did she . . . did she take her? Did she take Nicky?" The words echo in my ears. It can't be. Can it?

"No, of course not. Look, I don't know what's going on, but I'll get answers for you. I swear it. Just give me a few hours."

"A few hours?" I shake my head. "No, that's too long. We could be giving them time to get away. No, I have to call Detective Kent. What if they're both hurt? There's no time to waste—" My voice cracks, and I take a shaky breath. "I can't lose her, Tyler."

"You're not going to lose her," he replies. "But calling the police will only make matters worse. You know that, don't you?"

How does he know this? Does he think Marissa is responsible, and that's why he doesn't want the police involved? "What if you can't find her?"

"Where's this note they left?" he asks.

I glance into the kitchen, terrified to show him because it'll only raise more questions. "I threw it away. I was scared and ripped it up. I threw it in the trash."

"Why? Why would you do that?" He sets his hands on his hips. "There could've been DNA or hair or something, I don't know . . . they could've tested it."

It's getting harder and harder to keep my secret. How can he help if I don't tell him the truth? And if I do? Will he turn me in to the police himself? Never mind what happens to Marissa and Nicky.

Something about his tone, his certainty, puts my senses on alert. I study his face, searching for . . . something. His expression is steady, his eyes sincere, but can I trust him? Do I dare? "I know, but I told you what it said. I still have the music box. Maybe that'll have fingerprints or something on it."

He meets my gaze without flinching. "Okay. Like I said, just give me a little time to see if I can find Marissa. If you want to reach out to that detective after that, you should. Don't let me stop you. Hand over the music box. Tell him everything. But in the meantime, I can try to do my part to help."

"Yeah, okay."

His brow furrows. "I understand what you must be going through right now. You're scared. I get it. This is at least something that I can do for you instead of sitting on my thumbs. But you do what you need to do, Evelyn."

I nod, but my thoughts are already spiraling. Part of me clings to the notion that Marissa is just out there somewhere with Nicky, taking her for ice cream or at the park. I gloss over the fact that Nicky's things are gone. I have to for now.

I drop to the edge of the couch, glancing at Ben as he sleeps. My hands are trembling again, and I clasp them together to stop the shaking. "Okay. A few hours. I'll keep trying Marissa too and if I still don't hear from her, then I'll have no choice but to call Detective Kent."

He nods, heading for the door. I watch him closely. But I can't shake the single thought running through my head. Did I just let someone walk away with my child?

CHAPTER 34

I have only hours until Tyler returns. Hours until I learn whether my daughter is safe with Marissa, or . . . Trust has again become my worst enemy. And now I wonder whether I've placed that trust in the right person.

Why didn't he insist on calling the police? That's the most logical step when a kidnapping occurs.

I glance at Ben, who stirs on the sofa where I've let him sleep. I've lost my job and my child on the same day. How the hell can this be happening? My only solace now is looking at my son, certain he is safe. But are we? If they came for Nicky, will they come for us, too?

"I have to leave. I have to get answers." Dragging Ben around with me, letting him see my worry and fear — I can't do that to him, but I have no friends here. No family. And after what happened, do I trust to leave him with a neighbor? "No. Not a chance. He's not leaving my side."

I walk into the living room. "Ben? Sweetheart, we need to take a drive, okay?"

He sits up on the couch. "Where are we going?"

"Just for a little drive, okay?"

"Are we going to get Nicky?" he asks.

Tears prick my eyes, and I do my best to hold them back. "Soon, baby. We'll get her soon."

I help him with his shoes and pack a few snacks and water. If I didn't know any better, I'd say we were planning on a day trip. Instead, I'm taking my son with me on the hunt for the truth.

"All right. Let's go." I take his hand and walk outside, locking the door behind me. Securing him into the car, I head out. The first place? Downtown.

We head toward the highway, driving beneath a sunny sky. It's a beautiful spring day, yet noticing such things should be left to those mothers who haven't lost their children. Not me. I remain laser-focused on finding my baby, and that starts with finding out if Tyler Mitchell is who he says he is and how else he might be connected to Marissa Warren. The sister of one of his staff? Maybe. But I take nothing for granted now.

It's almost three in the afternoon. My former employer's office is just ahead. But I'm not going there. I've come to find out more about Tyler's new office.

I park in front of the building and glance back at Ben. "I'm going to step outside for a minute, okay? I'll be right there." I point toward the building. "You'll be able to see me."

He nods, fidgeting with one of his favorite Lego figures.

I step outside, peering around as if someone is watching me. I approach the storefront and lean close to the window, shielding the sun's glare with my hands. Inside, I see a couple of desks. No computers. In fact, there isn't much here at all. If he's in the process of moving in, it's taking him a while.

I walk back to the car and climb inside, entering the building address on my phone. My fingers hesitate for a split second before hitting search. The results pop up — commercial listings, mostly. No mention of a business occupying this space, much less one tied to Tyler Mitchell. My throat tightens as I refresh the page, hoping I've missed something, but the answer is clear. No office, no business.

I glance at the building again. The unease rolls in my gut, and I switch gears, typing in Tyler's name instead. "Tyler

Mitchell." The results come back instantly: hundreds of Tyler Mitchells scattered across the country. LinkedIn profiles, news articles, random mentions. I scroll through them, but nothing stands out. "Damn it," I mutter, rubbing my temple. This isn't getting me anywhere. I pull up my contacts and scroll until I find Chuck's name. My thumb hovers over the call button for a second before I press it. The phone rings twice, and he picks up.

"Hey, kid. What's going on?" His voice is gruff but steady, like always.

"Chuck, I need your help," I say, trying to stay calm. "I'm sitting outside this office building, which a man I met claims he leases, but I see no evidence of it. Hardly anything inside and no signage out front. I can't find anything online about it, either. I don't want to believe he's lying to me, but past events suggest he could be."

"What's the address?" Chuck asks, already sounding like he's moving toward his computer.

I read it off to him, and I hear the faint clicking of keys on his end. "Okay," he says after a moment. "I'm not seeing anything legit tied to that address. It's listed as unoccupied in the public records."

"Can you . . . can you check his name? Tyler Mitchell? He's an accountant. Has a CPA license and owns a business somewhere near here, but I don't know where."

"Sure. Hang on."

More typing. I grip the steering wheel, my eyes darting to the rearview mirror to check on Ben. He's still absorbed with his toy, unaware of my gross error in judgment.

Chuck makes a noise, something between a grunt and a sigh. "Evelyn, I've got something here."

"Go on."

"The name Tyler Mitchell . . . it's popping up, but it's connected to a completely different location. You got a picture of this guy?"

I close my eyes, the weight of Chuck's words settling around me. "Not handy. What are you seeing?"

"Let me send this to you. Hang on. I'm texting it now."

I hear more typing and then a moment later, my phone pings with the message. I open it to see the photo Chuck sent. My heart sinks. "That's not him. Chuck, that's not him."

"The other people with the same name are nowhere near you. No one with that name owns an accounting firm nearby, either, so I have to assume . . . the man you think you know isn't who he says he is. It's like your Tyler doesn't exist. Or . . . he's using someone else's name."

The air feels like it's been sucked out of the car. "Are you sure?" I ask, already knowing the answer.

"I'm sure. Whoever this guy is, he's not who he claims to be, Evie. What are we talking about here? Some random guy from a dating site?"

"No, though that would be easier. Uh, you ran that background for me on Marissa Warren."

"I did," he replies.

"Can you see if she has anyone connected to her under the name Tyler Mitchell? A relative or something."

"Hang on."

I wait for what seems like an eternity.

"I'm afraid I got nothing here, kid . . ."

Tears sting my eyes. "So I have nothing."

"Well, I wouldn't say that," Chuck adds. "You know this guy's not being straight with you. That's probably what you ought to be worrying about right now."

I won't tell him about Nicky. He doesn't know the truth of it all, and that's how it has to stay. "I wish that was my biggest problem right now, Chuck. I appreciate everything you've done for me."

He hesitates a moment. "Why do I get the feeling you're saying goodbye, kid? Do I need to get you some help?"

"No. No, I got this. I'll be in touch again soon. I promise." I end the call, ready to scream. I can't, but I want to. Once again, I've been lied to by someone who wants something from me. And all I can guess is that they want my child.

CHAPTER 35

When I return home, I do my best to keep Ben occupied, not letting him see how rattled I am. Tyler hasn't returned, nor has he called. So, either I let the man who may have helped in the kidnapping of my daughter get distance, or he's doing what he said he would do. But that's hard to imagine, given what I know about him now.

Chuck didn't find much of anything, so whoever Tyler is, he knows how to hide his true identity. The same thing could go for Marissa, too.

Not knowing where Nicky is tears me apart. I don't know how to function . . . how to go about finding her when I can't think of anything except wondering whether she's safe.

The more I think about it, the more I realize it could ultimately be Riley's family behind all of this. I have to find out more about them. Was all of this one big set-up? I must know who they are, where they live . . .

Is it possible Tyler and Marissa were involved with Riley when she had Nicky in foster care? Could one or both of them have been Nicky's foster parents, intending to adopt her? It's a logical explanation, though it doesn't excuse what's happening now.

The answers must lie with Riley's family. They're who I need to talk to, without revealing that I was the one who murdered their daughter. I'll be forced to walk a fine line between my truth and whatever Riley told them.

But who do I turn to who can help me find this information? If I involve the police, they'll soon discover I lied to Detective Langston back in Beaufort, and even if they find Nicky, they'll still take her from me.

There is one person I could turn to. He's already helped so much, sometimes at the risk of his career. It would mean that he'd have to be told everything. No secrets. But he has access to information that I don't. And I know — if I asked — he'd cross that line for me. That line from which there is no return.

"He's my only shot." I retrieve my phone and dial him again. Closing my eyes, I pray that he answers.

"Well, hello again, kid."

"Chuck, hi," I say, hesitation marking my tone. "You deserve to know everything because I need your help."

"'Bout time. But not over the phone. I can be there tonight. Send me your address, and I'll get on the first flight."

"This can't wait until tonight, Chuck. My baby's gone."

He hesitates a moment. "And I take it, you don't want the police involved, otherwise, you and I wouldn't be having this conversation."

I pull back the front room curtain and look outside. "Right."

"Okay, here's what we're going to do," he begins. "This Tyler Mitchell character . . . we know he's lying about who he is."

"Yes," I reply, anxious to hear his plan.

"That means he'll either be in the wind, never to return, or he'll keep playing his game, stringing you along for reasons we have yet to uncover. So, this is what I want you to do . . . get his ID and send me a picture of it, okay? I'll run it through every goddam database I can to find out who he is. Because

I'll tell you this — unless he's some master spy working for a foreign government, I'll peel back the layers and get to the truth. Now, if you're afraid of him, then—"

"No," I cut in. "I'm not afraid of him. I can convince him that I believe what he's telling me. I'll keep playing his game if it means finding Nicky. I can do this."

"Good. Send it to me as soon as you can, and I'll jump right on it. But in the meantime, Evie, if you feel you or your son are in any danger, you gotta promise me you'll pull the plug. You'll go to the police, all right? No matter what. Don't risk your lives."

"Yeah," I whisper. "All right."

"Then I'll keep watch for that image. Stay safe, Evie. I mean it," Chuck adds.

"Thank you. I will." I pocket my phone and peer through the front window again. Dusk is settling over the neighborhood. It's been hours, and I still don't know where my baby is. But as I gaze out, headlights come into view.

As it nears, I recognize the vehicle. Tyler's back. He parks in front of the house, and I drop the curtains. Ben is still playing with his toys on the living room floor, so I walk to the door and open it before Tyler has a chance to knock.

He's alone. I stand in the open doorway, wrapping my arms around my chest as though it's cold outside, but it isn't. In fact, it's warmer than I expected. He walks toward me, his face wearing disappointment, and I'm all but certain it's a lie. On the plus side, he's returned, which I admit, I wasn't sure about.

"I'm sorry, Evelyn," he says, making his way toward me. "I've looked everywhere. Called everyone. No one's seen her."

My eyes flood with tears as I stifle my cries. I expected these words yet hearing them makes this all too real. He steps inside and pulls me into an embrace. I flinch, but he doesn't seem to notice. If this is a game to him, then I have no choice but to play it for as long as it takes to get Nicky back. I won't end up like Chelsea.

155

"I suppose we have to call the police," I say, pulling out of the embrace and closing the door.

He places his hands on his hips and shakes his head. "If I could just get a little more time. If the police get involved, I don't know, Evelyn. I feel like this whole thing could turn on a dime."

Should I be surprised by his answer? He doesn't want the police involved for far different reasons than mine. Meanwhile, I'm left to wonder where my child is and why Marissa has taken her, which has become the most logical conclusion at this point. Just stick to the plan.

I take a deep breath to steady my nerves, feeling the weight of uncertainty pressing down on me. "You're right, of course. I just feel so powerless not knowing where Nicky is or if she's okay. But involving the police could make this worse."

Tyler nods, seeming relieved that I'm not pushing to call the authorities just yet. His eyes flicker with an emotion I can't quite place. "I understand, Evelyn. I know this is impossibly hard for you, but I meant what I said — I'll do everything I can to get Nicky back safely."

I force a small, grateful smile, though inside I want to scream at him. "Thank you. I appreciate that more than you know." My voice comes out too calm for someone in my position.

He approaches, and I see he's coming in to kiss me. The thought of his lips on mine is repulsive, but I can't pull back, no matter how much I want to. He's lying to me, and he must know where Nicky is, so I let him believe I'm putty in his hands.

He presses his mouth hard against mine as though he's proving a point. I can't pull away as my gut churns with anger. Instead, I do my best to focus on finding a way to get his wallet from him. When he pulls away, I regard him, searching for any crack in his facade. "What do we do now? Just wait? Hope and pray?"

I realize that the only way this works is to persuade him to stay here tonight. And when he sleeps, I can take a picture of his ID and send it to Chuck. So, I propose the idea, desperate to sound convincing.

"I'd like you to stay with me tonight. Will you do that? Stay here? Maybe she'll call you. Maybe she'll turn up. I don't know, but I can't be here alone. Please." Playing to his ego is all I can think to do.

"Of course I'll stay," he replies, rubbing my arm in what he probably thinks is a comforting gesture. "I wouldn't leave you to deal with this alone. I feel responsible, Evelyn. I thought I knew Marissa. I mean, I don't want to fully believe this is her fault, but I have to start to face facts. I'm so sorry this is happening."

"Me, too."

CHAPTER 36

Marissa

I peer through the curtains of the motel room window, wondering if we'll be safe here. The baby fusses a little on the bed, surrounded by pillows in a sort of makeshift crib. The sound echoes in this uninviting space. The only other noise comes from the distant cars on the highway.

I drop the curtain and return to the bed, staring at the perfect child who looks back with a wonderous gaze. "It's all right. Mommy's here. We'll be just fine — the two of us." I lean forward, my face hovering above hers. "It's just us. Just you and me. No one can take you away from me here. They don't understand, do they? But that's okay, baby girl. I'm here now."

I brush my hand over her head, in awe of her perfection. My smile can't be contained. "You're perfect. My perfect little angel." My voice drops to a near-whisper. "I saved you. I finally saved you. And no one will ever take you away from me. I won't let them."

The baby's soft whimper breaks the stillness, and my mood shifts in an instant. I pick her up, cradling her. "Oh, shh, shh," I say, rocking her gently. "Are you hungry? How about we get you a bottle?" I carry her to the diaper bag resting on the dresser. I'm prepared for this. Bottles, diapers, clothes. Even a few jars of her favorite food, sweet potatoes. We have everything we need right here.

There's no way to warm the milk, so I'm left to offer her a cold bottle. When I sit on the edge of the bed, I place a few drops onto her lips, hoping she'll open her mouth. "I know it's cold, honey. I'm so sorry." Finally, she takes the bottle.

My gaze drifts to the mirror next to the dresser. For a moment, I stare at my reflection, my head tilting as if inspecting who I've become. "I had to do this. There was no choice."

I turn back to Nicky, my voice soft again. "We'll be safe here, little one. No one will find us. I've thought of everything. Well, almost everything."

The baby's small hand flails, catching a strand of my hair. My smile widens, and I bring her tiny fingers to my lips, kissing them gently. "See? You know me. You know I'm the only one who truly loves you."

My phone rings inside my purse, which lies on the nearby chair. I know who it is, but I won't answer. He'll only tell me to bring her back, but I won't. I can't. I've been through too much to get here, and I won't give her up. Ever.

When the ring silences, my shoulders drop as though the worst has passed. I know it hasn't. In fact, I have a feeling the worst is yet to come.

CHAPTER 37

Evelyn

We have dinner, the three of us, like we're some happy family. The clinking of utensils is the only sound for a while until Ben looks up with innocent eyes and asks where Nicky is. My heart clenches, and I'm forced to make up a story — a lie — something about Nicky staying the night with Marissa. The words taste bitter as I'm forced to keep the truth from him. Meanwhile, Tyler Mitchell — though I know that's not his real last name — plays along, nodding and smiling as if everything's perfectly normal.

After dinner, I tuck Ben into bed, listening to his soft breathing as he drifts off to sleep. My heart aches as I walk by Nicky's room, the door slightly ajar. I pause there, peering inside at her empty crib. The silence in the room is deafening, and I can hardly contain my emotions. What if she's crying right now? What if she needs me?

Then I feel him — Tyler. He stands behind me, his hands cupping my shoulders with a grip that feels smothering.

"We will get her back, Evelyn. She'll be safe and sound back in your arms soon," he says.

I place my hand on his, pretending to appreciate his support. So often, I've told Ben monsters aren't real, but I don't think that's true anymore. Monsters surround me.

"Does she wonder where I am?" I ask.

He pulls me close and begins kissing my neck. Each touch sends fear and repulsion through me. The man who, only the other night, I'd willingly given myself to, now makes my skin crawl with every caress.

They won't hurt her — I need to believe that. It's the only thread of hope that will get me through tonight.

"Let me take you to bed," he whispers against my ear. "I can be who you need me to be, Evelyn, if you give me a chance."

* * *

I lie perfectly still, my breath shallow as I stare at the ceiling in my bedroom. Tyler's snoring is steady, like he's already in a deep sleep. My pulse is anything but steady, each beat throbbing in my ears. I need to do this. And it has to be now.

Sliding the covers off me, I inch out of bed, careful not to let the mattress move. Tyler shifts beside me, mumbling something incoherent, and I freeze. A moment passes. Then another. He settles, his breath leveling out again.

I place my bare feet on the cool floor. The room is dim, moonlight spilling through the gap in the curtains. I spot his pants crumpled in a heap by the window. Perfect.

Every step feels loud in my ears as I cross the room, even though I'm not making a sound. When I finally reach the chair, I crouch, hands trembling, and pick up his pants.

I rifle through the pockets as quietly as I can. Keys. Crumpled receipts. A breath mint wrapper. And finally, his wallet.

Got it.

I flip it open, scanning for his ID. There it is. Tyler James Mitchell — or so it says. His face stares back at me from behind the plastic sheathing. Chuck will be able to look up his license number and confirm if it's legit.

The weight in my chest loosens as I pull out my phone. I need to take a picture. I angle the ID against the faint light coming through the curtains. My hands shake as I line up the shot. I press the button — and the flash goes off.

A burst of light fills the room. My stomach plummets, and my gaze darts to the bed.

"Evelyn?" Tyler's voice comes out groggy.

My eyes are glued to him. With every movement he makes, I ready myself for the inevitable.

He props himself up on one elbow, squinting at me. "What . . . what are you doing?"

Think fast.

"I—" My mind races, trying to cobble together an explanation. "I, uh . . . I couldn't sleep, and I saw your clothes on the floor. I was picking them up. Then my stupid phone fell out of my robe, and when I picked it up again, I pressed the camera button."

Even as the words leave my mouth, I know how ridiculous they sound. It's plausible, but the explanation is too long and sounds rehearsed. I pray he's too tired to make any sense of it.

Tyler frowns, but his head drops back onto the pillow. "Come back to bed."

"Okay."

He sighs, muttering something about being tired, and rolls back over. Within seconds, his breathing steadies again.

I stand there, fixed to the spot, my hands clutching his wallet. After a moment, I slide the ID back in, return the wallet to his pants, and tiptoe back to bed.

Sliding under the covers, I clutch my phone against my chest, my heart still racing. The picture is saved. Chuck will have it by morning.

* * *

162

Dawn emerges through my curtains, a gentle glow radiating over the room, and I find Tyler still asleep. This is my chance. Ben will be up soon, and I must send the image to Chuck before the day begins.

I slip out of bed, wrapping my robe around me as though it will somehow offer protection, and head into the hallway. Quietly closing my door, I continue toward Ben's room and peek in on him. He's still nestled under his covers, looking peaceful. I won't be taking him to school today. In fact, I won't let him leave my side until I get my daughter back.

I don't bother looking in Nicky's room again; the pain is too fresh and raw. Instead, I head downstairs to do what must be done. As I reach the kitchen, I type the message.

Here it is. I hope you can work your magic.

With a deep breath, I hit send and feel a weight lift from my shoulders — hoping that I'll have answers soon.

Ben's light footfalls sound on the staircase, each step echoing in the quiet house. I quickly tuck my phone into my robe pocket and plaster on a smile as he enters the kitchen. "Good morning, sweetheart. You want some breakfast?"

"Yes, please." He looks at me with wide eyes, tilting his head in curiosity. "Why aren't you dressed, Mommy? Don't you have to take me to school and then go to work?"

A pang of guilt shoots through my gut. "Not today, baby. We're going to stay home today, all right?

"No school?" he asks with a hint of disbelief and some excitement.

"No, buddy. Not today." I pour him a bowl of cereal and then make a pot of coffee, trying to focus on the mundane tasks. The thought of seeing Tyler again terrifies me — he's in my house, and last night . . . last night happened.

I'm in too deep to back out now; this has to be seen to its end.

CHAPTER 38

Marissa

The road extends out before me, a black ribbon winding between the trees. I've been driving for hours, watching dawn break through the darkness. The baby stirs in the back seat, her whimpers cutting through the droning of tires on the road.

"It's okay, sweetheart," I say, glancing at her in the rear-view mirror. Her face is peaceful again, eyes closed, her little fist clutching the corner of her blanket as if it's her most valued possession.

We're finally here. I gaze at the stately home perched at the top of the lengthy driveway. Its black shutters stand in stark contrast to the white-painted siding. Red brick steps lead up to a welcoming wrap-around porch, though I know better now. Nothing is welcoming about this place, yet it's the only place I could think of going. However, uncertainty gnaws at me — will she take us in? She doesn't know what I've done.

Surely, everything will be forgiven the moment she sees her. But questions will be raised. These are issues I should have considered more thoroughly before coming here. Every mile I place between us and Evelyn feels like a win, but then doubt consumes me. I went against the rules. Against the plan. What will my punishment be? I wrap my fingers around the steering wheel, my knuckles white with tension.

The gas gauge shows a quarter tank, a reminder that I can't keep driving forever and I have to find a place for us to stay soon. Cash is drying up fast. I check the rearview mirror again as if the baby can sense my worry. But she looks as peaceful as she did moments ago.

Maybe it's better to stay somewhere else in town until I've figured out my next move. But who am I kidding? My arrival here has already been detected. I imagine she's looking at me now through one of the windows, judging me, wondering if I've come alone.

I can't keep Tyler in the dark forever. He needs to know where I've gone; maybe he's come to his senses and will understand why I did what I did.

"This is a mistake. I can't be here." No doubt, she'll already be on the phone, making the call, alerting Tyler herself. So, I press the ignition, turn around, and head back toward the city. I didn't think this through; that much is clear to me now.

It isn't long before I arrive at a local diner, one I haven't been to in a long time. I take the baby out of her car seat and carry her inside. A smiling waitress, too old to still be forced to work, gestures outward.

"Take a seat wherever you like, honey."

I nod, certain I must look like every other haggard new mother who has no idea what she's gotten herself into. At the back of the diner, I see the perfect spot. I set down the car carrier in the booth and slide onto the green vinyl seat beside it.

The baby peers at me. Her perfect blue eyes and near-toothless smile warm my heart, reminding me this was all worth the risk. "I'll never let you out of my sight again. I'm so sorry to put you through this, sweetheart."

The waitress approaches, her gaze drawn to the baby. "Well, look what we have here. Aren't you a little cutie-pie?" She looks at me. "How old?"

"Eight months."

"Oh, a petite little thing, for eight months." She looks me over. "Must get that from her momma."

I smile at the first nice thing anyone's said to me in a long time. "Maybe so."

"All right, what can I get you, sweetheart?" she asks, holding a small notebook.

"A coffee, cream and sugar. And, uh, I don't suppose you have any bananas?"

"I sure do." She leans toward me. "I can smash 'em up for you if you like."

"That would be great, thank you."

She pulls back. "I'll have that up for you in a flash."

After she leaves, I retrieve my phone, scrolling through social media. Everyone seems to be going on with their lives as if nothing's happened. I suppose nothing's happened to them — just me.

When the waitress returns, she hands me a small bowl of mashed bananas. "Here you go. I'll bet the little one will love these." She sets down my coffee. "And one coffee, cream and sugar. You sure you don't want anything else? Toast? A muffin?"

I wave her off. "No, I'm good. Thank you, though."

"All right. Enjoy."

I take a sip from the mug, then reach for my phone to open Tyler's contact. I have to tell him we're okay. He's called several times and texted just as many. But I needed distance. He would've done everything to convince me not to do it, so I didn't give him the chance.

But I have her now, and I'm never letting her go.

CHAPTER 39

Evelyn

He'll be up soon. I've been standing in my kitchen, staring at my phone, willing it to receive a message from Chuck, but so far — nothing. I know how this works, and I know he needs time, but I don't have any left. I need to find my daughter.

I think back to the stuffed animal on the curb — the disturbing message scrawled on its chest. The music box and the note inside. Never mind the fact Chelsea died right out front of my house. I still don't know how she ties into it or whether she's a victim. Did Marissa really kill her? Did Tyler? Why? What did Chelsea know? Or was it that they simply wanted her out of the way?

They must've orchestrated all of it. Once Brenda decided to kick my kids out of her facility, that was when they went to work. Ruining everything in my life to force me into this position. Who could do that unless they had money and connections? Who the hell are these people?

I naively believed Chelsea was out to blackmail me, ignoring the obvious warning signs. But how did they find her? I rack my brain for answers, fighting off the rising tide of guilt.

Now, I have to find a way to be around Tyler and not let him see what I know — that he isn't who he says he is. Marissa isn't either, so whoever helped them do this knew exactly how to keep their identities hidden. But Chuck is good. If anyone can get to the truth, it's him.

Tyler walks into the kitchen, dressed and ready — for what, I don't know. "Good morning," he says.

"Morning. I just made coffee. Care for a cup?" I force a smile through the heartbreak, trying to hide the truth of my furtive actions.

"Coffee sounds great. Thank you."

He doesn't seem to pick up on my nervousness, so I pour him a cup as he heads over to Ben. I don't want him near my son, but I say nothing.

"Hey, buddy." He kisses the top of Ben's head. "That cereal looks tasty."

"It is," Ben replies. "It's yummy. You want some?"

"No, thanks. Maybe next time." He approaches me, wrapping an arm around my waist and kissing my cheek as if the son of a bitch owns me. "Hey. How are you holding up?"

"Not great, Tyler." I turn and hand him his cup. "We need to find her today."

"I know," he says, taking a sip. When he swallows it down, he looks at me again. "I have a plan."

"And what's that?"

"I'm going to go see a few people. People who know Marissa and might know where she went. But I think it's best if you and Ben stick close to home. There's no telling if she might just show up, realizing the mistake she's made."

I already don't like this plan; it sounds an awful lot like what he told me yesterday. If he leaves, I risk him not returning, and Nicky will be lost to me. But I hold out hope that if Chuck gets the information I need, I'll have the time to put together my own plan for finding my daughter. Maybe it's worth the risk. "How long will you be gone?"

He shakes his head. "A few hours. It shouldn't take long. I need to make a few stops around town."

I look at Ben, knowing we're probably safer without Tyler here. "Yeah, okay. Ben and I can stay here and hope for the best."

He places his hand on my cheek. "I can't imagine what you're going through, Evelyn. But I'll do everything in my power to bring Nicky home. I just need you to trust me, okay? Can you do that?"

There's that word again — trust. Something I lost in anyone long ago. And the moment I thought it'd returned, the rug was pulled out from under me once again. "Yeah, I can do that."

I sip on my coffee, going about my morning rituals, waiting for Tyler to leave. I keep my phone in the pocket of my robe, clutching it for dear life. If Chuck were to choose this moment to reply, this little game of mine would be lost.

Tyler grabs his car keys from the counter and smiles at me, a kind of solemn smile that I'm certain he thinks will convince me he's on my side. Instead, it makes my chest burn with rage. He's the reason Nicky's gone, and Chelsea's dead, but I don't know why.

"I'll see you soon," he says, offering a slight nod before walking out the door.

When I hear the click, then the turn of his car's engine, I feel like I can breathe again. With Ben still eating his breakfast, I pull my phone from my pocket and open the messages. Still nothing from Chuck. "Okay, I need you now, old friend. I don't know how much time I have."

Waiting for something to happen leaves me feeling hopeless like I'm nothing more than a feckless woman who relies on others to come to her rescue. That can't be who I truly am, though past events suggest otherwise.

If I leave, I might as well say goodbye to Nicky forever, but it would ensure Ben stays safe. Both our lives are at risk by staying. Nevertheless, I can't bring myself to give up my baby. No, leaving isn't an option. Instead, I have to convince Tyler that I trust him — that he is our savior. And when I do get to the truth, I'll find a way to use it against him.

* * *

The morning seemed to drag on forever. I did my best to stay occupied, having taken a shower and gotten dressed. I made Ben a snack and got him cleaned up, too. While I was upstairs, it took every bit of energy not to go into Nicky's room and sob my eyes out. Doing that would serve no purpose and would only frighten Ben more. I have to stay strong for him.

"Mommy?" Ben looks up at me as we sit on the sofa together.

"Yes, honey?"

"Can we have lunch now?"

"Yeah, sure. I think it's about that time." I stand up and offer him my hand. "Come on. Let's get you something to eat."

We walk into the kitchen when my phone buzzes in my pocket. My heart soars at the idea it could be Chuck. "Sit down, bud. I need to answer this, okay?" And when I see the screen, I want to cry. Instead, I answer, "Oh boy, Chuck, you have no idea how glad I am you called. Please tell me you have some news."

"Not yet," he replies.

Defeat weighs on my shoulders as I close my eyes, an audible sigh escaping me.

"Just hear me out," he continues. "Look, I'm getting close, all right? I think I found a connection to Medford, but I'm still ironing out the details. When I do, I should be able to ID this guy for you."

"How much longer?" I ask.

"As long as it takes me, Evie. Can you stick it out with me? I need you to stay strong here."

My eyes sting with tears because I feel my resolve slipping away with each passing moment. Instead, I swallow my emotions. "Yes, of course. I can keep doing what I'm doing. Tyler went out, saying he had a few more people he could talk to who might know where Marissa is."

"And you believe him?" Chuck's words are laced with his usual skepticism — a quality any good PI possesses.

"No," I reply. "But I don't know what the hell else he could be doing. Or maybe I just don't want to think about it."

"Best you keep focused on sticking to the plan, Evie, you got that? I can do this. I just need a little more time."

I nod as though he can see me. "Okay. You're the only one I trust with this, Chuck."

"Then I'll get you what you want. But keep in mind, if he's around, don't you dare risk answering my call or texts. Put your phone on silent. Don't even look at it until you know you're somewhere he can't see. We don't need to raise his suspicions while he's in your home."

"I know. I have Ben to consider, and if something starts to feel off, we won't stick around. And listen, thanks for this, Chuck."

"You got it."

He ends the call, and I pocket my phone. The hope I felt only moments ago has vanished, replaced by the familiar fear and anxiety that have devoured me since all this started.

"Mommy? You said you were going to make me lunch," Ben says.

"Of course. Yes." I clear the emotion from my throat. "I'll do that right now."

While Ben eats, I wipe down the kitchen counters and empty the dishwasher. Anything and everything I can do to keep my mind off the fact that my baby is in the hands of a woman I hardly know for reasons I know even less about.

As the afternoon drags on, I wonder when Tyler will be back. I'm desperate for Chuck to contact me before he arrives. I don't know what will happen if Tyler catches me digging into his background, but I imagine it won't be good.

I hear a car in the distance, and my heart stops. I strain to hear if it pulls onto my driveway. Is that him? Is he back? Does he have her? I feel like I already know the answer to that question, but I remain hopeful.

I pick up my phone, swiping open the screen to Chuck's text messages. "Please. Please text or call. It has to be now, Chuck. I need it now."

"Mommy, who are you talking to?" Ben asks, still sitting on the bar stool, coloring in one of his books.

"No one, honey. No one." I find my feet again and walk to the window overlooking the front yard. It's Tyler. He's here.

I pocket my phone and walk back to the kitchen sink, turning on the faucet as if I'm in the middle of something — I don't know what.

He knocks and opens the door. "It's just me, Evelyn. I'm back."

A moment later, he appears in the kitchen. "Hi," I say, forcing myself to appear grateful he's arrived. "Any news?"

He continues inside, tousling Ben's hair as he passes him by. "Hey, buddy."

"Hi." Ben shakes his hair back into place.

"I'm not having any luck, Evelyn." He glances down. "I'm so sorry. I'd hoped to have better news. No one's seen or heard from Marissa."

My phone buzzes in my pocket. Tyler hears it, too. Jesus. I thought I'd put it on silent. A careless act that could cost me everything. And I already know who it is — the only person who would be calling or texting me right now because I have no one else.

I keep my gaze on him, and he looks at me, tilting his head and narrowing his gaze. "Aren't you going to answer that?"

"Oh," I say, feigning surprise. "Of course." I retrieve my phone and try to angle the screen away from him. Chuck's name appears in big bold letters.

Tyler walks toward me. "Who's that? A friend? Because I'm not sure you should be talking to friends right now. They'll sense you're upset and start asking questions."

"Yeah, no. I get that. He's a friend. And you're right. I'll let it go to voicemail." I press the button to decline the call, and before I have a chance to set down my phone, a text arrives.

I glance at it, the notification appearing on the screen. The first line of the message appears.

I know who he is. Call me ASAP.

Tyler regards me, a darkness swimming in his gaze. He sees it, too. I give him a sideways glance while various escape scenarios run through my head. I check Ben's location. How far away from the door are we? Can we both get past him?

"Evelyn, what does that mean? Who sent this to you?" Tyler places his fingers under my chin, turning my head toward him. "You have something you want to tell me?"

CHAPTER 40

Tyler stands inches from me, peering at my phone. My stomach churns. The way he's looking at me — eyes narrowed, jaw tight, like he could explode at any moment.

"Who have you been talking to, Evelyn?" he asks, his voice low and razor-sharp.

I see him clearly now. I see the monster. "Chuck is . . . just someone I used to work with. An old friend."

Tyler grunts. "A friend? A friend who's doing what? The message says he knows who *he* is. Who's he talking about?"

The room closes in around me. I glance at Ben, who doesn't take notice of our conversation, keeping crayon to paper. "Look, he's no one, all right? Just a friend who I asked to look into Marissa for me."

"Look into? What, is he a cop or something?" Tyler snatches my phone and turns the screen toward my face to unlock it. "Let's just see what ol' Chuck has to say, huh?" He swipes open the message.

All I can do is stand there while Tyler reads what I haven't read yet. It only takes a moment, and then a tight smile forms on his lips. He raises his gaze at me.

"Looks like Chuck knows a lot about me, Evelyn. What'd you tell him? Does he know I've been trying to help you get your daughter back? That I've agreed to keep the police out of this for your sake."

Agreed? He insisted I keep the cops out, and I agreed for my own reasons, which I suspect Tyler must already know. Nevertheless, Chuck must've learned the truth, leaving Tyler on edge, which is a bad sign for Ben and me. "Where is she, Tyler? Where's my daughter?"

His smile grows into a full grin, teeth and all. "Your daughter?"

He snatches my arm, digging his fingers into the soft underside. "Stop. You're hurting me." I try to keep my voice low, not wanting to frighten Ben.

Tyler takes a step closer. "Do I need to worry about Chuck, Evelyn? Is he going to call the police? Is he going to come here and try to save you?"

Save me? My breath hitches as fear presses in. "No. He doesn't know where I live." That part is true, but knowing Chuck, it wouldn't take him more than five minutes to find out where I've been working and look up public records to see that I've purchased this house. Which, now that I consider it, is probably how Tyler and Marissa found me. But I still don't know who they are. The answer rests on my phone, which I doubt I'll ever see again.

I try to steady my breathing and keep my face calm even as my pulse races. "I'm sorry, Tyler. I was getting desperate for answers. I had to know if Nicky was safe."

He stares at me, his expression twisting, disbelief giving way to something darker. He laughs — a harsh, unamusing sound. "Safe?" he repeats. "Safe? I have more interest in Nicky's safety than you'll ever know."

"Tyler, please—"

"You should've just listened to me," he snaps, making me flinch. "I told you I'd fix everything. I told you I'd find Nicky and bring her home."

I glance again toward Ben. I have to protect him. "Tyler, we can talk about this," I say, my voice coming out cracked. "I just . . . I made a mistake, okay? I shouldn't have involved Chuck. But right now, you're scaring me."

"Good," he says flatly. "You should be scared. Maybe you'll stop doing stupid things if you listen to me from here on out."

I edge back, my body trembling as I try to put distance between us. The front door is too far, and I'll be damned if I'm leaving without my son. I need to keep Tyler calm and keep him talking.

"I'm sorry." I shrink down, making myself small . . . less of a threat to him. "I thought I was doing the right thing."

The veins in his neck bulge, and he's breathing loudly through his nose. He looks like a coiled spring about to snap. "I've been trying to protect you, Evelyn. Now, you've made it very difficult for me to continue to do so."

He takes another step closer, and I force myself not to flinch. "I can fix this," I say quickly. "I'll tell Chuck it was a misunderstanding. That you've been helping me, and I was just second-guessing the both of us."

He doesn't believe me. "Tyler," I say, keeping my voice calm, though my hands are shaking. "We can do this together, okay?" I do my best to play on his attraction toward me. "Just bring Nicky home and you and me? We can be a family."

His expression falls, and I sense I've said the exact wrong thing.

"You and me? We're not a family. We're nothing. You and Ben mean nothing to me."

I look at my son, who raises his gaze, having picked up on Tyler's words. And now I see fear in his eyes.

Tyler doesn't move or blink, and I realize with horrifying clarity that he's already decided what he's going to do. His grip on me tightens.

"Please, Tyler. I'll do what you say, just don't hurt my son."

Without another word, he pulls me into the living room.

176

Ben looks at us, a confused expression masking his face. "Mommy?" he asks, darting his gaze between Tyler and me.

"It's okay, sweetie." I don't know what else to say. I don't know what Tyler intends to do.

"We're going on a little trip, Ben," he says. "You, me, and your mom. It'll be fun."

My heart sinks. I can't leave here. Staying here is the only shot I have at Chuck finding us. He's the only person who can.

"You and your mom are going to pack a few things, and we'll leave in an hour, okay?" Tyler continues.

Ben slides off the barstool and heads toward the staircase. "Okay."

Tyler finally lets go of my arm. "Get your things together. Now."

* * *

The car's engine hums low, almost soothing, if not for the fact that every muscle in my body is wound tight. Tyler's hands grip the wheel, and his eyes focus on the road ahead. Beside him, I sit rigid, my heart pounding so loud I'm sure he can hear it. Ben is in the back seat, chattering about something he saw out the window, oblivious to the tension around him.

"Where are we going?" I ask, trying to keep my voice steady. Casual. But it comes out small and thin.

Tyler glances at me. "You'll see," he says, his tone light, almost teasing. But I know better now.

I force a smile, turning slightly in my seat to look at Ben. He's grinning, pointing out the window at the trees rushing past. "Look, Mommy! That one's huge!"

"It is," I say, my voice too bright, too cheerful. "Maybe we'll see even bigger ones soon."

Tyler smirks at that like he knows exactly what I'm doing. He doesn't say anything, just presses his foot a little harder on the gas. The car surges forward, and I grip the edge of my seat, nails digging into the fabric.

I glance at the road signs, and my stomach drops. We're heading toward Medford, the place where my nightmare first began. I haven't been back there since I learned the truth about Riley and Derek and found out why she followed us to Beaufort. The name pierces my thoughts like shards of glass — Riley Dittrich.

This isn't a coincidence. Tyler knows her. But how? Is this where my daughter is? My throat tightens, and I swallow hard, forcing myself to focus. All I want is to get Nicky back, to hold her, to know she's safe. Whatever Tyler is planning, I have to keep it together for Ben.

"Ben, sweetheart, why don't you tell me what you did in school last week?" I say, turning toward him. Distraction. Keep him talking. Keep him from noticing the fear in my voice.

"Oh, we learned about dinosaurs," Ben replies. "And how some eat plants and trees and others . . ." His voice fades as I nod and smile, my eyes darting back to Tyler. His jaw is tight, the muscle in his cheek twitching.

I've never felt so helpless. But I can't let Tyler see that. I can't let Ben feel it. I press my hands into my lap, forcing them to stay still.

"Tyler," I try again, keeping my tone light. "If we're going to be in the car much longer, we might need to stop for a bathroom break. Unless you want an accident . . ."

"We're not stopping," he says flatly.

My stomach twists in knots. I peer through the passenger window, trying to calculate how far we are from Medford — the place where everything fell apart. From the memories of the days and months that followed, memories I've been desperate to bury.

Tyler's voice cuts through the silence. "You turned quiet, Evelyn. Something else on your mind?"

I regard him, my smile plastered in place. "Just wondering how much longer. You know how kids are with long car rides."

He doesn't respond, his lips curling into a faint smile, taking pleasure in my fear.

All I can think about is Nicky. Her little laugh, her tiny hands. I have to believe she's okay. Whatever Tyler's game is, I pray she's not in danger.

But as the road lies out ahead, taking us closer to Medford, closer to the past I've been running from, I can't shake the feeling that Tyler's leading us straight into a trap. And I don't know if he'll ever let us out.

CHAPTER 41

As the surroundings grow more and more familiar, so, too, does the dread in the pit of my stomach. The sun curves to the west as the afternoon wanes. Tyler has said nothing. I do my best to keep Ben happy by playing I Spy and other road trip games. I can't let him see how scared I am.

Chuck will wonder why I haven't responded to his message. How long will it take him to realize that what he feared might happen — has?

"Where are we going?" I ask again, doing my best to sound confident and unafraid.

Tyler glances at me. "You'll see soon enough."

"How long are we staying?" I'm aware I'm pressing my luck by questioning him, but I need answers. I need them so I can find a way out for all of us.

"As long as it takes, Evelyn." He shoots a look at me. "Now, why don't you keep doing what you're doing, all right? Ben's happy, and I'm sure you want it to stay that way."

"Who are you?" I ask, desperation tinging my words. "Why did you come for me? Why did you take Nicky?"

"You think I took her?" he asks. "Marissa took her, Evelyn. Not me."

"Maybe so, but you can't pretend you're trying to help me any longer. I think we're well past that now. So why her? Did you know Riley Dittrich? Were you and Marissa Nicky's foster parents, or were you planning to adopt her?"

"That's not her name," he says, cold and flat.

"What?"

"Her name isn't Nicky — Nicole — whatever the hell you've been calling her."

"Riley called her Jenny," I reply.

He scoffs but says nothing more.

"I saved her," I add. "Did you know that? Riley tried to kill her, and I rescued her."

He glares at me but quickly sets his eyes again on the road ahead. "And you just thought you'd be okay to keep her, huh?"

"Riley killed my husband. I shot her, trying to save him, but I was too late. Riley lied about who she was. She tracked down my family after we left Medford." I turn away, disgusted by the entire situation. "She did this. You're angry at the wrong person."

"We're here," he says, turning sharply down the street of an older neighborhood.

I don't recognize it. Not this part of Medford. "Is this where you live? Is Marissa here too, with Nicky?"

He pulls to a stop, and his eyes darken. Before I know it, he slaps me across the face. "I told you to stop calling her that."

Shocked, I press my hand against my stinging cheek. The sound startles Ben. He looks at me and starts to cry. "It's okay, baby. I'm okay. Don't cry. Please, don't cry." It's all I can do not to cry myself, but I have to be strong for him.

"Get out," Tyler says.

I stare at the house in front of us. "What is this place?"

"I said, get out." He opens his door and walks around to the passenger side.

For a moment, I consider climbing into the back seat, unbuckling Ben, and both of us running for it. But no sooner does the thought enter my mind than Tyler opens my door and yanks me out.

I stumble over my feet, almost losing my balance. "Please, just tell me what's going on and why you're doing this."

"Get Ben. Now."

He follows closely behind me as I walk around the car and help Ben out of his booster seat. "We're going inside. Stay calm. If you scream, I'll hurt him."

I know he's telling the truth, so I don't risk it. Instead, I walk toward the two-story house. It appears lived in and cared for, though not particularly nice.

I clutch Ben's hand as Tyler ushers us up the front steps. My heart pounds, fear and adrenaline coursing through me. But I force myself to stay calm for my son's sake.

The inside of the house is dim. A hazy glow hovers over the old furniture and outdated decor. Tyler leads us through a living room and down a hall. I scan everything, searching for some clue as to where we are and why. But there are no photos on the walls, no personal items that give anything away.

At the end of the hall, Tyler unlocks a door and guides us down a set of creaky wooden steps. *A basement.* Descending into the darkness, I sense what's about to happen, and I clutch Ben's hand tighter.

It's unfinished. A concrete floor and cinder block walls. No carpeting, just a rug under an old sofa and table. A fluorescent light fixture hangs from two chains fixed to a wood beam in the center of the ceiling. A plastic folding table stands a few feet away, where a TV might be placed. Along the side wall, metal shelving hangs from rusted brackets, boxes and papers stacked on them. I'm instantly reminded of our basement in Beaufort, and I feel like that's the intended effect.

"Have a seat," Tyler says, motioning to the couch.

I lower myself, pulling Ben onto my lap. He clings to me, his small body tense.

"Please," I say, looking up at Tyler's imposing figure looming over us. "Tell me what's happening. Why did you bring us here?"

"I haven't figured out what to do with you yet." He pulls out my phone from his pocket. "We're going to answer that message. Tell your friend, Chuck, that you're fine and this was all a misunderstanding."

A laugh unexpectedly escapes me. "He'll never believe that."

He moves closer, squatting low to meet my gaze. He glances at Ben, offering him a smile, before looking at me again. With cold resolve, he continues, "Make him believe, Evelyn, or your son will be the one to pay the price." He stands up again, waiting for me to relay the message. I realize now that he won't let me see the phone . . . see what it was Chuck discovered about him.

With a deep breath, I begin. "Tell him this . . ."

Hey Chuck, sorry for the radio silence. Everything is okay now. It was all just a big misunderstanding with Tyler. He was trying to help in his own way. I overreacted, but it's all good now. Anyway, no need to worry. Ben and I are doing fine. I'll check in again soon.

My stomach turns as he hits 'send.' I know Chuck pretty well, and I don't think he'll buy it. What that means for us — I'm not sure. I could've just sealed our fate.

"Good girl," Tyler says, pocketing my phone once again.

I survey the cold and uninviting space, filling my head with scenarios of what might happen here. "What are you going to do with us?"

Tyler smirks. "Nothing at the moment. Right now, I'm going to get my wife."

CHAPTER 42

Marissa

I push open the diner door with my shoulder, the baby balanced on my hip like she weighs nothing. Her head rests against my chest, her belly full of mashed bananas. The warm air brushes against me, carrying the scent of exhaust from the nearby highway. It mingles with the aroma of stale coffee and fried food from inside.

My sneakers scuff against the pavement as I step into the parking lot, the neon *Open 24 Hours* sign buzzing behind me. I don't know where to go. My car waits as though I have a plan, and it's ready to do its part. But the idea of sitting behind the wheel with no destination — it makes my stomach twist into knots. Tyler hasn't called since yesterday. Not one word. I expected him to, and now that he hasn't, I can't help but wonder why.

Where is he? What's he doing? The questions irritate my skull, rubbing it raw with each step I take toward the car. I imagine him with Evelyn — her perfect hair, her smooth voice, and her gifted intellect. Maybe they're somewhere laughing about me. Calling me crazy. Maybe they're in bed together.

The thought cuts through me, tearing open old wounds that never really healed, and I shift Nicky higher on my hip to stop my hands from quivering. What if he never calls? What if he's gone, not just for tonight but for good? What if he's chosen her over us?

I don't want to cry. Not here, not with the baby pressed against me. She's the only thing keeping me grounded, but the tears come anyway. I blink them back and open the car door, placing her gently into the car carrier. Her little body goes slack against the straps, her head lolling to the side as she drifts off again.

I close the door and grip the roof of the car, leaning into it as if it can somehow absorb my worries. I need to hear from him to know what's real and what's just in my head.

I stare at my reflection in the car window — my face pale, my eyes red-rimmed, and my hair disheveled. I'm almost unrecognizable. "Where do we go now?"

I wait for an answer that doesn't come. Instead, I consider another hotel as I'm forced to play this waiting game, hoping Tyler doesn't abandon us.

I slide into the driver's seat and start the car. Looking out at the road ahead, the truth is that I don't have a plan. I don't have anything left except for one undeniable certainty reflected at me in the rearview mirror: "I have you, sweet baby. I only have you."

Just as I'm about to leave, a text appears on my phone. And when I look at the screen, relief washes over me.

I have a plan. Tell me where you are, and I'll come to you. We'll do this together, you, me, and the baby — just like it was supposed to be.

CHAPTER 43

Evelyn

A damp smell lingers in the air. The walls around us, gray and cold, confirm any effort to escape would be wasted. I have no sense of time because there isn't a single window in here. Basements are supposed to have a secondary egress — an emergency escape route. Not here. Not this place.

What's worse is that we have no bathroom. The bucket and toilet paper in the far corner are supposed to be an acceptable substitute.

The door is locked. Of course it is. I've already tried pounding on it. I don't recall the neighboring houses being that far away when we arrived, and I'd hoped someone would hear me, but no. Nothing.

My wife.

His words echo in my ears. Marissa is his wife. I suspected as much, but how could he have so willingly slept with me? I wonder if she knows. Could I use that to wedge a divide between them?

I'm led to believe, then, that Tyler and Marissa knew Riley and must've been promised her baby or had been taking

186

care of her. That would explain why Riley didn't turn up with Nicky until the night of my brilliant plan — the one that backfired spectacularly, resulting in my husband's murder. She must've taken Nicky from them.

A part of me feels sorry for the couple, but why would they have chosen to go about things this way? Why not come out with the truth when they tracked me down? Then again, would I have willingly handed Nicky over to foster parents? Parents who wanted to adopt her? No. I don't think so. Nicky is Derek's daughter. Maybe Tyler realized that me handing her over would have been an impossible ask, so he made other arrangements. And someone ended up dead. I'm not sure that was part of his plan. But if it was, it reinforces the idea that he wouldn't hesitate to kill again.

Ben is curled against me as we sit on this old, ratty sofa. It took me a while to get him to stop crying. I'm pretty sure he cried himself to sleep. I wrap my arms around him, pulling him close, trying to keep him warm. It's cold in here with no heater. I can't imagine what it's like down here in the winter. But where is *here*? What is this place? We're in Medford, but in an area I don't recall.

His face is buried in my shoulder, and his tears have soaked through my shirt. I rock him gently, the way I used to when he was a baby, back when I thought we were safe.

I glance at the bottles of water and granola bars lying on the folding card table. Our captor was kind enough to provide us with some sustenance. I scoff. Twice now, I've let myself be taken in by men who turned out to be different than I thought they were. As a lawyer, I should have better instincts than that. Instead, I have a startling inability to thoroughly assess a person's character. Tyler isn't the man I thought he was.

I force myself to move, gently laying Ben down on the couch and walking to the table. I grab a bottle of water and twist the cap off, my hands shaking so badly it almost slips away.

I return to Ben, whose eyes flicker open. "Here, sweetheart," I say, holding it to his lips. "Have a sip, okay?"

He takes it, his small mouth moving slowly, and I feel some semblance of relief that he's at least drinking. But it's fleeting as my gaze shifts back to the locked door at the top of the stairs. How long will he keep us here? What will he do to us? What will become of Nicky?

I shake away the thoughts, trying to focus. I have to keep it together. My son needs me. But every creak in the house above us makes me flinch. Every minute that ticks by feels like I'm a minute closer to losing my son.

"Mommy?" Ben's voice is small, almost a whisper.

"Yes, sweetie?"

"Why are we here?"

My throat tightens with emotion. How do I explain something I don't understand myself? "I don't know yet, sweetheart. But we're going to get out of here. I promise." It's a lie that I tell him and myself.

I don't dare let him see the truth in my eyes. The truth is that I'm not sure we'll get out of this place at all.

* * *

When I'm certain Ben is asleep, I drape a tattered blanket over him and get up from the sofa to wander inside this new prison. They found us. Now, I've lost Nicky, and I could lose Ben, too. "So what are you going to do about it?" I challenge myself.

I feel like I'm right back where it all started — inside the basement of my home. Every second of that night floods my thoughts, but I push them aside, trying not to let them rattle me.

Right now, getting my son and me out of here is all that matters. Then . . . then I'll find Nicky, and I'll get her back.

I walk the perimeter of the room, running my hands along the masonry walls, searching for any weakness — a crumbling block, loose enough to wedge free. Something I can use as a weapon. But no. I'm not that lucky.

I move on to inspect the wooden stairs leading up to the locked door. They creak under my weight as I climb. Upon reaching the door, I examine the hinges and the frame, pushing and prodding, looking for any weaknesses. But it's solid. No give at all.

Ben stirs in his sleep, and I halt, wondering if he's having another nightmare. I'm not sure I have the energy required to bring him out of it. But I wait. "Please, not now," I whisper.

Thankfully, he settles again, and I continue my search. Gazing up at the ceiling, I notice exposed pipes and ductwork hanging from metal brackets. It's all too high, and the openings too narrow to provide an escape route. However, if I can somehow knock one of the pipes free, I could use it as a weapon when Tyler returns or cause enough commotion so that he'll have to come down. I must consider the prospect of attacking him, even killing him in front of Ben.

Returning to the folding table, I sort through the meager provisions Tyler left. I shake the table's legs, wondering if they'll break free. But no.

My sights land on a pile of old magazines stacked beside the table. I reach for one and scan the date — two months ago. So, wherever we are, someone has lived here recently.

"I need something that will help. Please, God. Help me find a way out before he comes back."

My gaze roams around the room again, looking for anything I might have missed. The bucket, the food, the dingy couch. Wait . . . the couch. I march over and start running my hands along the fabric, checking under the cushions. And that's when I feel it — a loose spring. I dig my fingers in, twisting and turning the soft metal until it snaps off.

Examining it, I see it's only a few inches long, but it could be useful. I climb the stairs and stand in front of the door. "Let's see what happens." I insert the spring into the lock, jiggling it around. It's stubborn, but I don't give up. I keep maneuvering the improvised lock pick, feeling for the pins inside. It refuses to disengage. "Goddam it." I hold back the tears that are desperate to break free. Overwhelmed with anger, I throw my weight against the door and only succeed in hurting my shoulder. But then I hear something beyond the door. Noises inside the house. "He's back."

I rush to the sofa and sit down, doing my best not to appear as though I've been attempting an escape.

Footfalls approach. I hear a key inserted into the door and the click as the lock disengages. The door creaks open. I don't dare look back. I already know it's him. His footsteps sound heavy on the worn stairs. And when he appears, I glimpse him from the corner of my eye but refuse to look directly at him.

"What have you been doing, Evelyn? I hope you're being a good girl."

CHAPTER 44

Marissa

I sit on the couch, setting the carrier on the floor next to me. The house feels cold and unfamiliar. Tyler says it belongs to his family and was a rental that was abandoned a few months ago. I can't imagine anyone having lived here. It's worse than the hotels where we've been holed up. But it doesn't come as a surprise. Tyler's family is . . . different. Almost disconnected from the real world. Tyler wasn't like them, or so I thought when we got married.

Outside, darkness has settled over the neighborhood. I wonder if I'll be able to sleep tonight. Not just because of this house but because Evelyn and Ben are being held captive in the basement just below my feet. I know what Evelyn did, but Ben — his eyes wearing a wide, frightened gaze — it haunts me. I know this is a mistake, but Tyler didn't hesitate to remind me that it was a mistake of my own making.

In the short time I've known Evelyn and Ben, I've come to adore the boy. A part of me even thought that Evelyn could've been a friend in another life. She was only trying to protect her children. I'm no different. But instead of finding solutions, we've only tangled ourselves further in this web. I should've listened to Tyler and followed through with his plan, but how could I when she was right there? My baby — in the arms of another woman.

Downstairs, the creak of footsteps echoes, followed by Tyler's voice — a low rumble with an edge that worries me. What might he do? When he came for us tonight, I saw a change in him. His demeanor.

I glance at Jenny, still sleeping in her carrier. With a soft touch, I stroke her cheek; she stirs. My sweet girl.

The basement door swings open, and Tyler emerges alone. I search his face for any hint of what transpired below, but it's a blank slate. "How are they?" I ask.

Tyler's shrug is casual as he approaches like we aren't keeping two people down there against their will. "Scared."

I cringe at the thought of Ben's fear. "What are we going to do with them, Ty? We can't keep them down there forever."

"We'll figure it out," he replies.

His words are unconvincing. I've heard him sound more certain about lesser things than this colossal mess we've created. "Do you think she'll stay quiet?" I ask.

He squats low and brushes back Jenny's fine hair with a tenderness that seems at odds with the situation. "I think so. She won't risk anything happening to Ben."

"What are you going to do with them?" I press, needing more than just vague assurances.

He stands up again, his face heating with anger, his composure slipping. "What do you want me to say, Marissa? You were the one who took Jenny. I told you to wait. That I would handle it. All I needed was the goddam DNA results back to be certain, but you couldn't wait. You put us in this spot, all right? Now, I'm the one who has to get us out."

I stare at him a moment longer, searching for something — remorse, guilt, anything — but find nothing other than defensiveness. He's hiding something else, and I think I know what it is. "Did you sleep with her?" The question escapes before I can stop it.

192

He narrows his eyes and swats his hand dismissively. "Oh, for God's sake."

I don't want to admit what that means; his reaction tells me more than words ever could. Instead, I focus on Jenny. She's all that matters right now, and I'll do whatever it takes to keep her safe.

"How long are we supposed to stay here?" I press again, feeling defiant despite my fear of his behavior. Despite being certain he's betrayed me.

"As long as it takes to be sure no one finds her," he replies. "This Chuck guy she contacted — we have to know if he'll come looking."

"And if he does?" I ask.

He raises his chin. "Then I'll make sure he doesn't find her."

CHAPTER 45

Evelyn

Will he leave us here alone all night? I heard muted voices upstairs earlier. That must mean Marissa is here and Nicky, too. The thought of my baby being so near makes my heart soar. If only I could get to her. I need to get her away from these insane people. I need us all to be free of them.

Ben managed to eat one of the granola bars. So did I. But I have to ration them because I don't know Tyler's plan. Will he bother providing more for us, or will he leave us to die from a lack of water or food?

I inventory my surroundings once again. A gas water heater stands on the side of the staircase; it rumbles and moans as though on its last legs. A rug lies beneath the sofa and table that has an old industrial-type pile and no padding. That's where the damp smell comes from, and I'm left to assume that the basement was never waterproofed.

I look toward the staircase. The old wooden treads appear in various states of rot. I peer at the banister. Could I break it without destroying the steps and without alerting Tyler? Maybe pieces of it.

I head toward it, wrapping my hand around the railing and testing it. It's sturdy enough to shift only slightly under the push and pull of my grip. But if I have all night, I could loosen it enough to break a piece of it free, splintering off, rusty nails and all.

First, I have to be certain Tyler won't come down here again tonight. It's too soon to know whether he's fallen asleep or is merely quiet upstairs. My best guess is that we've been down here for four, maybe five hours. It was nearly dusk when we arrived, meaning it must be getting late in the evening. Ten o'clock at least.

Will he sleep? That — I can't answer. I'll have to trust my instincts.

* * *

I shoot up from the sofa, awakened by Ben's screams. It's black down here, so I feel around for him. Relief consumes me when I touch his socked feet, though his legs kick. "Baby, it's okay. Shhh . . ." I slide closer to him, pulling him against me to stop his movement. The noise is too much, too loud, and I don't know if they can hear him.

"It's okay. I'm here. You're safe." It's the first time I've said those words and didn't believe them. "Honey, I need you to settle down. Please, baby." Tears sting my eyes. How can I comfort him when we're in this place?

I rock him back and forth until he settles and becomes quieter — until it's nothing more than heart-wrenching moans. "I know. I know, but I'm here, sweetheart. Please don't cry," I whisper.

When he's finally quiet, I listen for noise upstairs. I don't know how long I slept. I have no idea of the time. But after several more minutes, I'm certain that Tyler isn't coming for us. Not right now.

With Ben nodding off once again, I let my feet swing to the floor. The cold, rough carpet fibers poke through my thin socks. I stand, using the arm of the couch to balance as I rise. Without the ability to see my surroundings, my equilibrium is skewed. I feel dizzy and wobbly on my feet.

I carefully navigate the room. Arms out, fingers extended, searching for obstacles. My foot scrapes the leg of the coffee table, bending back my pinkie toe.

I clamp my hand over my mouth to stifle the scream as pain shoots up my leg. I take a deep breath, holding it for distraction. The toe throbs and I'm certain it's broken. As I stand there, I listen for Ben but hear no movement. At least I didn't wake him.

After the initial shock wears off, I take another step and gingerly carry on toward the staircase. I could turn on the light; in fact, that would probably be easiest, but if I awaken Ben, he'll talk or maybe cry. I can afford neither, so I'll have to work in the pitch black.

Finally, I reach the staircase, confirmed by my hand clinching around the banister. I feel around for a loose spindle. If I can break one free, I can use it as a weapon. So far, each seems well secured, but I won't give up. I can't, so I keep searching.

I stand on the bottom step and wiggle the spindle before climbing each step to check the next one and then the next. I let out a gasp as I grip one that moves. I wiggle it again, and I almost want to cry. This is it. This is the one.

With both hands wrapped around the square spindle, I push and pull. Push and pull. Harder and harder. It begins to loosen under the strain. The nails squeak with each tug and echo around me so loudly that I wonder if they can hear me upstairs. But I press on. Tyler could be down here in a matter of hours, maybe less, and I have to be ready.

I pull with all my might, widening my stance and bracing myself for leverage. Then I hear a crack beneath my feet. My eyes widen, trying to take in light, but there is none. With a resounding thud, I fall through as the tread splits, scraping my calf so hard it feels like someone's taken a potato peeler to my shin.

I stifle my scream, covering my mouth. The sound of the crash still echoes around me, but all I can think about is the pain. Warm blood trickles down my leg, soaking through my pants and socks. My breaths sound in my ears as I try to calm myself.

"Mommy?"

Oh no. He's awake. "I'm right here, Benny. Shhh." My voice comes out shaky. "You're okay. Go back to sleep, baby."

"Where are you, Mommy? I can't see you."

Hot tears stream down my cheeks from the pain in my leg and the fear that Tyler will hear him. "I'm on the stairs, honey," I whisper. "Go back to sleep. Everything's fine."

Everything isn't fine. I'm injured. Badly. And I'm Ben's only hope of escape. Gripping on to the railing, I lift my leg out of the hole. The wood creaks, splintering farther apart. A piece breaks off and tumbles down the stairs. *Goddam it.*

Finally, my left leg is freed and throbs even more. I turn around, using the wall and railing as I put all my weight on my right leg. Slowly descending the steps, I pray another tread doesn't fail. When I reach the bottom, I hobble toward the sofa, feeling the blood still spilling from my wound. My pants are torn, and the air hits my raw flesh, stinging it as though someone is pouring alcohol over it.

I feel around for the sofa, calling on my memory to guide me along the same path I first traveled. I can afford no more injuries since the ones I've already sustained will hamper any chance of getting free.

"I'm right here, baby." I lower myself onto the sofa, finding Ben pressed up against the other side of it, curled into a tiny ball of fear.

"When can we go home?" he asks. "I want to go home, Mommy."

Hope drains from me. "Soon, honey. Mommy's doing everything she can to get us out of here."

I raise my leg, hoping my eyes have adjusted enough to see the damage I've done. "I'm going to have to turn on the light, okay, baby?"

"Okay."

Now, I have to get up again, but I remember where the light is, and I know the path is clear. I limp toward it, still using my hands to guide me. When I reach it, I flip the switch, and the fixture illuminates, burning my eyes with its harsh white glow.

I wonder if Tyler can see the light from under the basement door. Have I awakened him? I return to the couch and gingerly pull up my pant leg. As I look down at my injury, my eyes widen with shock. Bile rises as my gag reflex kicks in. Flesh hangs down inches above my foot, still clinging but mostly peeled away from my shin.

Whatever emotion I'd been able to hold back is bursting now. Tears fill my eyes as I look at Ben. He sees it too, and the look on his face . . . "I'm okay, baby. I'm okay. Don't cry. Please, don't cry," I whisper.

A faint blue light shines from behind the stairs and captures my gaze. "I'm here. Honey, I need you to stop crying. I need you to be brave for me. Can you do that? Can you be brave for Mommy?"

He nods, wiping his tears with the back of his hand. "You're hurt."

"I hurt my leg, yes, but I'll be just fine." I glance over my shoulder at the light. "Stay here. Take deep breaths and calm yourself down. Can you do that for me?"

"Yeah."

"Good." I stand up and realize I'm losing feeling in my left leg. I assume shock is setting in as I feel drained of color and woozy. But I need to know what that light is and where it's coming from.

I shuffle toward it, dragging my leg, putting all my energy into balancing on my right side. Finally, I reach the stairs. The light is coming from inside the step that broke. I move around behind the staircase where the wall is. "Storage . . . There's a storage closet here."

I continue to inspect the area, and I see something as I peer through the broken tread. "Is that . . . a pump?"

A sump pump closet would be logical. Which would mean there could be a tool or something I can use against Tyler. Something I can hide. I have to get in there somehow.

I walk around again toward the wall under the staircase, looking around for some sort of access door. "There must be one here." I run my hands along the wall, pressing here and there, looking for the door. And then I hear the click. I found it.

I press on the opening, and the door swings out. I see the blue light. It's a sump pump. I bend to crawl inside the small opening. My leg throbs and burns, but I can't let it stop me. I must know what's in there.

The light in the basement hardly reaches here. It's dark. But I follow the blue light, feeling around the cold concrete floor until my hand stops on something. Wrapping my fingers around it, I immediately know what it is. "A hammer."

CHAPTER 46

He didn't hear me — Tyler. It must have been an hour, and I've heard nothing from above. I don't know that I would've had the strength to fight him off, even with my newfound weapon. I'm weak. Tired. In pain.

The idea of killing someone — again — leaves my stomach churning. But I know it's either him or us. And I'll do anything to protect my son. I've found nothing else of use inside the small sump pump closet. A way out would've been nice.

Instead, I sit on the sofa next to Ben, who doesn't seem to have it in him to sleep any longer. At least he's quiet. I don't know how he's able to do what he's doing at only five years old, but I'm grateful. God knows the impact this trauma will have on him. I fear the little boy I've known is gone, replaced by a child who will shut himself off from the world, wall up his heart, and never let anyone in again. To be honest, I'll probably do the same.

My calf has swollen. Most of the bleeding has stopped, but the raw flesh is still exposed. I need to cover it to prevent infection. I can't use the blanket. It's the only thing I have to keep Ben warm. There's nothing else down here to use except the clothes I wear.

Maybe this is my way out. If I can get Marissa to hear me when Tyler comes down again, I can plead for medical help. I don't know if he'll let us go upstairs, but it's worth a try. Then again, a hammer won't easily hide under my clothes. "Damn it."

"Mommy, you said a bad word."

I can't help but smile. "I did, baby, and I'm sorry." Even in a time like this, Ben reminds me that I'm his mother and we're still a family.

I don't know how much time has passed, but I now hear sounds upstairs. It must be morning. I hope it is, anyway. I wonder if Chuck has come looking for me. The message I sent him didn't sound like me at all, so I'm banking on his skills as a private investigator to pick up on that. But what can he really do? Well, if he knows who Tyler is, he'll probably find out where he is. But until then, it's on me to get us out of here.

I glance up as the noise above grows louder. I can't believe I'm so close to Nicky, though it might as well be a thousand miles. Will Tyler come down to check on us?

It occurs to me at that moment to turn off the light. Tyler doesn't know one of the steps is broken. If it's too dark to see, he might fall, giving me a precious few moments to use the hammer against him. I don't want to kill him in front of Ben, but I may not have a choice. *It's him or us, Evie,* I remind myself.

I do my best to hurry to the light switch, though my leg is almost completely numb from pain. "Benny, I'm going to turn off the light for a minute, okay? I want you to stay exactly where you are and not move. You understand me?"

"Yes," he says, his voice tiny and afraid.

"Okay." I flip the switch, casting us in complete darkness once again. I hold the hammer and carefully move toward the stairs, standing between them and Ben.

Tyler's footfalls draw near, and the door handle rattles as though he's inserting a key into the lock. My heart races, and I instinctively glance back at Ben. He's unaware of what's about to happen. Then again, I'm not entirely sure, myself.

The door opens, and light from above spills in. The broken tread is still cast in shadow. He might not see it or might not see it in time. I tighten my grip around the hammer, and for a fleeting moment, I wonder if I have it in me to strike at him. *Him or us. Him or us.*

He steps on the first tread, closing the door behind him. He won't see the broken step now. But when I see a flashlight — or maybe the light from a phone — shine down, my hope that he'll fall to the bottom fades. As does my hope that we'll get out of here.

Still, I hide beside the staircase.

"Evelyn?" Tyler calls out. "It's awfully dark down here, and somehow, I don't think you're still asleep."

I turn toward Ben, still only seeing a slight outline of him. I just have to hope he'll remain silent. Maybe it doesn't matter either way.

Tyler continues descending the steps, the light he carries, aimed down. And then he stops. Damn it. He's seen it. "What the hell happened here?"

He aims the light into the room, scanning around, searching for me. "Evelyn, where are you?"

My throat dries, and I squeeze the hammer. I say nothing, praying Ben says nothing, either.

"Are you hurt? Is Ben? What happened to this step? How did it break?"

I refuse to speak. If he wants to find us, he'll have to come down here.

"Goddam it." Tyler returns the light to the steps and carefully avoids the broken tread. But he doesn't notice the missing spindle.

If this doesn't work, the spindle could be my backup, unless he decides to kill me for coming at him with a hammer. Still, I'd hoped he'd fall down the staircase to make things easier for me. Looks like I won't be that lucky.

When Tyler reaches the bottom, his light sweeps across the room, landing on Ben. Still in shadow, Ben squints, but he remains silent. *Good boy.*

"Hi, Ben," he says. "Are you okay? Where's your mommy hiding?"

Ben says nothing.

"Okay." Tyler moves toward the wall switch, sweeping his light back and forth. "There's blood on the floor. Evelyn, you must be hurt."

If he turns it on, he'll see me. I'll be left with no choice but to rush him.

The light floods the basement. He sees me. I freeze, the hammer behind my back.

"Oh my God. Your leg." He regards me. "Let me look at it. You're obviously hurt. I don't know what you did, but it's bad, Evelyn."

"Don't come near me," I say.

"For God's sake, look at you."

He starts walking toward me. Adrenaline shoots through me like a bullet. I have to do this. There's no choice. I can get past Marissa. I can get Nicky, and we can all leave. He looks down at me, his gaze landing on my arms before he stops. He knows I'm holding something. The time is now.

A guttural roar climbs up my throat, escaping in the haze of rage. His eyes widen as I lurch toward him, dragging my leg behind me, moving as fast as I can. The hammer falls to my side, and as I begin to raise it, he sees it.

Tyler stumbles back, raising his arms in defense. I hear Ben crying behind me, but I can't think about that now, so I press forward, moving as quickly as I can while Tyler continues to step backward. He's surprised. Maybe surprised enough that I can get in a swing, landing on him hard enough to buy us time to get upstairs.

With all the strength I can muster, I bring it down, the hammer cracking against his forearm. He yells out in pain. I raise it again, ready to let it fall, and as it does, he clamps his right hand onto it, stopping it mid-swing.

"Stop!" he yells.

His hand shoots out, taking my wrist in a vice-like grip. The hammer clatters to the floor, and his other hand slams into my chest, sending me sprawling backward. My head hits the concrete with a thud, and stars explode behind my eyes.

"Mommy!" Ben screams, his voice shrill with terror.

"Stay back, Ben!" I manage to choke out, even as pain radiates through my skull. I try to scramble to my feet, but Tyler is on me, his weight pinning me down. His face is a mask of fury now.

"You think you're tough?" he growls, his breath hot against my face. "You think you can take me?"

I struggle beneath him, my injured leg splitting open and spilling fresh blood. "Let us go! You don't have to do this!"

"Goddam it, stop struggling!" he shouts. "You're not getting out of here, Evelyn. You or your son."

CHAPTER 47

We're on the couch. Ben is calm. Tyler looms over me while Marissa wraps my leg in a bandage. I glance at him, pleased with myself when I notice the bruising and swelling in his forearm. At least I got in a decent hit. Not that it did anything for Ben and me. We're still here. Still trapped. And now, I no longer have the hammer.

"Why won't you let us go?" I ask Marissa, my tone soft and low. "Please. I've done nothing to you."

She glances up at me, then returns her gaze to the bandage. "You have no idea what you've done."

"Then tell me!" My voice raises, drawing Tyler's attention.

He steps toward me. "Shut up, Evelyn, or you and Ben won't make it out of here alive."

"So you plan to let us go?" I press, raising my chin in defiance.

Marissa glances back at him but doesn't say another word. I sense she doesn't like this any more than I do. Can I use that? Can I use her? I'm out of options, so I'd better think of something.

"Ben needs to use the bathroom," I say. "He's got a stomach-ache, so unless you want a big mess down here, I suggest you let me take him upstairs to use the toilet."

Tyler's narrow gaze darts between Ben and me. "Is that true, Ben? Do you need the bathroom? Does your stomach hurt?"

How will Ben respond? Will he sense that I need him to lie? My God, can I really expect him to help in such a way? I have no choice.

He's quiet and doesn't answer.

"Ben?" Tyler asks again.

His eyes dart up at him. They're filled with tears. Finally, he nods, and relief washes over me. *Thank God.*

"Then I'll take you." Tyler offers his hand.

"No," I shoot back. "Let me do it. You'll only scare him more, and he won't go. It has to be me." I look over at Ben. "Come here, sweetheart. I know your tummy hurts."

Marissa glances over her shoulder at Tyler. "Please just let her take him."

That did it. I got to her. Whether it's enough to get her to help us, I don't know, but she's on my side with this one. It's a start.

"Fine. But I'm going up with them," Tyler says.

My heart soars at the prospect of us getting out of this dank basement. I can scope out the house, try to get a sense of our location. Anything I can use to aid in our escape. "Thank you."

He helps me up, and I take Ben's hand. "Come on, buddy. We're going upstairs."

"Go," Tyler says. "But give me Ben's hand. I'll walk him up and make sure he doesn't hurt himself on the step."

I should've known it wasn't going to be that easy. Still, there's a chance. "Fine." I start up the steps, my leg feeling only mildly better. Though with nothing to dull the pain or reduce the swelling, it still hurts like a bitch.

We reach the top of the stairs, and I stop at the door and try the handle. "It's locked."

Tyler walks in front of me, and I have the perfect opportunity to push him down the staircase. But it wouldn't be enough. And if I try to attack him again, he'll probably kill me. Then what good am I to Ben?

Instead, I take Ben's hand. "It's okay, buddy. You can use the bathroom in just a minute." I smile at him, squeezing his hand as if telling him I know what I'm doing. But that couldn't be further from the truth.

The door swings open and Tyler steps through. "All right. Let's go."

We walk into what looks like the kitchen as he keeps his hand on the knob, holding it open. The smell of fresh air hits me first. The sun is shining through the windows, forcing me to squint. It looks like it's still early in the morning. But with the sunlight beaming through, I can't see outside. I don't know where we are. I don't see her — Nicky. She must be here. Where else could they have taken her?

"Hurry up, Evelyn," Tyler says. "Bathroom's that way, down the hall." He aims his finger to the right.

"What is this place?" I ask as we begin to walk.

"Nothing to you. Just keep quiet, all right?" he says.

"Yeah, sorry."

"It's that door on the left."

I open it and turn on the light. Peering inside, I notice that the bathroom is old and dirty. Mold lines the grout in the pink tile around the tub. The vanity top is laminated and has yellowed with age. The faucet has plastic crystal-looking knobs from decades ago. I remember my parents' house had them too.

"Well, go on," Tyler insists. "Take him inside."

As I usher Ben in, Tyler grabs my arm, spinning me around. "If you try anything, Evelyn, I won't hesitate to kill you."

"All right. I get it," I reply. When I close the door, Tyler's voice calls out.

"I'll be standing right here, waiting."

I close my eyes for a moment, then look at Ben. "Are you doing okay, buddy?"

"I don't have to poopoo, Mommy."

"Yeah, I know. I'm sorry I made you lie about a tummy ache. I- I just needed to get us out of there so I could see where we are," I whisper. He doesn't understand any of this. How could he?

"So I don't have to try?" he asks.

"Well, do you have to go at all? Anything?"

His face twists and his brow rises. "I can try."

"Good. Okay." Anything is better than sitting on that bucket like we did yesterday. And now I have a minute to think. What can I do? How can I get us free from this nightmare?

I pull back the shower curtain and see a window. It's small and high, and no way could I fit through it. Ben might be able to, but I have no idea what's outside that window. Plants, dirt, gravel. I don't know, and I'm not going to risk it.

So what else is there? In a matter of minutes, we'll be forced back into the basement, probably for the rest of the day and night. I raise my gaze. *God, how am I going to get us out of here?*

Tyler knocks on the door. "Let's hurry it up in there."

"He's almost done," I call out. Ben jumps off the toilet and pulls up his pants. "All good, buddy?"

"Yeah. I went peepee."

"Good job, sweetheart. Wash your hands." I lift him so he can reach the sink. I'm almost out of time, and I still have no plan. After he dries his hands, I set him down again. I grip the handle, out of time and out of options.

"Mommy?" Ben looks up at me. "Aren't you going to open the door?" I hear the sound. Faint, almost indiscernible, but I know what it is. "Nicky?" A sudden surge of hope rushes through me. She's here. My baby is here.

"Let's go," Tyler says, his voice raised. "Now."

I take a breath and open the door. "Sorry. I wanted Ben to wash his hands." I take his hand and step out of the bathroom. Nicky's cry still sounds in the distance. I look at Tyler.

He knows I can hear her — my baby. "All right. Back into the basement."

I take a step forward while Tyler presses his hand against my back. Ben is a step in front of me. Nicky's cry grows distant. She must be in a bedroom at the back of the hallway. Only feet from where I now stand.

My chest pounds. Sweat lines my neck. I have to do it. I have to try again.

I stop cold, forcing Tyler to run into me. I ram my elbow into his gut, knocking the wind from his lungs. He stumbles backward as I turn around. Before he has a chance to regain his balance, I shove the palm of my hand in an upward motion, connecting with his nose. Blood spurts as he stumbles back again.

I turn toward Ben. "Run!"

Ben dashes down the hallway. Tyler comes at me, rage in his eyes and fists curled. I can't let him get to Ben, so I charge toward him, head down, ramming him in the gut like I'm an NFL linebacker.

We tumble to the floor, sending white-hot pain through my leg as the bandage slips down, exposing my raw flesh.

"Mommy, Mommy!"

I hear Ben pulling on the front door handle.

"I can't open it!" he cries out.

It takes all my energy to keep Tyler at bay. Ben has to find the deadbolt, which I'm sure must still be locked. Tyler takes a swing, clipping my jaw. I turn in time before he can do any real damage, though it still throbs. "Why are you doing this?" I plead as he grips my wrists.

"You did this!"

Tyler flips me over, straddling my body, pinning down my arms. "Stop fighting. You'll only make things worse."

"Run, Ben, run!" I scream. But all I hear is him crying and tugging on the door handle. He can't escape. Even if he did, where could he go? Are there any neighbors around? Anyone at all who could help? The thought of him being out there alone terrifies me, but not as much as dying here with me does.

Footsteps sound in the living room. And then I hear her, too. "Nicky!" She's crying, and I hear movement but can't see around Tyler as he keeps me pinned down. I writhe and twist, but he's too strong. I can't break free.

Tyler glances over his shoulder. This is my shot. I bring up my good leg, kneeing him in the lower back. It doesn't do much except draw his attention to me again. "Get the fuck off me!" I scream.

Then I hear the front door. Ben screams for me. Nicky is crying, and then the door slams shut. "Marissa. No! No!" I thrash under Tyler's weight. "Get off! She's taking them. Tell her to stop! Tell her to come back!"

"Shut the hell up." The back of Tyler's hand lands across my face. Everything turns black.

CHAPTER 48

When I come to again, I regain my focus, and it only takes a moment to realize where I am — back in the basement, tied up this time, hands behind my back. I scan the area around me. "Where is he? Where's my son?"

Tyler sits on a chair across from me. By the look of his face, I got in a few good shots. A bruise covers his cheek. His bottom lip is cut. I got my share, too, as the throbbing in my face worsens. My leg has been rebandaged. But the entire house is quiet. "Where's Marissa?"

Tyler stands and walks upstairs again, saying nothing in response.

"Where is my son?" I scream. "Give me my son!" I yell as loudly as I can, but he doesn't return. Not for several minutes. Then the footsteps come.

He's holding a box, and he walks to the folding table. "This should last you a few days," he says. "After that, you're on your own."

"What?" Panic surges in my chest. "What are you doing?" I try to stand, but my ankles are bound, as well as my hands. "Tyler, give me my son. Tell me where he is. He's not part of this — whatever the hell this is."

211

He sets his gaze on me. "You took my child. Now, I'm taking yours." He starts walking toward the stairs. "Don't come looking. It won't end well — for you or Ben."

"Wait! No . . . You can't just leave me here. Tyler, wait!" I hear the basement door slam shut. "Tyler! Give me my son!"

Everything around me spins. My thoughts churn. Fear consumes me. Now, these people have both my children, and they're gone. Tears stream down my cheeks. Dread and panic build in my chest. How do I get out of here? He won't leave me here to die — will he?

Then I remember that he has everything he wants now: Nicky, Ben, and me out of the picture. I have no way out — no phone, and food and water that might get me through a week.

I don't know where they're going. If I had a way to get in touch with Chuck, he could tell me the truth about Tyler. Then I might have a fighting chance, but I have to get out of here first. "How the fuck am I going to do that?"

Each moment I'm stuck in here is another moment for them to get farther away, taking Ben to God knows where. And Nicky. My head sinks low as defeat rests on my shoulders. I don't know who these people are or why they're doing this to me. But if I don't find a way out, my children will be lost to me forever.

I struggle against the ropes binding my wrists, but Tyler has tied them too tight. The coarse fibers dig into my skin, chafing it raw as I try in vain to loosen the knots.

My eyes catch the spindle I'd managed to break free from the staircase. Nails extend from it, rusty, but sharp. Is it possible to use it to cut through the ropes? I don't know, but I have to try.

I manage to stand without falling over. The odds of me face-planting onto this concrete floor are better than I'm willing to wager. So, I take slow baby steps, shuffling along toward the spindle.

It takes several minutes, but I make it. Now, I turn around and bend backward to reach it. My back cracks, and my legs ache from the awkward position, but I think I'm getting close.

I spread my fingers out, searching for the old piece of wood, desperate not to knock it over where it will only be that much harder to grasp.

There it is. I feel it. "Come on. Just hang on to it, okay? You can do it." I still have no idea if this will work, but it's all I have. It's the only hope I can cling to.

Finally, it's in my hands. I shuffle back toward the sofa. Now, to figure out how to get the three nails on the bottom of the spindle to cut the rope. Am I crazy? This is never going to work.

But I try anyway.

Holding the spindle behind my back, I lower it to the ropes around my ankles. They've already cut into the wound I suffered from the staircase, but I think I've lost all feeling in it now. That's probably a good thing.

The ropes are thin — almost like decorative jute, which can unravel if I wedge it between the twists. It's my only shot.

I push the nails between the ropes, wriggling them around to loosen the fibers. But as I do, the rope cuts into my injured leg that much deeper, sending fresh pain through me. "Just keep going. You can do this," I remind myself. "This is how you get out of here." I ignore that this is only the first step and probably the easiest. After this, I have to find a way out of the basement, which presents a whole other set of problems. "One thing at a time. Come on, Evie. Focus."

I continue to wriggle the nails, feeling the fibers loosen a little. I keep going. Keep pressing harder and moving more until the nails slip. The skin on my heel splits open, one of the nails slicing right through it.

My head grows light from the pain and the loss of even more blood. I feel like I'm going to . . .

* * *

My eyes flutter open. For a moment, confusion reigns as I struggle to remember where I am. Darkness surrounds me, and the cold seeps in. "The basement." I'm on the floor next to the couch. I must've fallen. My head throbs. Yep, I fell hard. "Oh God." I try to use my hands but am quickly reminded that they're tied behind my back. So, I raise onto my elbow and push myself upright. "What time is it? How long was I out?"

Not a soul is around who can answer my questions. "Help! Help me!" I scream. But I'm only answered with more silence. "Oh God. Please get me out of here. Please." The tears come, and I can't stop them. Not this time. Defeat presses down on me, and I feel like I might die in here. "Benny," I cry. "Nicky. I love you both so much."

I have no one to blame but myself. "No. Stop. This isn't over, Evie," I tell myself. "Don't you dare give up. Your kids need you." With a painful grunt, I leverage the sofa to get up, managing to sit on the cushions. "Halfway there." I rise on weak legs, pain shooting through them.

Now, I stand. "What next?" The wood spindle lies on the sofa, where I must've dropped it before passing out. "It can still work. You have to try again."

This time, I take hold of the spindle and sit down on the edge of the couch angling my legs outward. It should make it easier to control my movements.

Again, I wedge the nails through the jute, doing my best to fray it, let it unravel, and make it easier to slip off. With practiced patience, I do the work. I stay calm. Panicking again will end in more injuries.

Tears prick my eyes as I work cautiously against time. I have to break free from here, and I can't be certain, once I'm free of my binds, that I'll even find a way out. But I must take this a step at a time.

I feel the rope snap and look down. A piece of it has torn loose, leaving more behind, but it's a start.

Several more minutes tick by, and there's another snap. I wriggle my feet, trying to help the process, but it's still secured, so I keep at it. Thirst consumes me, and I have to pee, but

I'm not stopping now. It took me too long to get this far, so I carry on.

A final push and pull of the spindle and the last pieces of rope tear apart, unraveling what remains around my ankles. "Oh, thank God." My legs are free, but I need my hands too.

I walk toward the table where Tyler placed the box of food and water. I'm desperate for water, but I can't get to it with my hands still bound behind my back. So, I look around, praying my gaze lands on something I can use. "I'm so close. Please . . . there must be something in here."

I could try the spindle again, though it would be awkward to reach the ropes. But as I scan the room, I see nothing else that will help. No mirror I can break. No glass or piece of metal lying around. Tyler knew what he was doing when he brought us down here. He knew there was no way out.

Finally, I take hold of the spindle and bend my hands upward toward my wrists. I twist them, rubbing the rope back and forth over the nails. It's tedious work, the strands fraying one by one. My hands ache, and my shoulders burn from the strain.

Finally, the rope splits, and I pull my hands free with a gasp of relief. I walk up the stairs, careful to avoid the broken tread, reaching the door. But when I turn the knob, it's as I expected. Locked. Of course.

I press my ear to the door, straining to hear anything beyond it. Voices. Footsteps. The faint creak of the floor. Nothing. Only the low hum of silence. I know they're already gone. I just hoped I would hear something. Marissa's change of heart? But no. I'm here alone, and my children . . . Ben. Nicky. Their names catch in my throat. They're gone, too.

CHAPTER 49

I pace the windowless basement again. No vents. Just feature-less masonry walls and a single metal door at the top of rickety stairs, its hinges, rusted in place.

There *has* to be a way out. I need to think.

I run my fingers along the walls, my nails scraping the rough surface until the skin catches and splits. Blood smears across the gray stone, but I keep going. I don't stop until I remember . . . "The sump pump closet."

I go back to that tiny space where I found the hammer. Crawling inside, I look up. The ceiling is plastered over but it looks as though water had seeped through at some point. "What's above here?"

Could it lead to the kitchen upstairs? Any part of the house that I might be able to climb through and break free from this place?

I crawl back out again, finding my trusty spindle that so far has gotten me out of the worst of my jams. Now, I hope it can help one more time. I return to the closet, unable to stand at full height, and pound on the ceiling with the spindle. The dry wall breaks and a small indentation appears.

This is going to take more effort. I'm already weak from injury and lacking energy. But I need to dig deep and find it because this could be the answer. This could be my way out.

I thrust the spindle into the ceiling again. Over and over. Pieces of dry wall fall into my face and eyes. I squint to see as my eyes feel as though they're full of sand. But I'm making progress.

As the plaster breaks away, wood beams are exposed. It's the bottom of the floor upstairs. "Oh my God. I can do this. I can get through."

I stand up now, my head poking through the opening I created between the floors. Above, I see sheets of plywood — the underlayment of the floor. My spindle won't get through that. I need to cut it or break it apart. That hammer would come in handy right now.

"Hang on." I run my hands along the wood between the floor joists. "Nails. Nails are the only things securing the plywood to the joists." If I can push on the thin wood near the seams, maybe I can lift it. But the floor above might make that hard. "Goddam it."

I walk out of the closet, searching desperately for something that can break through the floor above me. Then I see it. "Are you kidding me?" I walk to the other end of the basement where the shelves are mounted on the wall — with metal brackets. "Leverage. That could work."

But I have to take down the shelves and pry off the brackets. It seems like every time I think I've found a way out, another obstacle presents itself.

I start yanking at the bolts, my fingers slipping against the smooth steel. The brackets won't budge. I grab the spindle and wedge it behind one of the lower brackets, throwing my weight against it.

The metal groans, bending just enough to loosen the bolt. I let out a cry and work at the others, my hands blistering and raw, until the whole shelf tips forward. It crashes to the ground with an earsplitting clang.

The brackets are free. I grab them and head back to the closet. My work is far from over. But hope emerges in me for the first time in days.

I wedge the bracket between the plywood sheets, lifting one of them. I push and push until a piece of the wood snaps apart. "I see it. The floor above. Jesus, I see it!"

I use the bracket to break apart the wood planks. Dust chokes the air as debris crumbles away, scattering at my feet. My arms ache, my vision swims, but I don't stop. I can't.

Finally, there it is — a hole barely big enough to squeeze through. I use the bracket to chip away at the edges, widening the gap until I can see through it. I laugh, feeling a mixture of astonishment and relief. "It's the kitchen. I made it to the kitchen." I only have to climb through the hole and I'm free.

I reach up with aching arms and grip the edges of the opening. Pulling with every ounce of strength I have, I rise off the ground a few inches. Not enough. "Come on. You have to try harder." For a moment, my thoughts return to my eighth-grade gym class where we were forced to do pull-ups in front of everyone. I failed miserably.

But there's too much at stake for me to give up. I'll be damned if I let myself die in here. So, I pull, harder and harder. I just need to get an elbow out for leverage. It takes several more tries and I grow weaker, but then . . . my elbow is free. I pull up the rest of the way, climbing out onto the kitchen floor.

I lie there a moment in disbelief, laughing and crying at the same time. I've made it out of the basement. Now, I just have to find Ben and Nicky before Tyler and Marissa take them forever.

I get to my feet, aching, bleeding, drained. But I observe my surroundings as I regain my balance. Taking a step, my foot slips on the debris strewn across the kitchen floor. Another step and then another, and now I'm running, well, hobbling, down the passageway toward the exit.

With an unsteady hand, I turn the handle and push the door open to the dusky sky. I stumble out into the open, drawing in great gulps of fresh air that burns in my lungs but fills me with renewed strength.

I glance back at the house. I have no car. No phone. My leg is injured. All I can do is walk. So that's what I'll do.

* * *

The never-ending road lies before me, a swath of cracked asphalt consumed by darkness on either side. I limp along the shoulder, each step jarring, sending fresh pain slicing through my leg. Blood sticks to the inside of my jeans, wet and warm, and every time my foot touches the ground, I want to scream. But I don't. Screaming does nothing.

The night presses in around me, heavy, damp air, with no street lights to guide me. The only light comes from the pale glow of the quarter moon, hanging low in the sky like it's barely strong enough to shine. The air smells like dirt and damp leaves, and the occasional rustle from the woods lining the road makes my stomach twist with panic. Keep going, Evie. Just keep moving.

I don't know where I am. I don't know where this road leads. But standing still isn't an option. Not after what I left behind.

The distant rumble of an engine sends my heart into my stomach. I halt, swaying on my good leg, and look over my shoulder. Headlights break over the hill behind me, cutting through the dark. My chest tightens. They've found me.

No, no, it's not them. It *can't* be them.

The lights grow closer, and the engine louder. I stumble off the road, into the grass and weeds, crouching low as the car passes. It's an old truck, the kind with rust eating at the wheel wells, and for a second, I think it's slowing down. My breath catches.

But then it roars past me, its tail-lights disappearing around a curve. I exhale, my body trembling with the effort of holding myself upright.

I should have flagged it down. But I can't. I can't trust anyone. Not after Tyler. Not after Marissa.

I step back onto the shoulder, my injured leg screaming in protest. I'm light-headed now, the edges of my vision blurring. I need to stop, but I don't dare. Not yet. Not until I find someone — something — that feels safe.

My mouth is dry, my tongue like cotton. I think about the water I left behind, back in the basement. The thought makes me want to laugh.

Another set of headlights appears on the horizon, this time coming from the other direction. My pulse quickens. The car is smaller, sleeker, its lights brighter than the truck's. I hobble farther off the road, keeping low, watching it approach.

As it nears, the car slows. Oh God, they're stopping.

The car rolls to a stop just a few feet away, its engine idling. The driver's side window rolls down, and a man leans out, his face shadowed.

"You okay?" His voice is deep, rough, but not unkind.

I can't move. My body locks up, the memory of Tyler's smile flashing behind my eyes. He sounded kind, too, when I first met him.

"Hey," the man calls again. "You need help?"

My instincts tell me to run, but I can barely stand. My leg wobbles, and I sway on the spot, clutching at the air as though it'll steady me.

The man gets out of the car, leaving the door open. The dome light casts him in a soft, golden glow. He looks normal. Jeans. A jacket. Dark hair. Not like Tyler. Not like Marissa.

But I've learned how monsters can excel at looking normal and trustworthy. "I'm fine." It's a lie so obvious even I don't believe it.

"You don't look fine," he says, taking a cautious step closer. His hands are up, palms out, like he's trying not to scare me. "Are you hurt?"

"Stay back!" I shout, stumbling away from him.

He stops. "Okay, okay. I'm not gonna hurt you." He glances at my leg, where the blood has soaked through the denim, and the tear reveals my injury. "You're bleeding. You need a doctor."

"I'll find one," I say, even though I have no idea where I am or where I'm going.

The man hesitates, then nods. "All right, miss. Suit yourself. But at least take this." He leans into the car and pulls out a bottle of water, setting it on the ground between us. "No strings attached."

I stare at the bottle, my throat aching with thirst.

He gets back in the car and drives away, his tail-lights vanishing into the night.

I wait until I'm sure he's gone, then hobble over to the water. My hands tremble as I unscrew the cap and drink. The cool liquid soothes my throat.

For a moment, I let myself believe it's a good sign. Not everyone is a monster. Maybe someone out there will help me. But as I start limping down the road again, I feel the familiar weight of doubt settling in my chest. And I wonder if I'll ever be able to trust anyone again.

CHAPTER 50

The cold night air seeps through my skin. I'm dressed in only a T-shirt and jeans. My pinkie toe is broken, and my foot swells inside my tennis shoe. The good news is that I'm pretty sure my leg has stopped bleeding, or I've lost all feeling in it. I've been walking for over an hour, still having no idea where I am or even which direction I'm headed.

As I continue down the side of the road, fewer and fewer cars pass me by. It must be getting late. I press on, making my way slowly, when I see the faint glow of lights over the horizon. It's not the sun rising. It looks like a town or city. It's civilization, and that's all that matters because I'm not sure how much longer I can keep going.

The light in the distance carries me farther than I thought I could go. It takes another forty minutes before I see the outskirts of this town. A few buildings — a storage center, a couple of old houses. I need a phone. A convenience store might still have a phone booth, though it's not likely. If I walk inside a place looking like this, they'll call the police. I don't want the police. I can't tell them the truth about what's happened because they'll know what I did with Nicky.

No, I need a phone so I can call Chuck. He'll help me. I carry on and begin to recognize my surroundings. "It's Medford." I run through the list of friends I still have here, but would any of them help? After what happened and our hasty move to Beaufort, probably not. So, I'm left to call Chuck. I'll figure out the rest later.

As I reach the city, I search for a phone booth. There must be one around here somewhere. Do I remember Chuck's phone number? I'm not sure.

I scan the streets, my gaze landing on a convenience store. "Please, for the love of God, let there be a payphone outside." But as I approach the parking lot, I search the front of the store and see nothing.

"Screw it." I limp inside, and right away, the cashier eyes me with a mixture of suspicion and concern. He's a younger man, maybe only in his late twenties. Round face with a full beard. I approach the counter. "I'm sorry, but do you have a phone I can use?"

"Lady, do you need a hospital?" he asks, scanning me up and down.

I can only imagine what I must look like to him. "I need to call my friend. He'll come pick me up and take me to a hospital." I'm left to make up something to help this guy feel better about my intention.

"Uh, there's a phone in the back office." He walks around the counter. "Come on. I'll show you, and you can use it."

"Thank you." I follow him to the back of the store.

He gestures inside. "There . . . on the desk. Please, help yourself."

I look back at him, forcing a smile on my face, though at this moment, I feel like crying. "Thank you." I walk inside and pick up the phone. The door closes behind me. I glance over my shoulder to confirm he's left me alone and isn't standing there, trapping me inside. I can't help but feel afraid of everyone I see.

I sit down, searching my mind for Chuck's number. I wonder what time it is. I look around the tiny office that seems to double as a storage closet, but I see no clock. The desk phone . . . There it is. I see the time on the display. 10:30 p.m.

It takes me a few minutes to clear my head and recall the number, and then I do. "Thank you." I sigh with relief at the small miracle. I pick up the phone and dial. One ring. Two rings. Three rings. "Shit. Please answer, Chuck."

He picks up. "Hello?" His voice is groggy like I woke him.

"Chuck, it's me, Evie."

"What?" His tone becomes clearer. "Dear God in heaven, are you all right?"

At that moment, it's all I can do not to completely break down. "It's a long story, but I need your help. I'm back in Medford. I don't have a phone or money or anything."

"All right," he says. "Here's what we're gonna do."

* * *

I walk out of the office and head back toward the cashier. "Thank you. I'm grateful for your help."

He regards me with sympathy in his gaze. "Take a bottle of water and something to eat."

I shake my head. "I don't have any money."

He waves me off. "Don't worry about it."

My eyes flood with tears at his kindness, and I swallow the lump in my throat. "Thank you." I take the water and a candy bar. "Thank you so much." I walk outside and wait for my ride. Chuck has called me a cab that will take me to a hotel. One he's already paid for.

Headlights approach and I see the familiar sight of a yellow cab. I raise my hand, wincing as my entire body radiates with pain. It stops in front of me, and I step inside. "St. Charles Hotel, please."

"Yes, ma'am."

As he drives off, I peer at the darkened road. The surroundings are familiar to me now. The university is only a few miles from the center of the city. Our old house is less than twenty minutes away. But I'm not going there. It's not mine anymore. This place isn't my home any longer.

"Ma'am?" The driver peers through the rearview. "We're here."

I shake out of my trance, as it seems he must've told me this already. "Yes, uh, thank you. I believe the ride was prepaid?"

"It was, Ma'am, yes."

I smile and nod before opening the door. "Thank you again."

He watches me get out, and I see the same look in his eyes that the cashier had. For a moment, I feel like maybe not everyone is out to hurt me. I continue toward the manager's office and collect my room key.

Walking down the breezeway, I find my room and open the door. I turn on the lights. My breath catches as I begin to realize that I made it out alive. But this nightmare is far from over.

CHAPTER 51

I don't want to sleep. I want to find my children. But Chuck won't be here until morning. It's already past midnight. I've washed my face and stripped down to my T-shirt and underwear. I have nothing to help with the pain, something I should've considered while the store clerk was feeling generous. The bandage on my leg is bloody, and I'm certain I need stitches.

All I can do is wait now. Wait until dawn for Chuck to arrive. Bring me fresh clothes and help me fix up my leg. He'll probably insist on a hospital visit, but there's no time. Being here already feels like a waste. I should be looking for my kids.

Tears stream down my face as I think about what could be happening to Ben and Nicky. Are they safe? Have they eaten? What must Ben think? I'll bet he thinks I abandoned him. Both of them.

I lie down, turning over and curling up into a ball, letting the tears come out hard and fast. I can't stop it now. I need my kids back, and I don't want to wait until morning. What if they're on a plane, going to some foreign country where I'll never see them again?

"Stop," I whisper. "You will find them."

* * *

The sunlight cuts across my eyes as it shines through the curtains in the hotel room. I shoot up from the bed, forgetting for a moment where I am. "Ben. Nicky." Panic fills my chest as I search the unfamiliar surroundings. It takes me a minute to get my bearings.

I spin around, setting my feet on the floor and glancing at the clock on the nightstand. "6 a.m. He's on his way." Testing my legs, I get to my feet. My leg still throbs, but thankfully, it's a little better than it was yesterday.

Then I hear the knock on the door.

"It's me, Evie. It's Chuck."

I didn't think he'd arrive so soon. I walk into the bathroom and grab a towel to wrap around my waist since I'm in only a T-shirt. "Hang on. I'm coming." I carry on toward the door, slowly, and peek out through the curtains, just to be safe.

A smile pulls at my lips, and I open the door. I can't even get out a word before his mouth drops.

"Dear Lord. No offense, Evie, but you look like hell."

"I feel like hell, Chuck. It's so good to see you." I step aside and let him in. "It's been a long time."

"Yes, it has." He sets down a duffel bag. "I brought you some clothes. Shoes." His gaze roams over me. "You okay to get dressed on your own?"

"Yeah, I am." I grab the bag and head into the bathroom.

"I'll be right here if you need anything."

I turn on the bathroom light and sift through the bag. I pull on a fresh T-shirt and a pair of jogging pants. I splash water on my face and then return to Chuck. "Thank you for this. It means the world to me."

"Don't thank me yet," he says. "I'm gonna need you to sit down to hear what I got to say."

"You didn't want to tell me on the phone last night, so, yeah, it's time to hear what you found." I perch on the edge of the bed.

Chuck leans against the credenza behind him. "Tyler's real last name is Dittrich."

"What?" The name echoes in my ears. "Dittrich?"

"Yes, ma'am. And look, whoever helped this guy hide who he really is knew what the hell they were doing because I could only find one former address."

"Dittrich?" I say again as if I misheard him the first time. "Wait . . . how are they related then? Cousins? Brother and sister?" I look away. "But that wouldn't make sense unless Riley had left Nicky with him—"

"Listen to me now," he says. "There's more."

Chuck takes a breath, and I already don't like where this is going.

"That former address, Evie, only reason I got it is because it belongs to a hospital. And not the kind that fixes broken bones, you understand me?"

"What?" I breathe out.

"I don't know how all this fits together yet, but Tyler Dittrich was institutionalized when he was barely eighteen. Stayed there four years. That's all I could get, but it doesn't put my mind at ease about this man. And I gotta tell you, I sure as shit didn't know that son of a bitch would be around when I sent you the information. I caused all this, Evie, and I'm damn sorry."

"This isn't on you, Chuck. Not even a little." I take a breath, letting this news settle around me. "Institutionalized. Given his behavior, it shouldn't come as a shock. Still, nothing about this makes any sense. What do I do? He took my kids. He and Marissa. I have to find them, Chuck. I don't know where else to turn."

"I hear you, kid, I do. I'm just so goddam thankful you're all right. You have no idea." He sighs. "Okay, look. I'm gonna have to reach out to my law enforcement contacts—"

"No, you can't," I cut in. "Chuck, please. I have to find them on my own. I can't have the police involved."

He folds his arms. "Why on earth not? What are you keeping from me, Evie? Come on, now. I thought we were friends."

"I — we are, Chuck." He's right. How can I expect him to help if he doesn't know everything? What I did in that moment with Nicky — I was certain it was in her best interest. I thought she was alone in the world. Is that an excuse? Will Chuck see it the same way? "We are friends, Chuck, so what I'm about to tell you, I have to trust will stay with you."

I go into it all. From the very beginning until this moment. And now, he's unreadable. Simply standing there, arms crossed, nodding.

"Then I think the best place to start is with Riley Dittrich's parents," he says.

I don't press him; I know better. This is how he is, and I have my answer. Chuck will back me on this. "Are they still alive?" I ask. "If they are, I can go to them, and they'll tell me where I can find Tyler."

He nods. "Yeah, that's our best shot at getting answers."

* * *

I've been instructed to sit tight while Chuck works to get us an address, the names of Riley's parents, and anything that will tell me where I can find them.

All I can do is stare through the window of this hotel room as though I'm waiting for my children to show up. As though Tyler will change his mind and come find me. I know that won't happen.

I told Chuck about Chelsea, too. I still have to prove that Tyler or Marissa was responsible for her murder. I wonder if Detective Kent is looking for me. What new evidence has he found, if any? Maybe Chuck was right to want to involve the police. At this point, I may be risking more by trying to take this on myself. Still, something tells me that if I call the police, Tyler will take my children and disappear forever.

Even if I get my kids back, the legal mess of it all, the kidnapping, the murder . . . chances are good that I'll still lose them. But the most important thing now is to get them well away from the Dittrichs.

The more I consider what Chuck said about Tyler going into a hospital, the more I understand that whatever he suffered from or continues to suffer, Riley must have, too. Both manipulated me. Got me to trust them, then took everything I loved away from me. But what about Riley's parents? Jesus, are they all insane?

The minutes tick away, but it isn't much longer before I hear the knock. I walk to the door, opening it to see Chuck on the other side.

"How are you holding up there, Evie?" he asks, holding two paper cups. "I brought you some coffee if you're interested."

I reach out for one of them. "Thank you. I need this more than you know. Come in."

He walks inside, closing the door behind him. "I should've gotten some food. You must be starving."

"I'm all right." I take a sip from the paper cup. "So, have they been looking for her? Riley's parents?" I glance away for a moment. "I guess I thought no one would care, that no one would come looking because she'd been living under the name Summer Burton."

"They did," he says. "Detective Langston recovered DNA and tracked down her family."

I expected it, of course, but to hear him say it . . . "Then where the hell have they been all this time? Why didn't they care about Riley when she was pregnant? When she'd asked her parents for help, and they disowned her?"

"I don't have an answer for you on that, I'm afraid." He takes a sip. "But I do have some information."

CHAPTER 52

Marissa

With the spoon in my hand, I scrape the last remnants of mashed sweet potato from the jar. Aiming it toward Nicky's — *Jenny's* — little mouth, she fusses and turns away, her lips clamping shut in defiance. I sigh, bouncing her gently the way she likes.

"Come on, sweetheart," I whisper, brushing a curl of blond hair from her forehead. "Just a little more, okay? You're almost finished."

Her round eyes, so impossibly big, blink up at me. Then, finally, she opens her mouth just enough for me to sneak in the spoon. I've won this battle, but my victory is short-lived when I hear the sharp click of high heels against the hardwood floor.

"Honestly, Marissa," Colleen Dittrich sighs as she sweeps into the room, her perfume cloying. "You're making such a mess. Here, let me."

I don't turn around. I don't have to. Her presence infects the air, filling every available inch of space with her expectations. Her *entitlement*. "I've got it," I say, keeping my voice even and controlled.

Colleen ignores me. She always does. She circles the kitchen island, her eyes sweeping over me with barely concealed disdain before settling on Jenny. Her expression softens — just a bit — but there's something else lurking beneath it — possession.

"Poor baby," Colleen says, reaching out. "She needs someone who knows what they're doing."

I shift back instinctively, putting space between us. "She's fine."

"She's covered in food," Colleen says, her tone curt. "And so are you, by the way."

I clench my jaw. I know what she sees — my wrinkled shirt, the faint orange smear on my sleeve, the exhaustion in my eyes. I don't look like the perfect, poised woman she expects. I don't look like her. But she hasn't been through what I have in the past few days. And it was all her fault.

"She's fed, she's clean, and she's calm," I say. "That's what matters." Jenny shifts against me, her tiny fingers curling into the fabric of my shirt. I shouldn't push. I know better than to push, but I don't have the energy to deal with her right now.

Colleen's lips press into a thin, pallid line. For a long, unbearable moment, she just stares at me, the air between us, thick with unspoken threats. Then, finally, she exhales, like I'm the one exhausting her.

"Fine," she says, waving a manicured hand. "If you insist on making this difficult, then by all means. But don't come crying to me when you realize you're in over your head."

She turns on her heel and leaves, her shoes clicking once more against the wood floor, each step reminding me of the bizarre family I married into. It wasn't until I had Jenny that the veil was lifted, my eyes wide open.

Colleen and her constant turning up at our home, insisting that I let her take care of Jenny because I 'needed sleep.' Sure. That was her reason. And Tyler didn't help. He practically grovels at his mother's feet.

She controls this family — Colleen — and I've done everything I can to keep from losing Tyler to her altogether.

But when Jenny was taken, I needed her, as much as I hate to admit it. The Dittrich family has money — the kind that forces people to listen and to do things they wouldn't normally do.

Tyler walks into the kitchen, holding Ben's hand. My heart breaks for him — the fear in his face is undeniable. His eyes are red from crying tears that have now dried. I wish I hadn't done it — taken Jenny. I wish I had waited like Tyler wanted. Maybe we wouldn't be in this position . . . any of us.

"Sit down," Tyler says to Ben. "I'll make you some lunch."

Ben hoists himself onto the kitchen chair across from Jenny and me. His gaze is downcast, his hands folded in his lap.

"How are you, Ben?" I ask with a softness in my tone. I wait a few moments, but he doesn't answer. "I know you're scared, but this is only temporary. You'll be with your mommy again soon."

I feel Tyler's gaze bore through me, but I don't look at him. He blames me for ruining his plan, but I couldn't wait it out. Now, I'm stuck here with Colleen. She frightens me, and I don't want Jenny around her, or Ben, for that matter. There's no excuse for what Riley did, but I can almost understand.

And the more I consider the lengths Tyler has gone to, the more I wonder how much like Riley he truly is. "What happens now?" I ask him as he stands in front of the refrigerator. "He needs his mother."

Tyler closes the door and turns toward me, shifting his gaze between Ben and me. "Who says you can't be that for him?"

CHAPTER 53

Evelyn

I hadn't seen Chuck in years, yet he didn't hesitate to help me, even saving my life, if I'm honest. And to see him again, it was as if no time had passed, except he is a little grayer, a little thicker around the middle.

When he said he was coming, I didn't want him here. I didn't want him to know what I'd done and how it backfired, blowing up my entire life. Now, I know I couldn't do this without him. My efforts, so far, have nearly cost my life and that of my children.

"Where are they?" I press, barely giving Chuck the chance to take another sip of coffee. "I have to find out if they know where Tyler is and how he's related to them."

Chuck sets down his mug on the credenza. "Langston told me he'd searched Riley Dittrich's apartment but didn't find any information about next of kin. It wasn't until the DNA came back that he tracked down her family. Her mother, specifically. That was how she learned about her death. Her father passed years ago."

"Did her mom know she had a baby?" I press.

He shakes his head. "He made no mention of a baby, so if she knew, she kept it to herself."

"Why the hell would she do that?" I stare into my half-empty cup of coffee. "I just need to know where she is. It's time to find out if she knows where my children are."

"Not alone, you're not. I'm going with you," Chuck says.

"If she knows where Tyler is — who he is — then that's all I need from her," I insist. "This is why I said you didn't need to come here. Don't get me wrong, I appreciate it more than you know. You saved my life as far as I'm concerned. But she won't talk to you, Chuck. No, if this is going to get me anywhere, I have to be the one to do it."

He sets his best fatherly gaze on me. "You tried dealing with this yourself, and you almost died, Evie. I know you don't want the police involved, and I get it. But going to this woman's house, a rich woman at that . . . It's hard to say whether she knows the truth about what happened. But I'd venture a guess she knows exactly who you are, and that could put you in danger again."

"I won't get you more involved than you need to be," I reply.

"Fair enough," he concedes. "At least let me get you a phone and install a tracker app on it. If I know where you are, I can help if I'm needed. Otherwise, they could do whatever the hell they wanted to you, and no one would be any the wiser."

"Okay. I can agree to that," I reply. "Just knowing you're keeping watch is more than I could ask for."

"Now, let's go get you a phone and a ride," Chuck says. "And we'll take it from there."

CHAPTER 54

Marissa

One minute, I'm fastening the clean diaper snug around Jenny's waist, and the next, Colleen Dittrich's voice slices through the air, icy and shrill.

"What *is* this mess?"

My shoulders stiffen as I grip the dirty diaper in my hand. Jenny startles at the sharpness in Colleen's tone, her plump legs kicking against the changing pad. I force myself to stay calm, to keep my body between her and the woman standing in the doorway.

"I was changing her," I reply.

Colleen steps forward. "Changing her?" she repeats, her mouth twisting as if the notion is offensive. "Look at this. Wipes everywhere. Powder on the table. And you—" She waves a hand at me. "You look like a wreck."

I swallow hard, desperate to keep from giving her the reaction she wants. I won't let her see how badly she gets under my skin.

Jenny lets out a small whimper, and Colleen sighs, shaking her head as if I'm the worst mother in the world. "Give her to me," she demands, holding out her hands.

I don't move.

Colleen's eyes darken. "I said, give her to me, Marissa."

"Jenny's fine," I insist.

She leans in, her perfume thick enough to choke on. "You *think* she's fine."

The sound of her voice grates on me, and my desire to slap her in the face grows with each word that comes out of her mouth. I know I can't. I know Tyler wouldn't stand for it, but that doesn't change how I feel.

Colleen tilts her head, studying me like I'm an annoying pest she wants to exterminate. "Do you really think this will last? That Tyler will keep you after everything that's happened? You ruined everything, Marissa. Tyler had it all under control, and then you decided to be selfish."

My pulse pounds, but I keep my face blank. I know what she's doing. "You weren't there, Colleen. You don't know how hard it was."

She steps even closer, her voice dropping to a whisper. "You think my son loves you? That he'd choose *you* over his family? Over *me*?" She snickers. "No, honey. Not even if his life depended on it."

I tighten my hold on Jenny, hoping she'll help calm my nerves, which stand on end.

"Do you know what will happen then?" Colleen asks, running her fingernail along the dresser beside me. "He'll tell the police what you've done. You and that bitch, Evelyn Moore. Assuming she lives."

Everything around me turns red. "I—"

She cuts me off with a click of her tongue. "And when the police find her in that house? They won't come looking for me. They'll come looking for you." She leans in, her voice dripping with venom. "I'll make sure you never see Jenny again."

A cold rush of panic consumes me. She means it. I can see it in her eyes. She wants me gone. I'm beginning to understand why Riley left this family.

I press Jenny against me to shield her from her wicked grandmother, like we're in a nightmarish fairy tale we can't escape. "Tyler wouldn't—"

"Wouldn't he?" Colleen smirks. "You don't know him as well as you think you do." She turns and leaves the room as if she didn't just rip the rug out from under me.

Left alone in here, I look at Jenny, and I begin to wonder why I married Tyler. I didn't know Riley well back then because she was away at school. Tyler swept me off my feet, and the rest all happened so quickly. But now I'm beginning to see who these people really are. The horrors they're all capable of. And now, I'm not sure I'm safe here anymore.

CHAPTER 55

Evelyn

I'd wondered how it was Riley could afford to live in Beaufort. She'd had a nice apartment and drove a respectable car. Now, I know that her family has money. So even though she'd insisted that they had disowned her, I suspect she had been given a healthy allowance or trust fund.

The more Chuck tells me about them, the more inclined I am to think that, with all their money, they wield power too. Power to hide a murder, power to destroy my life.

That rundown house Ben and I were trapped in? According to Chuck, the Dittrichs bought it last year. They never rented it out. Their main residence is just outside of Medford. Not far from where we are now.

"So, did they know Riley followed us to Beaufort?" I ask Chuck as he drives away from the phone store. "And when did they find out she'd died? I suppose Langston would've told them about her apartment."

"Langston didn't get into much detail because he wanted to know why I was asking and who the hell wanted to know. So, I wish I had the answers you're looking for, Evie, I do," Chuck replies. "All I know is that the Dittrichs live nearby, and they're rich. Langston hasn't been in contact with them since they formally ID'd Riley's body. He had no reason to since the case was closed."

"Yeah, I suppose you're right."

The highway stretches on for another mile before Chuck pulls over in a parking lot. "There's a rental car place here. You take this one and I'll go inside and get another."

I turn to him. "So, I go to the Dittrich house, talk to the mother, and find out how Tyler Dittrich fits into all this. And pray she knows where my children are."

He reaches for my arm. "Listen to me now, Evie. I don't like you going alone, but I've made my position clear on that and it's your call. That said, you get a whiff of something that doesn't feel right, you get the hell out of there, you hear me?"

I see in his eyes that he's afraid for me. I can't say it makes me feel any better because I'm terrified too. "Yeah, okay. I know. I just don't want you involved any more than you already are, Chuck. I won't put you at greater risk."

He opens his door. "I'm not the one you should be worried about."

We step outside and he hands me the keys.

"If I don't hear from you in the next couple of hours, I'm coming whether you like it or not."

"Okay," I reply, watching him walk away. I don't know what I'll find when I get there. I don't even know if she'll have a clue as to why I'm there. But it's all I have to go on right now. So, I head out.

Colleen Dittrich. Riley's mother. A name that sits like lead in my stomach. She has to know something. About Tyler. About my children.

I've rehearsed a thousand ways this could go, none of them good. Maybe she'll scoff at me, slam the door in my face. Maybe she'll smile, all sweet and innocent, and tell me she *wishes* she could help but simply *doesn't know*.

Or maybe — maybe she'll know *exactly* where my children are. And *exactly* who I am, having no intention of helping me at all.

A fresh wave of fear rolls through me, and I tighten my grip on the wheel to keep my hands from shaking. I can't let myself spiral. I have to stay in control.

There's no phone signal out here. I glance at the screen, the little bars at the top — gone. It shouldn't come as much of a surprise. I'm in the middle of nowhere. Just miles of twisting, tree-lined roads, the kind that makes you feel like civilization doesn't exist, only nature.

It fits, though. People like the Dittrichs don't live among the rest of us. They exist in their own world, high above and looking down on us — untouchable. But I'll touch them. I'll break down their door if I have to.

As I exit the highway, a sign flashes past in my peripheral vision — Greensboro Lane — and my stomach knots. I ease off the gas, my pulse racing as I turn onto the long, narrow driveway. The trees seem to press in closer here, branches overhead, reaching out over the drive, blocking out the sun. My senses heighten as it becomes clear that I'm stepping into something I don't fully understand. And then, finally, I see it.

The house looms ahead, three stories of old money. The sun shines down on it, no longer blocked by the trees. The afternoon is fading fast, golden and warm, which should be soothing, but not right now. Right now, fear has me in its talons.

I pull to a stop. My hands stay glued to the wheel. I don't move. Once I step out of this car, there's no turning back. If Colleen Dittrich knows where my children are, I'll make her tell me.

And if she doesn't?

"She will." I step out. A small part of me wishes I was armed. I am not. So I have to pray that, if Riley's mom answers the door, she doesn't want me dead because I killed her daughter.

My feet crunch atop the gravel driveway as I climb toward the house, my leg throbbing with pain. My nerves are frayed, and my head aches from exhaustion and worry.

The house towers at the top of the hill, overlooking fields and forests. I had no idea about Riley's family, but knowing

Tyler was in a hospital makes me think it wasn't all sunshine and unicorns.

The house frightens me. Sounds ridiculous, I know, but something about this place . . . it's unsettling. And now, I wish I hadn't come here alone. Seems like Chuck was right to warn against this. But I'd feel worse for having him here with me.

I scan the grounds, and my gaze lands on the garage. "Oh my God." Tucked almost out of sight, the front end of a car sticks out beside it. "Is that the . . . the dark sedan? Jesus." My heart climbs into my throat. I'm not certain it's the same car, but it sure as hell looks similar. Now, the reality of my situation sinks in, and I question whether to continue, but I'm here, and I need answers, so I have to try.

The front porch wraps around the entire house. I climb the red brick steps and arrive at the door. Its black color matches the shutters. The rest of the house is white, a pristine white. The grounds are well maintained. Flowers rest in boxes below the windows. That should settle my nerves, but it doesn't. It only makes me feel that someone went to great lengths to make it appear that this is a happy home.

I curl my fist, raising my hand to knock, but I hear the lock disengaging. Someone is already standing on the other side. I steel myself, almost forgetting the throbbing pain still radiating from my leg. Pain caused by Tyler Dittrich.

The door opens, and an older woman stands guarded behind it. "Hi, please excuse my unexpected arrival, but my name is Evelyn Moore. Are you Mrs. Colleen Dittrich?"

She's well put together. Dressed in a cream-colored silk blouse and beige dress pants, she wears a full face of make-up, which looks a little too heavy for someone her age. I suspect she's in her late fifties or early sixties.

Her eyes roam over me, landing on my leg, which I'm still favoring. She doesn't seem to notice the bruises on my cheek. I did my best to cover them with make-up. "Ma'am?" I ask again. "Are you Mrs. Dittrich?"

CHAPTER 56

Marissa

Colleen put us in the room in the attic. She said it was best for us to stay out of view. Jenny sleeps in her crib. Tyler has left Ben with me while he does — well, I don't know what he's doing right now.

Ben is sitting at a small table, coloring in a handful of coloring books Colleen has had since God knows when. But I'm grateful she did. Ben has hardly said a single word. I don't blame him. He's terrified, and I'm pretty sure he didn't sleep at all last night.

A glint of light from the window captures my attention. I pat Ben on the head. "I'm just going to go look outside a minute." He says nothing in return.

I reach the small window, one barely large enough to climb through. Though with nothing below but hard ground, I wouldn't recommend it. A car has stopped at the top of the driveway, unrecognizable to me. It's not a police car, which I suppose is a good thing. What we've done is still kidnapping, and there's no other way to slice it.

I push my head against the screen to glimpse the porch below, but I can't see anyone on the steps. I didn't hear a knock either, yet I'm certain someone is here. Is Colleen at the door? She must be.

I strain to listen. No one knows we're here. No one knows who we are. So, who is she talking to? My attention turns toward the bedroom door when Tyler enters. I don't like the look on his face. "Who's at the door? Did you see?"

"Don't worry about it. Mom will take care of her."

"Her?" I ask, my heart dropping into my stomach. I glance at Ben. "Her, as in . . ."

He nods.

"Oh my God. What do we do?"

He moves in, raising his hands. "Let Mom handle this, okay? She knows what to do."

That's what bothers me, but I don't dare tell Tyler that. As far as I'm concerned, Colleen Dittrich is a tyrant, hell-bent on controlling not only her son but me and her granddaughter as well. Riley was right to leave, even if she ended up dead. I'm beginning to think that was a far better outcome for her than what I might be facing now.

I stand at the window, waiting to see her. Evelyn must be beside herself with worry, but does she know what she's done? To an extent, yes, but unfortunately, she messed with the wrong family.

"Just stay here," Tyler says. "I'll go downstairs and make sure we're good."

When he leaves, I look at Ben. He's only five, but I suspect he knows more than he lets on. I can't imagine what mental anguish he's suffered at our hands. I peer through the window again, still unable to see her. What could Evelyn possibly be saying to keep Colleen at the door? I know what Evelyn did, and my guess is, Colleen will never forgive her.

CHAPTER 57

Evelyn

Colleen Dittrich's evasive answers raise the hairs on my neck. She hasn't admitted as much, but I suspect she knows exactly who I am and why I'm here. "I knew your daughter, Riley."

"So you said," she replies, acting as if she doesn't know Riley's dead or that I'm the one who killed her. "Mrs. Dittrich, can you tell me what relation Tyler Dittrich is to you?"

"Why does that matter?" she replies.

Something about this woman terrifies me. Like she'd do anything to protect her family. Then again . . . "I'm looking for my children, and I'm certain he has them."

"Excuse me?" Her brows raise. "You think Tyler took your children?"

I pull back my shoulders. "I don't know how much you're aware, Mrs. Dittrich, but I once considered your daughter, Riley, a friend. Something happened along the way, and she turned against me."

"My daughter's dead, Mrs. Moore, and you killed her." She tilts her head, finally coming clean about her knowledge of events. "Do you think I'm unaware of who you are?"

"Oh, I'm certain you knew, and you were waiting on the right time to say as much," I reply. "Riley told me about you. How you and your husband disowned her. That you wanted nothing to do with her."

"Well, those were the words of a lonely and frightened girl who mistook discipline for a lack of love. I loved my daughter very much. Her father passed some time ago. It's a good thing because he didn't have to live with the pain of knowing his daughter was dead. So don't you dare stand there and tell me who Riley was. I'm all too aware. And I know who you are." She begins to close the door. "Now, if there's nothing else, I don't have to stand here and—"

I thrust out my hand to stop her. "Who is Tyler to you? Where is he? I will bring the police here if that's what you want."

Her lips curl into a sneer. "Oh, Mrs. Moore, I don't think you'll do that at all."

It's then that I realize she's aware of a great many things. Nicky, Ben, Tyler, which means she must know where my kids are being held. The leverage I thought I had is beginning to slip through my fingers.

Colleen Dittrich is part of this — that much is clear. If I stay and fight her now, I might not live long enough to see Ben ever again, let alone Nicky. Something in this woman's eyes tells me she's dangerous, just like Tyler, a fact I've come to realize far too late.

I look beyond her into the house. It's too dark to make out anything other than a staircase and a few pictures on the walls. "He's here, isn't he?"

She pulls the door closer to her, blocking my view.

"Do you know what he did, Mrs. Dittrich?" It occurs to me that there is only one logical explanation left as to Tyler's true provenance. He is not Riley's cousin, distant or otherwise. He is her brother. I see that same look in this woman's eyes as I saw in Tyler's.

"Why do you want the baby?" I ask. "Why come for her now when all you had to do was let Riley back into your life? Instead, all you've done is create pain and chaos for everyone."

Colleen stares back at me, cold and calculating, one hand still on the door. "I think you should leave now, Mrs. Moore."

I blink hard, shaking my head in defiance. "I'm not going anywhere without my children. If you know where Tyler is, you need to tell me. I will call the police if I have to."

"By all means, call them," Colleen replies, an icy smile forming. "I'm sure they'll be very interested to hear why you murdered my daughter. And kidnapped the child who didn't belong to you."

I feel the color drain from my face and a cold sweat forming along my brow. "Mrs. Dittrich, I'm sure you miss Riley very much. I miss my children too. Please, I'm begging you. I need my children back. You didn't want Riley's baby. I did. You don't get to change your mind later."

"Riley's baby?" she asks, a hint of a smile on her face. "Is that what she told you? That the baby was hers?"

My throat dries as I try to swallow the lump that's now lodged in it. "Yes."

She tsks, shaking her head. "And your husband — the supposed father of this baby?"

"Yes," I stammer, fearing what will come next.

Mrs. Dittrich steps outside, closing the door behind her. "I'll let you in on a little secret, Mrs. Moore. Your husband may have been a womanizing cheater, but what he wasn't? The father of the baby you took. That title, my dear, belongs to Tyler — my son."

My mind spins in confusion, and my stomach twists. "If Riley wasn't the mother, then who—"

"I believe you've met her already. Tyler's wife, Marissa."

I stumble back, thoughts swirling in my mind. "I-I don't understand."

"No?" she presses. "Riley stole Jenny right from her crib. Tyler and Marissa have been looking for her ever since. We

247

didn't even know she was dead until the police called me three months ago. The detective never mentioned a baby." She scoffs. "It took a good long while to realize you were the one who took their child. So, Mrs. Moore, do you want to call the police now, or should I?"

She's lying. She must be lying. I would've never — no, I don't believe her. "Why would he take my son?" My voice cracks with emotion. "Why? And if what you say is true, why not bring in the police to begin with?"

"I don't know what you're talking about. What son of yours?" she asks.

"This isn't happening." The world around me spins. All this time, I thought I'd been protecting Nicky. That she was Derek's child. But there must be more to this. Tyler didn't need to take Ben too. He could have let us both rot in that basement.

What am I going to do? She denies Ben is here, but I'm certain this woman knows everything about what her son has done. She's protecting him.

I'm numb, trying to process everything Colleen has revealed. If it's true, then I've made a horrible mistake. One that I can never take back or make right.

My legs feel weak, the persistent pain in my shin, unrelenting. I reach out to steady myself against the porch railing. Colleen watches me with dead eyes.

"I don't believe you," I say, but even I can hear the doubt in my voice. "Why would Riley lie about something like that?"

"My daughter was troubled, as I'm sure you know. Unfortunately, it runs in the family." Colleen sighs. "She was desperate for connection and created fantasies to feel wanted. The baby was never hers."

I shake my head, fresh tears spilling down my cheeks.

Colleen sighs. "Jenny was never meant for Riley. She took her, just as you did."

My chest aches as the magnitude of my mistake sinks in. I was so blinded by my grief and anger at Derek that I never questioned Riley's story.

Still, something isn't right. When Tyler tracked me down, why wouldn't he have called the police, insisting Nicky didn't belong to me? Why befriend me? Become a lover? Why bring Marissa into it only for her to have to watch me mother her child?

I can't leave here until I know where Ben is. I stare at Colleen, my mind racing. Something still doesn't add up. "If what you're saying is true, why did Tyler insert himself into my life under false pretenses? Why not just go to the police right away?"

Colleen shrugs. "I don't pretend to understand everything my son does. But I know he would do anything for his daughter."

I shake my head. "No. There's more you're not telling me. I'm not leaving here without answers."

Colleen's eyes darken. She takes a step toward me, her voice low and threatening. "I suggest you leave now, while you still can."

CHAPTER 58

Marissa

I hear the door close and rush to the window again. My breath hitches. There she is. Evelyn. "I knew it." I glance at Ben, knowing what we're doing is wrong. But if I try to intervene, I know what will happen to me. And it might make matters worse for Ben, maybe Jenny, too.

She's getting into her car. "Why are you leaving?" I whisper, careful not to let Ben hear. But I know why. Colleen. She must've spun a lie to convince her Ben wasn't here. I don't know Evelyn that well, but there's no chance she'd give up on her child. She will come back, and I have to be the one to make sure Ben stays safe until she does.

I hear the door close, and the sound of muffled voices drifts up. I glance at the crib to see Jenny still sleeping. Ben is watching cartoons. Well, he's looking at the television, but I'm certain he's being quiet out of fear.

I open the door and pad into the hallway. It's Tyler and Colleen — they're talking — there's no doubt about what just happened. Things are going to get complicated now, and I don't know what Tyler will do. We can't keep Evelyn's son.

I move closer in an effort to hear their conversation, careful to remain unseen. Their voices are clearer now . . .

"This has to end, Tyler. You got Jenny back, and it's the best I could hope for," Colleen says. "But if you think that woman will simply walk away, giving up on her son, then you clearly don't know her. I saw the look in her eyes."

"She deserves a taste of her own medicine," Tyler replies. "She stole my daughter."

"Don't forget her mother," Colleen says. "I love you, son, but I can only do so much for you. You did as I asked, but soon, they'll come snooping around about that girl. We need to keep Evelyn Moore away from us. She'll only bring more trouble."

My gaze narrows as I tighten my brow. Chelsea? Is that who she's talking about?"

"Marissa may be blind," Colleen begins. "But I see you. I know the truth. You will do as I say, or there will be consequences. I promise you, I won't lose that baby again."

Footfalls sound. It's Tyler. He's coming upstairs. I quickly retreat to the bedroom, quietly opening the door and closing it again. What the hell was that about? I look at Ben, but he hasn't moved. Jenny still snores lightly in her crib.

The door swings open, startling all of us. "I told you Mom would handle it. She's gone."

I want to ask him what Colleen meant, but if he knows I was eavesdropping, it won't end well for me. "Do you think she'll come back?" I ask, already knowing the answer.

"If she does, we'll be ready. Don't worry about that." He walks over to Ben, squatting low to meet him. "Hey, buddy. How are you doing?"

Ben slowly turns his head. "Where's my mommy?"

Tyler smooths Ben's hair. "I'm sorry, buddy. Like I said before, she doesn't want you anymore. She gave you to us. And I promise, we'll take really good care of you . . . and Jenny."

CHAPTER 59

Evelyn

Tears cloud my vision as I drive back to the hotel. I should've fought harder and demanded to know the truth. But Colleen Dittrich is a dangerous woman. She could still make sure Ben never gets back to me. So, I have to play her game. Whatever the hell game that is.

I dial Chuck's number, and he quickly answers.

"What happened? Are you okay? Do you have Ben?"

"No," I reply, my voice coming out fractured. "I'm on my way back now. Chuck — this woman — Colleen Dittrich — she's lying. She knows where Ben is. I don't know what to do."

"Evie, it's time to get the police involved. I should've insisted on it, but . . . never mind because I'm insisting on it now."

"I can't." I grip the steering wheel tighter. "She'll hurt Ben. I know she will. You didn't see her. This woman is insane, just like her daughter."

"Then what the hell are we going to do to get your son and daughter back?" Chuck asks.

I swallow the lump in my throat. "There's more to it than I thought. Nicky — Riley took her, Chuck. Took her from her real mother and father. Tyler and Marissa Dittrich are Nicky's parents."

"I — I don't understand. Are you sure? You say Colleen's off her rocker, maybe that's one of her lies."

"It's probably the only thing she said that made any sense to me. But it doesn't explain why Tyler took Ben. Revenge is a possibility, but I don't know. There's more. And I need your help finding out."

"Just get yourself back here safely, all right? We'll talk this through and figure it out. We will get Ben back, I promise you that."

"Thank you. I'll see you soon." I end the call and fix my sights on the road ahead. The afternoon is waning. Another day without my son. What he must be thinking . . .

But Chuck is right about one thing. This isn't over. Not by a long shot. I'll get to the truth, and I'll get my son back.

* * *

A knock on my hotel room door sounds, and I peer through the window. With a sigh of relief, I open the door. "Chuck. Hi."

"Hey, kid." He steps inside. "How are you holding up?"

"Not great," I reply, closing the door behind him. "He's there, Chuck. The more I consider it, the more certain I am that Ben's in that house, same as Nicky." I drop onto the bed, defeat pressing down on me. "What am I going to do? If I get the police involved, I'm afraid Tyler will do something — hurt Ben or Nicky." I wipe away the tear that streaks down my face. "I was afraid to get the police involved because of what I'd done — taking Nicky like I did. But now?" My head drops into my hands as my emotions spill over. "Now I can't because I don't know what he'll do."

Chuck sits down next to me, draping an arm over my shoulders. "Hey, hey now, listen here . . . I'm not going to let anything happen to your kids, you got me? We'll figure this out, without the cops."

I look at him, wiping away more tears. "These people, Chuck, there's something wrong with them. I don't know what it is, but they're hiding something. And they're dangerous people. I'm certain now that they're responsible for Chelsea's death. Maybe she stood in the way of them getting Nicky back. And Marissa — I don't see how she can be with them."

"But she is," he interjects. "Don't you forget that. She's the one who took Nicky, and now all this has snowballed, and maybe she can't figure a way out, either. But I don't give a good goddam about any of them, all right? What we need to do is figure out how to get back to that house and get those kids."

"I'm beginning to understand why Riley was the way she was." I shake my head. "I can't imagine what being raised by that woman — Colleen — must've been like for her." I grab a nearby tissue, gathering myself. "And what's worse is that Tyler is her brother. That's how this all ties together. Can you believe that?"

"Well, we knew there was a family connection, but no, I didn't figure that," Chuck replies.

"It makes sense, though, in hindsight," I continue. "Detective Langston contacted Colleen, telling her about Riley's death. She knew Riley had taken Nicky, and so when Langston never referred to a baby, well, she figured I'd taken her. And then Tyler went looking."

Chuck walks over to the table where he'd set down his computer bag. Pulling out a chair, he takes a seat and retrieves his laptop. "Okay, let's work with what we know." He lifts the lid and begins typing. "We have the names — Tyler and Marissa Dittrich." He begins to search for records. "I have to assume the Dittrichs filed a missing persons' report when Riley Dittrich took that child."

"Maybe, but it could be that Colleen wanted to keep it under wraps if she knew her own daughter took Nicky

254

— Jenny," I say, reminding myself of my mistake. I walk over to the table and join him. "It would make sense that they didn't file a report because surely it would've popped up on Langston's search for the family when Riley died."

Chuck raises his index finger. "That's a valid point. All right. So what else can we find?"

"Well, when I hired Marissa to nanny for Ben and Nicky, strange things happened. Like after the first few days."

"I'm listening," Chuck replies.

"I noticed things in Nicky's room had been moved around. Her baby monitor was positioned away from the crib. I noticed a swatch of Nicky's hair was gone — cut away. Marissa even took the kids for a drive to get ice cream, but never told me."

"Hang on." Chuck raises his index finger. "She cut the baby's hair?"

I nod. "She said it was because Nicky got paint in it."

He leans back, narrowing his gaze. "Sounds to me like she wanted DNA, though hair would be the harder option. She could've taken a used spoon or something."

"DNA?" I press. "Because they weren't sure Nicky was who they were looking for?"

"Possibly. So Marissa had the kids to herself for a good long while," Chuck says. "Going someplace you didn't know about."

"Right. And then . . . Marissa was gone and so was Nicky. And this was after poor Chelsea . . ." I trail off.

"And Tyler — where was he during all this?" Chuck presses.

"I don't know. I mean, we'd started going out." I close my eyes, sighing. "I didn't make the connection, of course. Tyler recommended Marissa, but that's all I thought it was, which was why I had you run background."

"And that came up sparkling clean," he adds. "Pardon me for getting personal, here, kid, but did you and Tyler . . . you know . . ."

My face flushes with embarrassment. "Yeah, we did. I made the mistake of trusting him."

"We've all been there, okay? We've all trusted people we shouldn't have, but that's what those types of folk are good at — getting people to trust them." He raises his gaze. "But you know what?" A smile tugs at his lips. "That is something we can use."

"How so?"

"Marissa — she's the weak link," Chuck presses. "We need to separate her from Tyler. She needs to know what you and her husband did if she doesn't already. She knows her sister-in-law took her baby, passing her off as her own."

"And she didn't like what Tyler did to Ben and me in that basement. I heard her talking to him about it," I add.

"All right. There you go." Chuck nods. "We can use all this because here's the thing — Marissa Dittrich may be the only sane person in that family. She's the one we need. You get through to her, she'll give you back your son."

"And Nicky?" I ask, already knowing the answer.

"Well, kid . . . she wasn't yours to take."

CHAPTER 60

Marissa

What don't I know? Tyler's keeping something from me and so is Colleen. They speak in hushed tones when they think I'm not listening, their words clipped, deliberate. Tyler keeps his phone too close. Colleen watches me too carefully. It's in the way they *pause* when I enter a room, the way their eyes land on me as though I'm intruding.

Something is *wrong*. And I'm going to find out what.

I wait until Tyler leaves, watching from the window as his car disappears down the long driveway. But he didn't tell me where he was going. Then, minutes later, Colleen grabbed her keys, muttering about running to the store. I smiled, nodded, and played my part.

Now that they're both gone, I make my move.

Ben and Jenny are napping upstairs or at least resting quietly. I have time. Not much, but hopefully enough.

I think back to the night Jenny was taken from us. It took until early the next morning before I realized she wasn't in her crib. I'd gotten up at the usual time. I'd only gone back to work a few weeks earlier, so Jenny's routine was new for the both of us. Tyler was in the shower. It was like any other day in our house.

I'd rushed into our bathroom to tell Tyler. He'd stepped out of the shower and dried himself off. And I was thinking, 'Why the hell aren't you panicking like I am?'

Once I proved she was gone, he changed. I'd started making phone calls to everyone we knew. Tyler called his mother, which I thought was strange, thinking we should be calling the police. But we never called Riley. Colleen had forced her out of the family and shunned her after something had happened at Medford University, where Riley worked. It wasn't until some detective called Colleen and told her Riley had been killed that things unraveled.

But Colleen offered to help us track down Evelyn to find out if she had Jenny. I couldn't wait for Tyler to get DNA back or whatever the hell he was doing, so I took her, and here we are.

Now, however, something seems off. Tyler said we can't go home or call the police because I kidnapped Jenny. I don't think that's true. She was mine to begin with. I think that's why he wanted to take Ben — to make sure none of us could involve the police. Mutually assured destruction.

Why?

I walk down the hall to the bedroom Tyler and I are sleeping in. I don't know how long he'll be gone, so I need to work fast. His laptop sits on his nightstand. I open it, but it's password locked. "Of course it is."

But maybe I don't need his laptop. I open mine and log in to our wireless carrier account, retrieving the phone bill from the month Jenny was taken. As I scan through the calls and texts, looking at some numbers I recognize and some I don't, I come across the day it happened.

It appears Tyler made several calls and sent a few text messages during the day to numbers I don't recognize. I exclude the ones from me. Then, I see several texts to Colleen. And . . . "Hang on." I snatch my phone and search my contacts, recognizing the number. "Oh my God. Riley called him that night." Then, I notice the time of the call. "Not that night. 4 a.m. the next morning." I cast my gaze through the window, my head spinning. "Why did you call your sister hours before I even knew our baby was gone?"

CHAPTER 61

Evelyn

We're losing daylight, and I can't bear the idea of going another day without my son, without my daughter. "How do we get her? How do we get Marissa Dittrich to come to our side after what I did?"

"Play to your strengths," Chuck replies. "You're both mothers. You thought you were doing the right thing by giving Nicky a loving home. You had no idea they existed because of what Riley Dittrich told you." He closes his laptop and peers at me. "Look, you said it seemed like she wasn't on board with Tyler's decision to keep you and your son in that awful basement."

"Right. She was pretty upset by it," I reply.

"Then she's not a cold-hearted, calculating kidnapper. So, now what we need to do is reach out to her. We make sure she's alone, first and foremost. Then, you try to talk some sense into her."

"How will I know if she's alone?" I press. "Tyler's a controlling man. I see that now. I'm not sure he'll let her out of his sight."

Chuck leans back. "Well, we know this son of a bitch is going to be looking out for you, right?"

"Yeah."

"So, how can we get him away from that house? And the grandmother?" He raises his chin, casting a sideways glance.

"Detective Bartz," I reply.

"And that is?"

"The man who investigated the death of Nicole Peterson," I reply. "My husband told me everything the night he was killed . . . about what happened to Nicole at the pool."

"Sure. I recall you saying something to that effect," Chuck replies.

"I relayed that information to Bartz. He had the case reopened, and the medical examiner found evidence that pointed to murder . . . murder committed by Riley Dittrich, who was already dead by that point."

Chuck nods. "I follow, but that doesn't tell me what this Detective Bartz can do for us now. And if you did open up a new can of worms with him, who's to say he won't come after you for taking the child?"

"He doesn't know anything about that," I reply. "He'll have no reason to look into it either. It's not his jurisdiction." I see a smile creep up on Chuck's face. So far, he's on board. "So maybe I make an anonymous tip about the Dittrich family, giving him cause to call Tyler in, and it'd have to be cause enough to get that woman — Colleen — in there with him."

"Well, you wouldn't need much time with Marissa, I'd hope." Chuck folds his arms. "It's a risk, but one I think you could minimize . . . with a little help from me."

I check the time. "It's almost three o'clock. Is it too late to do this today?"

"It might throw a wrench in the works for something like this to come out of the blue this late in the day. There might not be enough time to get them down to the police station. I will need a little time to pull some strings. See what I can get from Medford PD." Chuck reaches for my arm. "If you can stomach it, it'd be best to put this off until the morning. Gives me some time to do what I need to do. Can you hold on through the night?"

I close my eyes, feeling the sting of tears once again. "You don't know what you're asking."

"I realize that, Evie. I'm not a mother, but I do understand what you're going through. But we need time to do this right. You can turn Marissa. Of that, I have no doubt."

"Okay." I nod. "Then we do this in the morning. And I have to pray nothing happens to either of my kids before then."

CHAPTER 62

Marissa

Colleen made dinner. Here we are, sitting around her antique dining table like we're one big happy family. Ben hasn't touched his food. I'm feeding Jenny mashed sweet potatoes, and Colleen has decided to offer her two cents as to why I'm giving her too much of one thing. But it's all she seems to want to eat, so I brush off my mother-in-law.

Tyler is eating his dinner. Meatloaf and baked potatoes. Not my first choice. The house is quiet, apart from Jenny's gurgling and the occasional scraping of silverware on plates. It's all I can do to keep my mouth shut. I want to ask the question that burns my tongue, but I can't. Not in front of *her*.

As I look at my husband, I realize that I no longer recognize him. He's not the person I married. Since Jenny went missing, he's become someone different. I don't know — maybe he was this way before she was taken, but I was too wrapped up in being a new mother. I didn't pay much attention to him or anyone during my pregnancy. I mean, does any new mom?

And now that I'm fairly certain he slept with Evelyn Moore, I recognize even less of him, if that's possible. But now that I know he'd contacted his sister, I have to find the reason why. Why that morning and so early before I made him aware of the horror that had occurred?

My thoughts scramble to make sense of it all, and one idea keeps rising to the forefront . . . a notion so outlandish that I think I might be the crazy one. But the only way to find out is for me to dig deeper.

"Why don't I take the kids upstairs?" I say. "I'm not that hungry, and I don't think Ben is going to eat. Maybe I can get him to drink a juice box or something. Jenny looks tired."

Tyler looks at me with a guarded gaze. He turns to his mother, who nods her approval. Thank God she approves. Wow. I couldn't stand it if she didn't. If she wasn't looking right at me, I'd roll my eyes so hard, they'd get stuck in the back of my skull. Instead, I offer a pleasant grin.

"Yeah, okay," Tyler says. "I'll be up later."

I push my chair away from the table and rise to my feet. "Thank you." Ben hasn't looked up once. "Honey?" I place my hand on his shoulder. "Would you like to go upstairs and watch TV?"

He doesn't move. He doesn't do anything.

"I can put on some cartoons or a movie for you," I add.

Finally, he sighs, climbing down from the chair and standing at the table like a statue.

I close my eyes, unable to stomach what we're doing to this poor boy. But I turn to Jenny and get her out of the highchair, perching her on my hip. I outstretch my hand to Ben, but he doesn't take it, so I start walking, hoping he'll follow. He does.

* * *

I managed to get them both to sleep. The baby monitor on my nightstand is quiet. The only reason Ben went down was because he was exhausted, no doubt. Now, I rest in our bed, not sleeping, only thinking about how to get the truth from

Tyler. Thinking of ways I can get us out of this hellscape. I wonder if we'll ever go home again.

The door opens and a sliver of light spills in from the hallway. I hear Tyler's footfalls on the wood floor as he steps inside, closing the door behind him. I pretend I'm asleep because it's easier this way.

When he climbs into bed, slipping under the covers, I don't move. I don't want him to think I'm awake.

It takes about half an hour, and Tyler's out cold. I'm certain Colleen is asleep. She rises before the crack of dawn and goes to bed early. I have another chance to learn more about what I suspect happened at 4 a.m. the morning my world turned on end.

I slip out of bed, snatching my robe from the nearby chair, and quietly tiptoe out of the room. The door creaks on stiff hinges as I close it. The noise makes me cringe, so I stop, listening for movement inside. When I hear nothing, I make my way into the hall. As I reach the bottom of the stairs, I notice a box in the utility room. Has this been here all along? I don't recall it, but then again, I don't spend much time here.

The utility room smells like detergent and a faint mix of bleach. I wouldn't have come in here if I hadn't noticed the box — I recognize it. It's from our house. There it is, sitting on the shelf above the washer, in front of some cleaning supplies. That fact it's here and not in my house is what draws my attention.

Tyler must have gone back home to get it. He must have dug through our things and brought this here. But why? A cold thought slithers around me, tightening against my chest. *Are we moving in with Colleen?*

I clench my fists. *No.* That's my paranoia talking, my exhaustion twisting things in my head. Tyler wouldn't — he couldn't. Would he?

I stare at the box, frozen with indecision. My body knows what my brain won't admit yet — I have to open it.

I pull it down and set it on the floor. The tape is already loose like it's been opened and hastily resealed. With desperate fingers, I peel it back. It's dark in here, so I open the door a little wider to let in the moonlight that shines down the hallway.

I rummage through the box. Files and papers. Medical receipts. And then I see it. About halfway down. A birth certificate. I raise it toward the moonlight.

Baby's Name: Jennifer Grace Dittrich
Mother's Name: Marissa Dittrich
Father's Name: Tyler Dittrich

This is Jenny's birth certificate, but why is it here? Why did Tyler bring this back from our house? But it's what I find beneath it that causes my heart to jump. "What is this?" I whisper. "Another birth certificate?"

Baby's Name: Summer Nicole Dittrich
Mother's Name: Riley Dittrich
Father's Name: Unknown

I freeze. My vision tilts. Across the top of the paper is a stamp.

Draft copy. Not official until filed.

No. No, no, no. I don't understand. My mind races, trying to find an explanation, a rational way to piece this together, but — there isn't one. I pick up another document.

Death Certificate
Name: Jennifer Grace Dittrich
Cause of Death: Sudden Infant Death Syndrome

A sharp ringing fills my ears. My baby. My Jenny. She . . . *died?* Then *who—*

I clutch the paper so tightly it crumples. Tyler did this. He lied to me. He took Riley's baby and gave her to me.

Jesus. This Jenny . . . the Jenny upstairs, she's not mine. She's Riley's.

But why? Why would Riley allow this? I don't understand. My God, I didn't even know she was pregnant. Did Riley willingly give Tyler her child, or did Tyler threaten her? And then, what? Riley came back for her?

I stagger back, my thoughts coming fast, too fast. The floor leans. My hands shake. I want to scream, but no sound comes out. My baby is dead. The one upstairs . . . she doesn't belong to me.

CHAPTER 63

Evelyn

A distant buzzing echoes in my ears. My eyes are closed. I'm being pulled from sleep. Now, the sound grows louder, and I realize it's coming from my phone. For a moment, I don't know where I am; then I see the clock. It's midnight.

I grab my phone to peer at the screen, squinting at the brightness. The caller is unknown, but something tells me to answer. "Hello?" My voice comes out groggy.

"Evelyn, it's Marissa."

The name rings out in my head. *Marissa.* "Ben." I bolt upright. "Where's my son? Give me back my son, and my daughter. I don't care what you say, she's—"

"Wait," Marissa cuts in. "Please."

I breathe as though I've just finished a marathon. In the darkened hotel room, my eyes widen to absorb the dim light. "What?"

"Ben is safe. You should know that first," she says. "And . . . I can help you get your children back."

Did I just hear her right? As the fog of sleep clears from my head, I need to be sure I understand what's happening here. "Help me? You're going to help me?"

268

"Yes," she whispers. "Look, I don't have much time. Tomorrow . . . I should have some time alone here at the house where you came today."

My expression falls. "You saw me? You were there with my children?" I ask, my emotions rising to the surface. "How could you let me walk away like that?"

"I had no choice, Evelyn. I'm so — so sorry." Her voice falters. "Please, just give me till tomorrow to work this out. I promise you . . . I'll give you your children back, no matter the cost to me."

"Wait. Did you kill Chelsea?" I press.

But the line clicks. She's gone. I stare out into the dark room, my thoughts churning. I knew Ben was there, yet I walked away. I told myself I had no choice, but I did. I could've stayed and fought to get him.

I get up out of bed, pacing the small room, still in the dark. Marissa knows something. And that something has to do with my children. My son and daughter. But what?

I want to scream, to run out of this hotel and drive back to that house. Tears sting my eyes as I'm tortured by my own mistakes. Still, this isn't over. Chuck is going to get answers, but I may get them sooner.

* * *

The sun is rising. Finally. I couldn't fall back asleep. Instead, I paced. I showered. I watched television. All while losing my mind. But it's here now. A new day. And it's time for me to get my children away from Tyler Dittrich and his mother.

I still don't know why Marissa had the change of heart, but it doesn't matter. What matters is that she can arrange to be alone in that house. That's where I come in, taking my children away from those people.

But what happens after that remains unclear. Will Tyler call the police? I suppose that depends on what Marissa knows. She knows enough to tell me the children are mine, so she uncovered something deep and dark. Something Colleen Dittrich, no doubt, never intended to see the light of day.

I clutch my phone, staring at it, willing it to ring. How long do I wait? It's barely 6 a.m. But I'm crawling out of my skin, desperate to make my move — to get my children out of that house. If I jump the gun, I risk exposing Marissa's plan, and right now, she's my only shot at ending this insanity.

Chuck could still help, but it means alerting the police. No matter what he says, it's a risk I'm not willing to take.

My phone lights up as a text message arrives. "Oh, thank God." I swipe open the screen and see the same unknown number Marissa called from in the night.

10 a.m. I'll be alone. If you bring the police, bad things will happen.

CHAPTER 64

Marissa

I can't imagine Evelyn slept much last night. I know I didn't. The shock hasn't yet worn off. And now, as I stand at Jenny's crib, it's all I can do to keep from crying. Ben is still curled up on the small mattress we placed next to the crib. Although I suspect he isn't sleeping.

Before Tyler got into the shower this morning, he said he had to go take care of some things back at our house. I don't know if he's lying, and I no longer care. I just want him gone.

As far as Colleen goes, I plan to ask her to run out and pick up more diapers. No doubt she'll suggest that I could've told her yesterday when she was out, and that it's very inconsiderate of me to put it on her to take care of Jenny.

Still, nothing she says matters to me anymore, either. Both she and Tyler knew the truth and kept it from me.

The memories flash through my mind in sharp fragments — what happened to Jenny. *My* Jenny. SIDS. I remember now. This was her crib. The shock of losing her, I couldn't accept it. I refused. I don't remember when this Jenny came into our lives. I don't remember why I didn't make the distinction between her and my own daughter. But I'm not sure I could have. We'd tried so long to get our girl.

I feel sick looking at her now, despising myself for accepting what Tyler had done, for not questioning any of it. He thought he could pass Riley's baby off as our own. And he did. It's all I can do to keep from collapsing to the floor. I feel like I've lost my baby all over again.

But something prompted Riley to come back for Jenny, and I don't know what that was, but I know I can't keep her. I don't deserve her. This family doesn't deserve her. Evelyn does.

I change the baby into a fresh diaper and balance her on my hip. I look at Ben. "Honey, are you awake?" He doesn't answer. "Ben? Are you hungry? I'm going to make breakfast. Do you want pancakes?"

Still, he says nothing, pretending to be asleep. He must be starving and thirsty. The child has been through far too much. "Okay. You stay here and rest."

I head downstairs. The television blares from the living room, and I know Colleen is awake. As I reach the bottom, it's all I can do not to launch into a tirade when I see her sitting on the sofa. "Good morning."

She barely acknowledges me. "Morning. You mind making coffee?"

"Sure." I walk into the kitchen and put the baby in her highchair. I don't want to call her Jenny. I can't. This baby's name is Summer.

I head toward the coffee machine and fill it with water, adding the grounds. I open the fridge and grab the carton of eggs, placing them near the stove. Then, I reach for a frying pan in the bottom cabinet. All the monotony feels comforting and normal. But I know it won't last.

I crack the eggs into the pan, watching the yolks break apart like tiny sunbursts before dissolving. My hands are steady, my movements precise, just like every other morning. Because nothing has changed. At least, that's what I need Tyler to believe.

Behind me, the coffee machine hums, filling the kitchen with its rich, bitter scent. Toast pops up from the toaster, golden brown, perfect. The baby babbles on, having a conversation only she can understand. I smile at the wonder of her, but my heart is broken.

Tyler steps into the kitchen, stretching like a man who has nothing to hide. "Smells good," he says, his voice light and fresh. He presses a hand on the small of my back as he passes, and it takes everything in me not to recoil.

I pour his coffee, just the way he likes it, and slide a plate of eggs and toast in front of him. Just smile. Because if he sees even the smallest crack in my mask, I'll never make it out of this house alive. After all, I know he murdered that girl, Chelsea, despite his insistence he had nothing to do with it. I was naive, and that ends now. I can't trust anything that comes out of Tyler's mouth.

I stir sugar into my own coffee, though I have no intention of drinking it. My stomach is a tight ball of knots, my body locked in fight-or-flight mode. I know the truth now.

That baby isn't mine. She never was.

And Tyler — he did this. He lied to me. He built our life on a grave I refused to acknowledge. When Riley came back, when she wanted her daughter — he let her take her. I can't deny that part of me wishes he'd just killed Riley then. I never would've known the truth, continuing to pretend she was mine. I don't want to admit I would've preferred it that way. And Evelyn never would've lost everything that mattered to her in this world.

But he didn't do all this alone. In fact, he would've needed help with getting that girl out of the way. *Colleen.* She knows people. People I wouldn't trust to follow me into a dark alley.

In hindsight, I wonder if Tyler was worried Riley said something about the baby to Evelyn. And maybe Tyler was desperate because he needed to hide his tracks.

When Evelyn leaves with Ben and the baby today, one thing is certain: I won't be needed anymore. I can feel it in the way Tyler watches me. The way Colleen lingers just a little too long, eyes sharp behind her polite smile. They won't let me walk away from this.

I swallow against the growing weight in my throat. Maybe Tyler will do it himself. Maybe Colleen will slip something into my drink. Maybe they'll make it look like an accident.

It doesn't matter. By the time the sun sets, I'll be dead. But I won't give them the satisfaction of keeping these children.

If this is my last day, I'll spend it pretending I never learned the truth. But that doesn't mean I won't try like hell to change the outcome.

CHAPTER 65

Evelyn

My stomach rumbles, and I know I should eat. It's been two days since I had food. The last time was back at that convenience store. My leg still aches, the wound gaping but scabbing over, and the worst of the pain has subsided. Though the mild swelling suggests an infection.

Now, I wait for Chuck to arrive. I told him what Marissa had said on the phone. He doesn't think I should go, so I'm certain he's coming to convince me not to. But there's nothing he can say that will make me change my mind.

The rumble of a car's engine sounds outside. I peek out the window. He's here. Chuck steps out of his car, dressed in a white button-down, sleeves rolled up, and black dress pants.

I open the door before he has a chance to knock. "Chuck, you didn't have to—"

"The hell I didn't." He steps inside. The way he puts his hands on his hips — I know he's about to chide me. "Do you have any idea the risks you'll be taking?" He wags a finger at me. "And not just with your life, but with those kids, too?"

"Chuck, no one else will be there except Marissa," I reply.

He raises his brow. "Look, I know we talked about getting her on our side, but this feels a little too convenient, don't you think? This could be a trap, Evie. Come on, now. I thought you were smarter than that. Now, let me do what I said and—"

"No. Chuck, I'm sorry, but I'm doing this whether you agree or not. This is going to happen."

He rubs his face, turning around, shaking his head. "Then I'll be damned if I let you go alone."

"I can't let you do that."

He raises his hand. "Too late. You're going to be stubborn, then I'm going to be stubborn right back. We can both play this game." Chuck looks at his watch. "What time did you say this is going down?"

"Ten," I reply. "She said everyone in the house will be gone at ten, except for her and the kids."

He paces the room. "And she didn't tell you why she had this change of heart?"

"No. I imagine something happened, but I don't really care. I want them both back and she's willing to give them to me."

"And what happens afterward?" Chuck folds his arms. "That man isn't going to be happy about his wife's actions. He'll come for you, Evie. As sure as the sun shines in the sky, that man will come for you."

"I thought about that," I say, lowering myself onto the bed. "And the only way we all stay safe is for me to go somewhere he won't find us. And with your help, I can start over with them."

"Damn it, Evie." He sighs, still shaking his head. "Let's just make sure this whole thing isn't some big set-up, all right? I'll come with you. Check it out, and make sure that woman's alone. We'll go from there."

I grab my things. "Then let's go."

We walk out to his car, and I toss in my bags.

The morning sun obscures the road ahead as Chuck drives. Glare bounces off the hood of the car, reflecting through the trees and buildings. Chuck grips the wheel, his jaw tight, eyes shielded with dark sunglasses. I sit beside him, my fingers tangled together in my lap, my stomach coiled into knots.

"We get in, we get the kids, we go," Chuck says, his voice firm. "No room for doubt. No room for hesitation."

I nod, though my pulse pounds hard enough to shake me apart. Marissa said she'd be alone. That she'd hand Ben and Nicky over without question. That she *wanted* this. So why does this still feel like walking into a trap? I don't dare tell Chuck I agree with him.

The Dittrich house looms in the distance, its sprawling porch bathed in the glow of the sun. It looks peaceful, almost welcoming, but I know better. The walls of that house possess secrets buried so deep they've poisoned everyone inside.

Chuck pulls up to the top of the driveway and kills the engine. The house stays silent. No movement behind the windows.

We step out, shoes crunching on gravel. My throat tightens as we approach the door, but before I can knock, it opens.

Marissa stands there, her face pale, despondent. Her eyes, dark-rimmed and hollow. Her auburn hair, disheveled. "Come in." She steps aside, her hands twisting together.

Inside, the air is laced with a hint of perfume, floral. I recognize it — it's Colleen's. I don't want to be here any longer than I have to. I just want my children, so I get to the point. "Where are they?"

Marissa nods toward the staircase. "Upstairs. They're ready."

I take a step, but Chuck grips my arm. He's not relaxed. He doesn't trust this. Neither do I. Marissa meets my gaze, and something flickers there. A warning.

"Take them and leave," she says, almost too quietly. "Quickly."

The urgency sends my pulse into overdrive. I rush up the stairs two at a time, Chuck close behind.

Nicky is in her crib. Ben is sitting on the edge of the bed, swinging his legs. When he sees me, his face lights up. "Mommy?"

I gather him up, breathing in his familiar scent, kissing the top of his head. "I'm here, baby. We're going home."

Chuck lifts Nicky from the crib and cradles her close.

We turn. Move fast. Get to the top of the stairs. And then the front door slams open. A heavy thud, followed by footsteps. I freeze. So does Marissa, who stands in the doorway.

"Oh God," she says, already knowing who those steps belong to — Tyler.

His voice slices through the house, sharp and edged with danger. "What the hell is going on?"

CHAPTER 66

Marissa

He must've suspected something. He wasn't supposed to be back for at least an hour. "Let them go, Tyler. I know the truth."

His eyes darken, and his chest heaves with long, deep breaths. His gaze snaps between me and Evelyn. "What is it you think you know, Marissa?"

"That Jenny was Riley's baby. That she gave her up to you and you thought you could pass her off as ours." I scoff. "My God, how could you do such a thing? How could you not help me get through the grief of losing our own child?" I raise my chin. "You let me grow close to her, then snatched her away. Was Riley threatening to tell me everything? Is that why you let her just take Jenny from me?"

"Shut up," he spits. "You don't know what the hell you're talking about." He looks at Evelyn. "You aren't taking them. Not a fucking chance."

"If you don't let them go," I begin. "I will tell the police everything."

"Then you'll go to jail too, Marissa, not just me. You kidnapped that boy. You held both of them hostage in that basement. Is that what you want?"

"Just let us go and there'll be no cops, all right?" Evelyn says. "I just want my children."

"Jenny isn't yours," he says, slow and deliberate.

"She's my husband's daughter. That's what Riley told me," Evelyn replies. "I didn't believe her. My husband didn't believe her. But since she killed him, and all this? I believe her now."

I start back down the stairs. "How could you let me think she was my baby? What kind of monster does that?"

"You were so grief-stricken, you didn't care," Tyler says. "Riley gave birth almost two months before you did. You knew she wasn't ours."

"Why did Riley just give up her own child?" I press, moving closer to him. Hoping to distract him long enough so Evelyn and the kids can escape while his guard is down.

"She didn't want that baby. From the moment she was born, Riley handed her off to Mom." He sneers. "And Mom gave her all the money she'd ever need in exchange."

"Then why the hell did Riley want her back?"

"Because she had a plan." He darts his gaze at Evelyn. "She'd planned to get back at the baby's father, attempting to destroy his life the same as he did hers. Only Riley was supposed to bring her back."

I glance at Evelyn. Her face is changed, masked in sorrow.

"But she never came back." Tyler aims a finger at Evelyn. "That bitch killed her and took Jenny. When we got that call about her death, I knew it was our chance to get Jenny back."

"But she wasn't ours to begin with," I say.

He thrusts his hand upward, toward Evelyn. "She wasn't that bitch's either."

Tears prick my eyes. "It's over, Tyler. We have to let them go."

CHAPTER 67

Evelyn

I can't believe what I'm hearing. This entire family is batshit crazy. I look at Chuck, both of us spinning our wheels, trying to figure a way out of here.

Marissa steps in front of the staircase, directly in Tyler's path. Her hands shake, but her voice is steady. "Let them go, Tyler."

His eyes flick to her, then to me. His expression shifts, something slow and calculating looming behind his gaze. "I won't let them leave with my kids." His tone is almost amused. "You think I don't know what you're doing?"

Marissa doesn't flinch. "They're leaving."

"No, they're not." Tyler moves toward the stairs, but Marissa lunges for him.

He doesn't expect it. Neither do I.

She grabs his arm, pulling, yanking, trying to hold him back. He shoves her, hard. She stumbles but doesn't fall. She blocks him.

"Go!" Marissa screams at me.

I don't think. I run.

Chuck is already ahead of me, barreling down the stairs, gripping Nicky tight. I clutch Ben to my chest as we tear through the house, past the ornate furniture, the floral-papered walls, toward the open door.

Tyler roars behind us, a sound that sends a chill down my spine. But Marissa fights him. She fights him with everything she has.

I don't turn back. I can't.

We explode onto the porch, racing for the car. Chuck yanks the door open, shoving Nicky into the back seat. I follow, pushing Ben in.

We are *so close*.

And then — Tyler is there. A blur of movement. A hand on my arm, yanking me back. I hit the car door with a resounding crack, stars bursting in my eyes.

"Evelyn," he yells, gripping my wrist. His fingers dig in, bruising, holding me in place. "You don't get to take them."

I twist, kick, claw, fight. I think of the truth. Of Jenny — no, *Nicky*. Chuck races behind me, trying to pull Tyler off me. One hard shove and Chuck is on the ground.

With a burst of strength, I slam my elbow into Tyler's throat. He gasps, stumbling back, just enough for me to break free.

Chuck is already on his feet again, already moving, already swinging. His fist connects with Tyler's face, a crack of bone against bone. Tyler crumples to the ground.

Marissa appears in the doorway, her face pale, blood on her lip. She looks at me, eyes wide, and I know — she's made her choice.

"Go," she breathes.

But Tyler comes back. Rushing at me hard, barreling into me. My breath is knocked from my lungs. I'm doubled over while he reaches into the car. "No!" I try to scream, but my voice comes out raspy.

I look at Chuck, who's scrambling to the other side of the car, trying to stop him from taking the kids. Still hunched over, I stare at the ground, my thoughts racing as to what Tyler will do. And that's when I see it.

A rock. Sharp and jagged. Large enough to do some damage — I hope. I pick it up. "Tyler! Get away from my children." I lean toward the car just as he's trying to pull out. Raising the rock, I bring it down hard on the back of his skull. It cracks, and blood spills, soaking his dark hair.

"You bitch!"

He turns around, and I swing again. The rock connects with his temple. His eyes widen, glazing over with surprise. Then the blood comes. It pours from his head, and when he blinks, he sways.

I don't chance him recovering, so I strike again, this time, knocking him to the ground. He's on his face. Not moving. I straddle him, bringing down the rock over and over, smashing his head as hard as I can. "Stay away from my babies!"

Even as he's stopped moving, I whale on him until I hear a voice.

"Stop. Evie, stop."

It's Chuck.

"He's dead. Evie, look at me!"

His words echo in my ears, and I stop. I stand up and see him only feet away. Blinking hard, I turn and peer into the car. Ben's eyes are wide, staring at me with fear. Nicky's crying, screaming, tears falling down her face.

And then I see Marissa. Hand over her mouth. Terror in her gaze. I gasp for air. We lock eyes for I don't know how long. And then the sound of a car approaching breaks our stare. She looks beyond me, and I turn around.

Colleen.

Marissa disappears inside. I look at Chuck. Neither of us seems to know what to do, but we know it won't be good.

When Colleen gets out of her car, she marches toward us. She doesn't see her son. Not yet. But when she does . . .

"No!" she screams. "No! What did you do?"

The door opens again. My gaze turns to Marissa. She cocks the rifle in her hand, aiming it at Colleen. "Get away from them, you crazy bitch!"

The world turns to slow motion as I look at Colleen. Her eyes widen with fear, and then the shot rings out. Colleen flies backward, then lands with a thud on the gravel driveway. I turn back to Chuck, his mouth agape, his expression mirroring mine.

"Go," Marissa says. "Go, now."

I dive into the car, slam the door, and Chuck peels out of the driveway, gravel kicking up behind us. Ben is crying. Nicky is wailing.

I peer into the side view mirror and see Marissa, the gun lowered to her side. She's sacrificing herself for me and the kids. Then again, it never had to come to this. She could've stopped it from the very beginning. Instead, she went along with Tyler's plan.

The Dittrichs took everything from me. All of it . . . caused by this family. But I have the kids. I know the truth. And we'll never have to hear that name again.

EPILOGUE

I'm lucky to be alive, or so I've been told. I gotta be honest, though, I'm just as surprised as anyone to be sitting here right now, peering at the walnut bookcases packed with historical case law. The leather-bound books radiate an intoxicating aroma that fills me with hope for the future. My future. One — by all accounts — I should have been denied.

Grant Calloway sits across from me. As the senior partner and the law firm's namesake, he makes the final decisions on new hires. I've gone through three rounds of interviews already, and this is the last hurdle. If he likes me, I'll be the next junior associate at Calloway and Associates. A dream come true.

Calloway studies my resume, repeatedly pushing up his reading glasses with his middle finger. I'm trying not to decipher any hidden meaning behind the gesture, but the thought of there being one makes me want to chuckle.

He breathes loudly through his pointed nose, which I imagine could be caused by a deviated septum. The sound is noticeable to the point of distraction. He seems too warm in his suit jacket, as evidenced by a tinge of dampness on his white collared shirt and a slight flushing of his round cheeks.

"You've had an impressive education," he says, tapping a finger against the page. "Graduated top of your class, clerked with Judge Ramirez. And now, looking to start your career as a trial lawyer." He glances up, smiling. "And nothing's been handed to you."

Pride swells in me. "No, sir. I've worked hard to get here with the support of my family."

Calloway nods. "That's more important than most people realize."

I smile. "Yes, it is."

His gaze sharpens. "You must've had an incredible role model."

"I did," I reply. "I've been shown what it means to stand your ground. To never let anyone take from you what they have no right to take."

The words settle between us, heavy with more meaning than he could know. More meaning than even I know because some truths are too dark to be revealed. Some truths were kept from me, supposedly for my own good. It's taken me a long time to accept that. Nevertheless, if you're not moving forward, you're standing still, and I have no intention of allowing that.

Calloway closes my file and extends his hand. "Well, Nicole, we'd love to have you on board. Welcome to the firm."

I shake his hand with steady resolve. "Thank you, Mr. Calloway. And, uh, everyone calls me Nicky."

* * *

I walk into the restaurant and approach the hostess. "Hi, I'm Nicole Moore. I have a reservation for two."

She searches her tablet and returns a smile. "Of course. Right this way. Your party is already here."

I follow her back through the rows of tables draped in linen. The light from the chandeliers sparkles on the gleaming floor.

"Right here, miss," she says.

"Thank you." I turn to see him. "Ben. You beat me here."

He rises from the table and pulls me into a tight embrace. "Hey, little sis. Long time no see. How you doing?"

"Great." He pulls out my chair and I sit down.

"Glad to hear it." Ben takes his seat again. "So, what's the big news? I didn't think we'd see each other until next week."

"I know, but I thought it'd be nice to have dinner with my big brother."

He smiles at me. I miss his smile. I don't get to see him much anymore. We both live busy lives now and even though he's only across town, it's like he's on the other side of the world.

"Same here, Nicky," he replies. "So are you going to tell me the news or do I have to guess?"

A grin tugs at my lips. "Well, I had my final interview with Calloway and Associates . . ."

He raises a brow. "And?"

"And you're looking at the newest junior associate."

His eyes widen, and his chin drops. "Oh my gosh, Nicky, that's great! Congratulations. Oh wow." He leans back. "Wow. I'm so happy for you. Did you tell Mom yet?"

I shake my head. "No, not yet, but I will. I was going to wait until we saw her next week for the . . ." I trail off, never really able to say the words.

"The anniversary," Ben says. "Yeah, well."

I study his gaze. His eyes hold more than he's saying. Then again, they always have. There are things he and Mom never told me. Things I don't think I want to know. "It's always hard on Mom — the day Dad died."

"Yeah," Ben replies. "Even after all these years, it still gets to her. I wish she would've found someone else, but she always said we were her priority, and she didn't have time for any other relationships." He looks at me again. "But this news will make her so happy. To have you following in her footsteps, Nicky, it's the best gift you could ever give her."

"I hope so," I reply. "I mean, she never went back and practiced law after I was born, but I know she loved it. I'm sure she missed it, too."

"She did," Ben adds. "But like I said . . ." He smiles. "This will make her beyond happy. You did good, sis. I'm proud of you."

"Thanks," I reply, picking up the menu. "So, what's good here?"

THE END

THE JOFFE BOOKS STORY

We began in 2014 when Jasper agreed to publish his mum's much-rejected romance novel and it became a bestseller.

Since then we've grown into the largest independent publisher in the UK. We're extremely proud to publish some of the very best writers in the world, including Joy Ellis, Faith Martin, Caro Ramsay, Helen Forrester, Simon Brett and Robert Goddard. Everyone at Joffe Books loves reading and we never forget that it all begins with the magic of an author telling a story.

We are proud to publish talented first-time authors, as well as established writers whose books we love introducing to a new generation of readers.

We won Trade Publisher of the Year at the Independent Publishing Awards in 2023 and Best Publisher Award in 2024 at the People's Book Prize. We have been shortlisted for Independent Publisher of the Year at the British Book Awards for the last five years, and were shortlisted for the Diversity and Inclusivity Award at the 2022 Independent Publishing Awards. In 2023 we were shortlisted for Publisher of the Year at the RNA Industry Awards, and in 2024 we were shortlisted at the CWA Daggers for the Best Crime and Mystery Publisher.

We built this company with your help, and we love to hear from you, so please email us about absolutely anything bookish at feedback@joffebooks.com.

If you want to receive free books every Friday and hear about all our new releases, join our mailing list here: www.joffebooks.com/freebooks.

And when you tell your friends about us, just remember: it's pronounced Joffe as in coffee or toffee!